Hunted by Angels
Line of Lilith Book One

by

R. A. Boyd

Hunted by Angels

Contact Information: info@thewildrosepress.com

Cover Art by *Debbie Taylor*

The Wild Rose Press, Inc.
PO Box 708
Adams Basin, NY 14410-0708

Visit us at www.thewilderroses.com

Publishing History
First Scarlet Rose Edition, 2018
Print ISBN 978-1-5092-2009-0
Digital ISBN 978-1-5092-2010-6

Published in the United States of America

**This she-demon is so hot
even the angels are chasing her...**

"Haines, please, help me." The tears that roll down my face sting my cheeks and chin. Everything hurts. It's as if my clothes should singe away from embers that should be oozing out of my pores.

"Perrian, I don't know what to do."

The ripping sensation intensifies until it feels like the top of my body will separate itself from the bottom; like my right side will tear away from the left. Like my insides are boiling. I close my eyes and wait.

Wait for it to stop. Wait to die.

Something seizes my body and yanks me upward. And the pain stops.

I don't feel anything. It's quiet. Only the sound of my breathing echoes in my head. Am I dead?

Haines' voice is soft. "Perrian? Baby, open your eyes." Though his voice sounds strong and grounded, a wavering tremble breaks though, and I can tell he's afraid for me.

My limbs are flat against a hard surface, but the pain is gone. I open my eyes and see Haines looking up at me.

And I'm looking down at him. Because I'm on the ceiling. Looking down at him.

Dedication

To my Belles.
Mommy loves you more than tongue can tell.

Chapter One

"I do," I say sulkily as the minister asks if I take this man standing next to me to be my lawfully wedded husband.

"You could at least muster *some* kind of joy over this," Haines says quietly as he squeezes my hand. "Your posture is disgusting."

"Shut-up," I snap at him.

For our friends and family attending our nuptials I have nothing but sweet smiles and kind words. But for this douchebag I have snark for days.

This is not the happily ever after either one of us was hoping for. And Haines is certainly not the man I wanted to end up with. But if I don't have a holy union —holy my arse!—with him all hell will break loose and blah, blah, blah. We're destined to be together. I despise him. He likes it. He's a demon. Figuratively and literally.

Haines is a full-blooded incubus, a male demon that feeds off the sexual energy of women. I am the female counterpart—a succubus. I also happen to be a cambion, a half-blood. *Perfect couple,* my parents said. *Marry him or you'll start murdering people. You won't hate each other forever.* Fat chance.

"Oh, my God," echoes the blubbering voice of my Aunt Rita amid the silence as the minister says the final lines of the ceremony. "She's. So. Beautiful!" She sure loves to be heard.

The minister smiles as he presents us to the crowd sitting in the church pews. "I now pronounce you husband and wife. You may now kiss the bride."

I turn to Haines and frown at him as he leans in and gives me a hard kiss on the lips. "Could you be more of a dick?" I say quietly while everyone stands and claps for us. "That hurt."

"Could you be happy about *something* for five minutes?" Haines says through gritted teeth, grabbing my hand as a show of affection. "Your parents should have let me train you years ago."

I look at him and scoff. "Are you insane?"

Haines is one of the yummiest men I've ever laid eyes on. He's just under six feet tall with broad shoulders, a narrow waist, and dark hazel eyes that complement his sun-kissed complexion perfectly. His chestnut wavy hair is cut fairly close but grown out just enough so that I can pull it when I get angry with him. Trust me. I've done it several times before. He pisses me off daily.

When my mother found out that I had inherited her demonic genes she contacted a soothsayer who did some witchy crap and found out that Haines was the man for the job. Again, we are fated to be together. There was a choice, though. Either marry Haines, apparently the only living, unattached incubus that has the power to help me control myself, or allow my need for sex and energy to take over. I loathe Haines, but I don't want to kill anyone.

Well, except Haines.

Before we walk down the aisle my mother stands up and addresses the crowd. "Please, everyone, listen for a moment. Mr. and Mrs. O'Neil Haines—"

I roll my eyes. "God, you have a stupid name…"

"—will be joining us at the reception hall after they take formal pictures. Please, head over to the hall, and they will be there shortly." She turns to face us. "Downstairs. Now."

Haines tries to take my arm and lead me down the aisle, but I pick up the front of my poufy white dress and walk off. "I gotta pee," I tell him over my shoulder.

****

"Come on, Perry," my mother says through the bathroom door. I've locked myself in. A girl has got to have privacy.

"Coming, Mother," I say sweetly, but I'm sure she catches the sarcasm.

I look in the mirror and see a not so blushing bride giving me the stink-eye. My dress is your typical A-line fit with silver embroidery leading to the bottom in long flowery lines. Since it's late November I opted to have a lace sheath that falls just below my elbows added to the top.

My hair is pinned up with real diamond pins and real silver ribbon laced through it. Haines may not be the man of my dreams, but my father is wealthy and this son of a bitch I just married is loaded. I insisted we do this in style. Why not? I'm not paying for it.

The make-up on my face is sparse and flawless and my platinum tear drop earrings make my neck look longer. I'm only five foot four and I'm not what you'd call petite. I have wide hips, child bearing hips my mother calls them, not so small breasts and a complexion of one who goes jogging in the sun every day. I'm a size ten, plus-sized model by today's

3

standards. I'm beautiful. Every succubus is. Most men don't want a demon that actually looks like a demon.

Haines may look like every woman's fantasy, but he is all demon. Ever since my parents found out he could help me not kill people Haines has been trying to get his hands on me. Those large, long-fingered hands that I'm sure can please anyone up for the challenge. *I'll teach you not only to control yourself but every person in the room who has eyes for you,* he said. *I already have a list of your duties in my home.*

I was sixteen and scared of my powers, but learning to control myself just enough to stay away from Haines' tyranny for as long as possible became my life's mission. It worked for ten years, and now the joke is over. I need help.

I eye myself in the mirror once more, unlock the bathroom door, and snatch it open. "Let's do this!" I say loudly as I walk toward Haines.

"You really do look lovely," he says, looking at my breasts.

"Suck it." I roll up my left lace sleeve.

"I fully intend to later." He knows that shit pisses me off.

"You're disgusting. Oww!" My mother grabs my arm and makes a minute but deep cut just below my elbow.

"Knock it off, Perry," she says, placing a small bowl under my arm to catch the falling blood.

"Mom, you could have gotten blood on my dress. I'm selling this bad boy on eBay when we're done."

Haines takes off his jacket and rolls up his sleeve. "Do you know how much I paid for that dress?" My mother cuts his arm.

I grin and shrug my shoulders. "Yes, husband, I most certainly do." My arm is starting to heal. Our union is already quickening. The church ceremony was my dad's and my idea. I'm a demon but I still wanted to have the beautiful church ceremony all little girls dream of, but it's the blood binding between Haines and me that will make it real. It will join us, bind us, and open me to all the help he is able to give. "Aren't we sullying the church by doing this here? Why haven't you burst into flames yet? I mean, you are a demon," I say, looking at Haines.

"The same reason you haven't burst into flames yet. You're half demon." Even though he's being a dick, his deep voice is like velvet and dark chocolate.

Feeling the pull of his demon to mine, I lean into him and inhale deeply. His scent is clean and warm, and beneath it rests one of my favorite scents—butter pecan ice cream. For a brief moment I can taste it on my tongue; the cold sweetness interrupted by the gentle crunch of the pecans. A fantasy of Haines dripping the frigid, beige cream onto my shoulder and using his warm mouth to clean it up fills my head. His lips shudder against my skin as he chews the pecans and nibbles the column of my neck.

I open my eyes and remember that we're in the basement of the church. "Damn-it! It's already starting. You did that on purpose." I feel drawn to him. I can't help it. An incubus' power lies in his sexual attraction. He can take the simplest of pleasures you may have, for me it's homemade butter pecan ice cream, and turn it into the most erotic experience you never knew existed.

He looks offended. "Mrs. Haines…"

"Don't call me that."

"Whatever do you mean? I didn't do anything."

I point at him and scoff. "Ice cream. I'm never eating it again." One less thing he can use against me.

"You would if I fed it to that pretty mouth of yours," he says, full lips curving into a half smile.

Hell yes, I would. "Absolutely not."

We've been married in the sight of God and now the blood-binding is kicking in. As an incubus, he calls to me. My body yearns to be touched by him, and now his blood calls to mine and tells me that I am his just as he is mine. Until we consummate our union, I will want him more than anything and despise him just as much. "Let's just do it here," I tell him.

"Absolutely not. I'm going to take my time with you, little girl."

"Eww," my mother says. "Join hands."

Haines grabs my hand before I can protest. My mother has soaked a thrice blessed sacred white ribbon in our blood. She ties it around our hands and puts the bowl on the counter behind her. "By the powers given to me, I bind thee. Perrian Ettis Haines, I bind you to O'Neil Haines. May you serve and tame one another. Blessed be." She unties the ribbon and puts it in the blood-stained bowl.

"That's it?" I say, snatching my hand out of his, instantly missing the warmth of his strong fingers curled around mine. "I thought there'd be more to do than just getting my arm cut."

"It's healing," he says, looking down at his arm.

"Shut. Up." I check to make sure the cut on my arm is fully healed and then roll down the lace sleeve. "Come on, husband. I'm hungry."

At the same time, Haines and I both inhale sharply,

and a faint moan escapes my lips. I look down at my hand that had been tied with Haines' to see the blood that was covering it, our blood, is now seeping into my skin. He's looking at me strangely.

Haines touches my hand and a flood of passion spreads through my body. The vision of him licking the melted ice cream from my bare shoulder comes racing back and a fury of flutters erupt in the pit of my stomach. I shake my head. "Knock it off." My voice is a little too breathy for even me to take seriously.

He comes to stand in front of me, gazing down with a grimace on his lips. "You will stop telling me to shut up. Do you understand, Perrian?"

"You two were made for each other," my mother says over her shoulder as she ascends the steps leading from the basement of the church.

"Curse your lips," I scream.

"Do you understand?" he repeats. He looks pretty pissed off. "I am five-hundred and twenty-six years old. To me, you—"

"Just shut up," I tell him as I walk away, leaving him standing next to the water cooler. And for good measure I turn around just enough to give him the finger.

****

"I feel like my skin is on fire. But in a good way." I'm sitting with my husband—barf—in the limo waiting for the driver to come around and open the door for us. I'm starving.

"Perrian, you need to calm down. Until I take you tonight—"

"Please stop," I tell him as I open the door my damn self. That driver is dragging ass.

Haines takes hold of my arm and pulls me back into the limo. "Enough!"

His energy bounces off the inside of the vehicle, and I moan loudly. His touch is an electric line leading directly to my core. I struggle against his grip, loving the feel of his fingertips digging into the bend of my arm. I hate him for making me want him so badly. "Don't." My voice is barely above a whisper.

"You want me to. I know you do." He traces his nose along the side of my neck and skims his teeth against my shoulder, and from his powers of lust I can feel the cold trail of the ice cream as if it were dripping from my shoulder. "There is no better sex than between incubi and succubae. You wanted this big wedding, you got it. But the more agitated you become the more trouble the human men will be in." He reaches inside the top of my dress and brushes his thumb across my left nipple. I lean into his touch as the oxygen is sucked from my lungs. "We are now joined in holy matrimony and blood bound. Your powers need a release that only I can give you. I told you I would take my time with you, and I will. So calm down. If not for my comfort then think of all your family and friends in there. Your ardor will set that room on fire if you don't compose yourself."

I try to think but his hands are in control of my thoughts. A moan breaks through my lips and I press my hips back against him. I can feel his erection through the ten layers of this dress. He grips my nipple between his thumb and forefinger, squeezing the already tightened bud and distends it away from my body. I want more. "Okay. All right. You have to stop before the driver…"

"He won't open the door. I thought I may have to give you some kind of release before we went in, so I pushed him to wait. I've been keeping a handle on your fervor since right after the ceremony, but I need your help now. You'll be fine if you calm down."

He pulls his hand out of my dress, and my thoughts clear. "God damn-it, if you ever touch me without asking—"

"What? What did I just say?" His voice is slightly higher and he sounds irate.

"What did *I* just say? Ask. Before. You. Touch."

He inhales deeply to settle himself. "I will not let you out of here until you are ready. Besides, tonight you *will* want me to touch you. And I will not release you until you beg for it. Now, will you relax?"

My lips draw up in a grin as I see the anger I've caused. I've still got it. "All right. I'm stopping. But you should be considerate. Tonight will be my first time. I'm a virgin," I say, turning to face him.

He looks horrified. I slide forward and open the door of the limo, peel me and my dress out, and slam the door behind me.

That little admission should shut him up.

****

"You two make a lovely couple," my Aunt Rita says. She's my father's older sister. Or only sister. He doesn't talk about his family too much and gets pissed off when I bring it up. "I didn't even know you were dating." She smiles and winks, giving me a knowing grin.

"We weren't," I tell her through a mouth full of mashed potatoes. I take a sip of champagne. "Shouldn't you be enjoying your food, Rita? Dad will bust a vein if you waste it. One-hundred and forty bucks a pop."

She looks perplexed. "Oh, I get it. You want to be alone with your sweetie!" Aunt Rita goes to walk away but then turns back to look at us. "Your father never thought you'd get married. I mean, you are twenty-six and we've never seen you with a man. Your cousin thought you were gay," she says, smiling at Haines.

I point my steak knife at her. "Go eat your food, Rita." She flitters off, and I notice Haines staring at me. "What?"

He looks me up and down and then takes a sip of bourbon from the glass tumbler. "I assume the reason you haven't been seen with a man is tied to the reason you've never had sex before. What is it?"

I take his bourbon from him and down it in one gulp. *Oh my God! My chest is on fire!* "Every time I've tried to have sex with a guy I wind up either taking so much energy from him he passes out, I don't do it on purpose of course, or he reaches his happy place before we can properly start. I just stopped trying."

He eyes me and then looks over to the waiter that stands waiting on our every whim. The poor guy is just for the bride and groom. He's already gotten me two helpings of mashed potatoes and three extra baskets of dinner rolls. Haines takes his glass from me and tips it up to the waiter. The guy nods and runs off to get another drink for him. Haines looks at me. "That's it? Nothing more."

"Nothing more."

"You're lying," he says, grabbing my hand. He pauses for a second and then lets go. Smart man. "In your early years your powers must have been like electricity. Who did you hurt?"

I look at him and he blanches. "Stop talking."

He doesn't listen. "That doesn't happen too often with a young succubus. You're very strong."

I take another sip of champagne and turn toward him. "So I've heard. I wish I was like my mom. She controls herself so well she was able to marry my father, who is human. If she was anything like me growing up she deserves a cookie. *That's* power. Mom and Dad love each other to death. He knows exactly what she is and he still thinks roses fall out of her..."

The waiter gets closer to us, sets the glass down in front of Haines, and then looks at me. "Miss? Would you like anything?" The waiter is gawking at me.

Damn-it, I'm doing it again. If I were in control of my powers his attention would be awesome. But now, for him, it's just downright deadly.

Succubae, like me, tend to go after the same man over and over again to gain control over and then suck the life out of them. And this is with protection.

"No, thank you." I turn to look at Haines, but the waiter stoops down next to me.

"I can get you anything you want—a drink, more food, anything?" His lips are slightly parted and he's completely ignoring Haines.

Waiter-boy's scent is changing. He smells like burning jasmine.

"This is priceless," I say, reaching out to touch his face. "No, I'm good."

"Do not touch him, Perry." I look up and see my mother standing behind the boy. My dad is quietly standing behind her. She gently touches the waiter on his shoulder, and he turns to look at her, like a viper following the most beautiful snake charmer he has ever

11

laid eyes on. Her power causes goose bumps to spread along his skin. I can see them on the back of his neck. "Young man, please, go get yourself a drink and take a break."

He stands up and gazes at her. She touches his arm, and I can actually see his release. It undulates along his skin, almost like a mirage drawing itself into its conjuror. She absorbs it, making it a part of herself. He shakes his head and walks away.

My mother looks drunk for a moment and then regains her composure. "You're not going to be able to stay much longer, Haines."

"Yes, Barbara." Haines stands up and takes his jacket off. "I'm keeping her powers as discrete as I can. But if she touches someone…"

"I'm sorry," I say looking between them. "I didn't mean to." I have felt a change since the ceremony, but this is too much.

"I know, darling," Haines says trying to soothe me. "We should leave soon. We'll have one dance, cut the cake, and leave."

"Why are you being nice to me?" I ask him.

"I'm always nice to you—"

"Bull-shit." I try to grab his glass of bourbon but he pulls it out of my reach.

Pulling the tumbler to his lips, he takes a sip and then pushes the glass toward me. "You didn't let me finish. I'm always nice to you, until you open your mouth. You're nice to look at, Perrian."

"You see, Mom," I say, standing and taking Haines' drink in hand. "This is the man I've married. You sure know how to pick 'em."

My mother inhales and closes her eyes. A small

'V' appears between her eyebrows. I'm getting on her nerves. "Perry, you need him. You don't know how to control your powers. More and more supernaturals are coming out and humans are getting more and more anxious. This may be a new day and age but if too many men start dying from unnatural causes the proverbial villagers will start hunting us with pitchforks and torches. Haines is doing us a favor."

I purse my lips. "Thanks Haines. You breaking my cherry is really going to help."

"Jesus Christ!" my father says, speaking up for the first time. He covers his whiskey colored eyes and shakes his bald head, the light above dancing around it like a halo. "I don't need to hear this. I need a drink." He walks away, carting my mother with him.

I watch my parents retreat and feel sorry for the both of them. My father is the innocent bystander in all of this, and he's being a real sport about it. My mother is just her normal cynical self. Everyone's got my best interest in mind and I'm just being a bitch about it.

Haines has rubbed me the wrong way since we first met. *You do know how to cook and clean, don't you? At least you are pretty to look at.*

"Come," Haines says. "Let's dance. I'll make an announcement that our flight was delayed but we have a chance to catch an earlier one. We'll have cake and then leave." He holds out his hand. "May I have this dance?"

I plant my hand in his and take a step toward him. "See how much easier things go when you ask before touching me."

We walk toward the DJ, and Haines makes the announcement. Everyone seems pretty disappointed.

My lovely Aunt Rita yells out something crass about us hurrying to be alone. She still hasn't cleared her plate. Too busy running her yap.

Chapter Two

"I could take you on a honeymoon," Haines says as the driver holds the door open for us. "Paris, London, the Caribbean. Your mother told me you've always wanted to go to Ireland."

"She's right. But I'd rather go with someone I liked. Besides, I go back to work on Monday."

He sighs and shakes his head. I don't know if he's at his wits end with me or if he just hates my guts. It's been a constant tug-of-war between us for years. His outdated, chauvinistic views bring out a hateful part of me that nothing short of homicide will quell.

The rest of the ride is in silence. Being this close to him with no one else around is causing me to restrain myself. I want him. My skin is burning with need for him. Keeping quiet and concentrating is the only thing that's preventing me from sexually molesting him.

And he knows it. I think it's getting to him too. He looks flushed and his breathing has sped up. I can actually feel his need for me as I'm sure he can feel mine. Every once in a while, he looks at me, and when he catches himself staring, he turns away and clears his throat. Good to know. Since we can't get along long enough to do so we haven't discussed the future dynamics of our relationship. When both of us have innate needs that stem from the sexual, things could get a little hairy. Every bone in my body tells me to reject him. Marriage is supposed to be about love and commitment. I need him so I won't start killing people. What is he getting out of the deal?

If our first meeting didn't go the way it did I might actually like him. But he was a prick, and I refused to tolerate it. We first met when I was sixteen years old. My mother knew I was a succubus by that time and sought the guidance from a witch not long after. The woman told her how to find Haines and once she finally met him she kept him away from me as long as possible. And when we did meet, let's just say it wasn't love at first sight. The prick. Even thinking about it pisses me off. He expected me to…

The car swerves, and Haines knocks on the tinted window that separates us from the driver. "Perrian, please stop." His voice sounds heavy. "Whatever you're thinking about…just stop. You're going to cause the driver to kill someone."

"Sorry," I tell him as I check out our surroundings. "Good, we're almost back to your house. We can get this over with."

He exhales deeply and rubs his eyes. "You don't seem to understand the severity of this arrangement. You don't want to live with me, I think you should. So does your mother. We will need to be able to get to one another when the need arises."

"I'm not giving up my apartment. It's rent controlled and in an awesome neighborhood. It's close to my job, the expressway… Nope, not giving it up." I live ten minutes from the major shopping areas and fifteen minutes from downtown Baltimore.

"You are most vulnerable when you are asleep. That's when the desires of men call to you. You'll feel compelled to answer those calls and you will hurt someone. I need to be able to keep an eye on you at night."

"I'll think about it, all right?" I say quietly as we pull up to his house. The desires of men haven't called to me yet. Why should it start now?

Once Haines found out I was supposed to be his lifetime sweetie he uprooted himself from Massachusetts to Maryland and moved into a small gated community in Towson called Cloister Vista. He lives in a beautiful brick single family home with columns that greet you as you walk in, granite tops in the kitchen and bathrooms, and striking hard wood floors. Maybe I'll move in just so I can claim his house as my own. My favorite feature is the breakfast bay that leads into the dining room. It has five bedrooms and five bathrooms. Maybe he thinks he's too good to have to share bathrooms with anyone if four other people moved in. I guess if I do choose to move in, fat chance, I could divorce him when this is all over and take his house.

The limo comes to a halt and I'm instantly nervous. I'm about to do it! This is disconcerting. I don't know what to do! We're gonna... What the hell was that? It feels like I just took a shot of whiskey.

A horrified whisper echoes from the front seat. "Oh. My. God. What was that?"

"We'll let ourselves out," Haines says to the driver who just creamed in his jeans. Haines scoots forward and opens the door. "In a rush to get my bride in the house," he says with feigned happiness. He turns to me and scowls. "Get out of the car, Perry."

I feel warm all over. And somewhat sated. "I didn't

mean to—"

"Get. Out." His voice is cold.

I lean over and pull myself out of the limo. This dress is a little overpowering. "I really am sorry. Tip the driver, please."

Haines gets out behind me and walks to the front of the limo. The driver rolls down the window and Haines hands him a few bills. One looks like a fifty. With everything I just put him through, he deserves a big tip. I don't think he knows what really just happened, but I'm pretty sure he's happy about it. Embarrassed, yes. But happy.

Each step I take toward the front door feels like a promise of punishment. I don't know what he has in store for me, but I don't think it'll be gentle. His face is angry as he gets closer to me. I would tease about carrying me over the threshold, but he doesn't seem to be in a joking mood. He just might pick me up and throw me over the railing.

"I suppose you'll need a key," he says coldly, using his to open the front door.

He ushers me in through the door and closes it behind us. I expect him to get right to it—maybe that's just what I want—but he walks past me and goes into the kitchen. "You should take a short vacation from work," he says. Haines has one of those glass refrigerators! I've always wanted one.

"Seriously, dude," I say, walking up behind him. He pulls two bottles of water from the refrigerator. Looks like I'm in for a workout! "I like my job, and you and I aren't doing anything next week."

He untwists the bottle top and hands it to me. "Drink. You're tipsy. I don't want you to blame alcohol for what we may be doing this evening." His eyes are dark and hold a look that makes me want him even more than I already do. "I'll make you a sandwich." He pulls out a large platter from the second shelf filled with lunch meats and cheeses. "You need to take off work. You see what you did to the driver? Do you want to bring your coworkers and patients to orgasm when you can't control yourself?"

"No," I mutter. "I'll take a few days off. Damn-it."

"Is that your favorite word?"

"Yes, *damn-it*. It sure is."

He rolls his eyes. "You'll need a few weeks."

My mouth hangs open in surprise. "Are you trying to get me fired? It's bad enough I'm going to take a few vacation days with such short notice, but a few weeks?"

He looks smug. "I tried to tell you. You wouldn't listen."

Bull-shit. "At no time did you say, 'Hey Perry, you're in danger of making everyone around you climax if you think too hard.' Yet another reason why I don't like you—failure to disclose. Why doesn't anyone tell me anything?"

He closes his eyes and takes a deep breath. "You need to learn to take subtle hints."

Smiling, I wave at him. "Hi, I'm Perry. Have we met?" I say sarcastically. "I need bricks thrown at me. Just say what you mean."

"Perrian, please go sit down at the dining room table. I'll bring in your sandwich. You are exhausting." He goes to the granite island and begins to make my sandwich.

I walk past the dining room and into the family room to check things out. The first time I came here he started telling me where I would stay and how he believed our relationship should be handled. He wanted to be my guardian. If I remember correctly I told him, '*I already have to deal with my parents and now I have to take you telling me what to do? You're gonna wait until I'm ready or until I explode.*' We instantly developed an aversion to one another.

"Haines," I yell while tracing my fingers along the fireplace mantel. The stone is cold and smooth. A vision of me face to face with Haines' hardened cock comes to mind. It's smooth and rigid, like the mantel. Or would it be ringed with veins that I could trace with my tongue while I look up at him? His eyes staring down at me as I suck the mushroom shaped tip into my mouth and hear him groan my name as he fists my hair. *Stop it, Perry.* "I'm going to get out of this dress. Where did my mother leave my overnight bag?"

There are no pictures of family or friends anywhere. Just little tchotchkes and keepsakes that range from antique to modern. Over five-hundred years of collecting stuff will probably do that to you.

"You don't do what you're told," he says as he rounds the corner, holding a plate with a massive sandwich, chips, and bottle of water. "I asked you to sit at the table."

"Again, my name is Perry…" He's going to hate me before the week is up.

"After you've sobered up I'm going to slowly take that dress off you." His voice is cold and smooth like the mantel. Walking closer to me he dips down and brings his lips so close to my ear I can feel his warm exhalations sweeping across my neck. "I am going to taste you until you scream, drinking in the passion I can already feel rolling off you. Then I'm going to ride you until the only thing you can see and taste and feel is me."

Well damn. I try to take a step back but the fireplace blocks me. My heart beats as if it will burst as a flood of heat seeps into my panties. My breath hitches in my throat, and my pulse slams to a stop as his lips draw closer to mine. God help me, I want to touch him. Have his delicious hands roam the curves of my body as he makes those pretty promises come true. Screw the sandwich. I want him now.

Haines' eyes are full of lust and they touch a part deep inside me that contracts my core and makes me think I could actually come from his closeness alone. "Once you've begged me to do so, of course. And you will plead," he says, taking a step back and walking toward the kitchen.

Son of a bitch. I want him right now, but I refuse to beg.

****

Three hours later and I'm still sitting here with this God-awful dress on. I would have taken it off eons ago, but I can't reach the gazillion buttons that line the back. And I don't know where he put my bag of clothes my mom left for me. So it's either walk around naked or wear his clothes. I'm thinking naked. Maybe he'd be faster at trying to get my goods if they are free for the pillaging.

"I love this show," he says, laughing at a recorded episode of Happy Endings.

It's one of my favorite shows, too. He's sitting three feet from me on the C-shaped, dark brown couch that complements the family room. He's taken off the jacket of his tux and the tie hangs loosely around his neck. The deep red cummerbund is hanging on the back of the beige recliner next to the fireplace.

He laughs. "The witty and crude dynamics of their relationships are just too comical. It's unlike any show on television."

"Yeah," I say looking at him sideways. "I liked it, too. Shame it was cancelled." I slide closer to him, grab the remote, and pause the show. "Haines, you may touch me."

He looks at me and laughs. "What did I tell you?"

"Dude, I don't beg. But I'm giving you permission. You. May. Touch. Me." I smile sweetly at him.

"Unlike mortal men I am completely immune to your antics. You will beg or you will as you told me before, *explode*. I am saying what I mean for a change. Goodnight, Perrian." He leans forward and chastely kisses my lips.

"Where are you going?" I whine.

"To my room. I'll put your bag in the hallway and you may pick any room that is not mine. Unless you're ready to supplicate me." He gets up from the couch, hands me the remote and walks off.

"Well, can you at least help me get this dress off? It's either that or I'll have to cut it down the middle."

"Goodnight, Perry."

I can't believe he's leaving. He thinks I'll follow him. Well, he has another thing coming because I'm not following him. He'll be back. Or not.

Well, at least he called me Perry.

****

I couldn't bring myself to cut the dress off last night. Waking up on the couch in a wedding dress is one of the most uncomfortable things that I have ever experienced. Well, on my twenty-first birthday I did get royally shit-faced and fell asleep on the porch swing face down and fully clothed. That was quite uncomfortable, but nothing compares to wearing a million layers of puffy fabric and a bustier that cuts off circulation. I must have fallen asleep deleting all of his recorded shows on his DVR. I will have my revenge!

I get up and start checking out the house. Outside of a closed door on the second floor is my overnight bag. I assume this is Haines' room, and he wants to be left alone. I grab my bag off the floor and head to the bathroom to brush my teeth and wash my face. Your average woman would look like stir fried hell right now, but I'm still looking all right. The perks of being half demon.

Oh, God. I have to pee. In this dress.

****

Twenty minutes later and I've managed not to pee *on* my dress. Before I locked myself inside of the church bathroom to be alone with my insidious thoughts of Haines, my mom helped me hoist the massive bottom up so I could use the bathroom. If I have to go again this dress may sustain unspeakable damage.

"That shower was so refreshing." Haines rounds the corner to the kitchen where I'm sitting at the breakfast bar eating a bowl of cereal. He's barefoot and wearing nothing but brown and black striped pajama pants. "I must say, Perrian, you still look lovely. I hope you slept comfortably."

"Bite me. Come on, help me get it off. I kinda like it and I don't want to ruin it," I say, pleading with him.

He puts a pod in the coffee maker and places a green coffee mug under the dispenser. "I knew you couldn't do it. At least I was hoping you couldn't. That dress cost me seventeen hundred dollars."

"That's not why I didn't cut it. It makes me feel pretty. But I gotta get it off!" I leap off the bar stool and go to stand in front of him. "Please, Haines, unbutton it for me."

"Are you begging?"

"Nope."

"Have you learned your lesson, Perrian? I will teach you to do what you are told. Or at least to be agreeable."

His smug look pisses me off, and I have the notion to punch him in the face. Do what I'm told? I walk to the knife block, grab the poultry scissors and begin to cut the dress, starting from my boobs and working my way down. "Do what I'm told? Fuck you!"

He stares at me in disbelief as I ruin the dress that cost *him* an ass-load of money. Haines is speechless.

Once I finish cutting it down enough until my hips and thighs are free I step out of my once pretty dress and hand the scissors to him. "I am not a child and you are definitely not my father. Do what I'm told? You must have forgotten who the hell I am." I feel great. Lighter. Free to pee! "I'm going to take a shower now and then I'm going to pick a room and go to sleep."

Chapter Three

After taking all the pins out of my hair, it kind of just dangles there just below my shoulders, and it still looks pretty good. I thought for certain it would be sticking up in different directions. Lucky for me. I spend a good amount of time in the shower rubbing the areas where the bustier left marks on my skin from me sleeping in it all night long. Seems as though the indentations are here to stay. And it's all *his* fault.

I feel completely exhausted after my shower. Forgoing the sexy lingerie my mom put in the bag I grab a tee-shirt, panties, and my thick pink and green fluffy socks. I refuse to beg, and he seems to be stuck on my doing just that. Maybe I'll stay a virgin forever. God, I hope not.

The bed is comfortable, and I lull myself to sleep with rancorous thoughts. I'll get that son of a bitch, one way or another. Deleting his saved shows was just the beginning. He'll learn. If anyone is going to learn a lesson it'll be him.

****

A warm caress and a kiss wake me. I open my eyes to see Haines kissing his way up my right leg. His eyes are trained on mine, and I fight not to look away. His lips are heated velvet, and each fervent kiss sends chills through my body and center in on my core. Damn him.

The room is quiet, save for the soft *swish, swish*

25

sound of the ceiling fan. The spinning blades carry a tender breeze along my exposed skin, but do nothing to cool the warmth that originates with Haines' kiss. I want to reach out and touch his hair, pull him closer to me, but I let him take his time. Electricity hums through me, and every kiss makes my stomach quiver. For a moment my chest constricts as if I've forgotten how to breathe. With every press of his lips I catch my breath and focus on him. Sweet, sucking kisses reach the apex of my thighs, and then he makes his way down my left leg, his lips leaving a trail of fire in their wake. Once he reaches my toes, he sucks each one into his lusciously supple, warm mouth. It tickles and my giggles give way to quiet sighs, his tongue darting out as he tastes every inch of me. Where the hell did my socks go? I should be fighting him, to let him know I mean business. But I can do that later.

Ripples of energy fill the room, reminding me of a hot summer day in a sunny parking lot. His power fills this entire space, and I clench my hands, trying to keep them from touching him. I don't know if it's his energy that makes me want him so badly, or if it's the attraction that's already there between us that fuels my desire.

Haines nudges my legs together and for the sake of the pressure on my sex I squeeze my thighs tighter just to feel the heaviness send a welcomed shock through me. "Can I have these?" he asks, gently tugging on the elastic of my blue panties.

My mouth is dry and my voice is weak. "Yes?"

I lift my hips as he pulls my panties down and he leans in to kiss my belly button. His kisses begin to descend as he runs his fingertips down the length of my thighs, his rounded nails skimming my bare skin, leaving a line of goosebumps. He grabs my ankles and pulls me farther down the bed, and then pushes them until my knees fall wide, and my feet lay flat on the bed. My breathing has accelerated and the anticipation for what's to come makes my heart hammer against my ribcage as if it threatens to explode through my chest.

As I watch, he uses his thumbs to part my inner folds and kisses the sensitive mound of flesh. His touch demolishes my resistance, and I give in to all he has to offer me; all he has to teach me. I inhale sharply and hear a deep rumble in his chest. He's laughing. Haines starts to suck and lick and bite, and I feel as if my body will shatter from this heavenly feeling. He kisses as if he were kissing my mouth, exploring, turning his head left to right, moving forward and backward.

I grip the sheets and focus on the pressure from his mouth and feel warmth blazing through my body. My hips roll to meet his tongue, his teeth, his lips. He hums and a delicious spasm makes its way through my entire being, singing across my skin, starting with his mouth sucking on my clit. He moves his hand and tenderly pushes one blessed finger inside me, and I bite my lip, trying to stifle the groan making its way up my throat. Without going too deep he hooks his finger and begins to move in a 'come here' motion, and at the same time he's still teeth and tongue and lips. My body feels like it's floating, and he's all the power I need to fly.

"Yes. Oh, Haines. Please." I barely recognize my voice as it escapes my lips. It's deep and wanton, mostly a groan instead of words.

And then it happens. The feeling that I've feared since I was a teenager begins to overtake me. His energy, his life force, is beginning to flow into my body. The first time it happened, I just thought that was what arousal was supposed to feel like—empowering, life-affirming, like the state of passion itself had descended and taken over my body. Until Linus, the first guy I tried to have sex with, passed out and was unconscious for two days. The doctors told his family it was a heart attack.

I grab Haines by his ears and pull him away from me. "Haines, stop it," I pant. Goddess that felt good. "It's happening, and I don't know how to stop it." Tears of frustration begin to build in my eyes. I may not like him that much, but I don't want to hurt him. This was what I've been afraid of all this time, and as much as I may fight it I was hoping he'd be the one to bring an end to it.

"Shh," he says, kissing my sensitive flesh once more, causing it to pulse as if begging him for more. Traitor. "This is how it will be between us. It's give and take. Our energy will sustain us." A wicked grin spreads across his face, and he continues pleasing me.

I didn't know this was how it worked. I relax and lay back, almost giddy in the feeling he's pulling from me. He sucks as much of me as he can into his mouth and wraps his tongue around my clit, massaging it, soothing it. "Oh, please," I say as I thrust my hips toward his face. "What is—" I begin, as an ardent, hot feeling grows in my center. "Haines, please." The feeling is building as he begins to draw an orgasm from me. My voice is getting higher and louder. Heat rushes to my extremities and it feels like the calm before the storm.

And then, he stops. He stops tasting. He stops

fingering. He sits up and looks at me. Haines climbs up my body and takes my top off. "I'll take care of this," he says as he kisses my left nipple. "And this," my right nipple, "if you would only beg me, Perrian. And if you don't, I will get up and walk out of that door."

Oh. My. God. I could kill him, murder him, commit homicide right now. My breathing is coming in gasps now as I try to wrap my head around the feeling that's now missing. "What? How could you? You son of a bitch!" I kick out with my right leg only meaning to get him out of my way, but when my foot connects with him he springs back about three feet, falling off the bed and onto the chest of drawers.

"Perrian—" he begins, getting up off the floor with a look of pure irritation.

"Holy crap. Did I do... I didn't mean to..." The kick was meant as an almost playful warning, not a full on assault. "Dude, I did not mean to do that. I didn't even know I could do that."

He stands up straight and cocks his head to the side. "It's our power. You've never been fed properly. When a succubus feeds her sexual appetite, she gains certain strengths. Didn't your mother ever tell you?"

"No." I look down at myself and blush. "Can we not talk about her since I'm naked and you're at full salute, which would be taken care of if you'd stop being a controlling dick?"

"Perrian, you will—"

I know what he's going to say and it hurts my ears before he even gets a chance to say it. Yes, he's supposed to help me. Yes, he knows things I don't, but this has to stop. I'm all for an alpha-male but I will not be treated like a child. This ends now. I won't allow him to make me feel like an incompetent fool who doesn't have the wherewithal to learn.

"No, Haines," I say, exasperated. "Just get out. I'm tired of playing this game with you." Damn-it, his mouth felt so good. "You want me to be a submissive little girl who you can boss around and do what's expected of her. That's not me. I've never been that girl." I pick up my tee-shirt and put it back on. "If you would have taken the time to get to know me you would have seen that I'm not that girl. I've tried to show you and you just keep pushing. So instead I've turned into a bitchy, irritated person who is attracted to and repulsed by you."

He sighs and rubs his forehead. "There are things you need to know. Things you have to be prepared for and I need to teach you. But…"

"But nothing. I will never bow down to you. You have to accept me as your equal, not your submissive. And I know you've got to help me get a grasp on my powers, but you've got to find another way."

He bites his bottom lip. "Will you be this strong when he comes for you? Most are not."

I feel a crease form between my eyes. "When who comes for me?"

"I was supposed to help you get control first, but…"

"When *who* comes for me?" I say a little louder.

"Samael. The archangel. When he comes to tempt you out of the hands of our Goddess, Lilith."

Where the hell did that come from? This conversation has taken a huge turn. I shake my head and begin to speak, but nothing comes out.

"And he will come, Perrian."

"I don't understand. I would never fall away from Lilith."

His smile is full of disdain. "Then why do you think She had to be redeemed?" He shakes his head and puts his shirt back on. *No! Leave it off!* "Why do you think there aren't many of our kind left?"

I shake my head. "I never thought about it."

"Of course, you haven't. Your mother kept this from you and maybe she was right. But now you're here with me." He walks closer to me and puts his hand on my chin, forcing me to look in his eyes. I let him do it. "If you're not ready Samael will drain you of all your power and leave you a shell of what you are. And then you'll die. Your rude ways may push me away, little girl, but he will not be that easy. There are only a handful of us left, and this is why. He helped create us. And now he wants to redeem himself in his own eyes. He wants us dead but he can't just kill us. We have to give in to him so that our powers, our life force, comes to an end."

My voice is unsteady and barely loud enough to hear. "I don't understand." He begins to walk away and I run after him. "Please, Haines! I don't understand."

He stops at the door and turns to look at me. "I'm calling your mother. There are some things only she can tell you." He opens the door, walks out, and closes it behind him.

An angel wants to kill us? Kill me.

My eyes dart around the room, making sure the window is closed; that the closet door is still set the way I left it. I hit the light switch to bring brightness to all the darkened corners. All of a sudden, I'm afraid to be left alone. I want to run after Haines, to stay close to him until I understand. But my pride won't let me.

Pride cometh before the fall, a voice echoes in my head.

I guess it's time for a family meeting.

Chapter Four

"Perry, I was going to tell you. The opportunity just hadn't presented itself." My mother looks flustered. I haven't said a word to her since she and my dad got here half an hour ago. I've learned from my father that the best way to make my mom spill her guts is to say nothing. "I knew you weren't in danger because you hadn't come into your powers yet."

Silently, I uncross my legs and tuck them both under me. I glance at my father to see him trying to hide a partial smile. He knows what I'm doing.

"A succubus doesn't develop all of her powers until she begins having sex and feeding her appetite." She takes a sip of water. "You know our Goddess is Lilith, but She didn't create us all by herself. Samael tempted her and she made love to him. That's how she and three other women became succubae, and how we came to be. Perry, please," she says. One word from me would shut down our 'sharing' session.

Haines looks at my father. "Kevin, would you join me in the kitchen? Perhaps we can..."

"Whatever," my father says, quickly rising from the couch. He feels the tension and wants to get away. My dad is a real sport at this supernatural stuff. He keeps his distance from all things weird and my mom does everything she can to help him do it.

I'm pretty sure she just wants to keep him safe.

He's mortal and too fragile for her comfort. She has never admitted it, but I see it. When other supernaturals started showing themselves to the world I thought she would shit a brick. She worried what my classmates and friends would do if they found out I was the daughter of a sex demon. By that time my powers hadn't manifested and I think part of her secretly hoped they wouldn't. She was hoping I'd be more like my father. Human. But my dad took it all in stride and told her to simmer down; that we would deal with whatever happened when it happened.

And here we are now. A succubus who doesn't know how to control herself, who just so happens to be the daughter of a secret keeping demon and a mortal father. The thought alone makes me sigh and shake my head.

My mother looks to my father for support but he only kisses her on the forehead and follows Haines.

"Perry, I'm sorry I didn't tell you. How do you tell your child that a man, an archangel no less, wants to kill her? The accepted idea is that he feels guilty for taking part in our creation. He had some kind of epiphany and for the last seventy years or so he's been picking us off. But our essence is so strong, we usually regenerate. We are hard to kill." She smiles at this. "I was able to resist him. It was hard, but..." My mother looks thoughtful for a moment.

I suppress a shiver and let her continue. Anything that scares her must be awful.

"I'm a full-blooded succubus and he wants us dead. He still comes to me sometimes," she says in a whisper, looking off to the kitchen to see if my father is listening. "It's like he's asking if I'm sure I still want to be alive. That's why most of us give in. Years of living off the lives of others takes its toll on your conscience. After years of living and watching your loved ones die…it just takes something from you. I don't know what I'd do if I didn't have you and your father. You two are the only things that make this life worth living."

All right. I can't take it anymore. "Then why would you leave me unaware of this? You should have been preparing me for his arrival, not trying to hide it from me and hoping I stay a virgin forever." My mother looks as if she wants to say something and then stops. "Mom, I'm scared. Really, really scared. You have to help me." I stand up and go sit next to her.

"I know, Perry. That's why you have Haines."

I scoff. "He makes my blood boil. I don't understand how he can help."

She smooths out my left eyebrow. "Then I'll contact the soothsayer who led us to him. I hoped you'd be like your father, but when I found out you were like me, I went to her to find out how to protect you. And she led me to Haines."

I shake my head. "But why? What can he do besides piss me off?"

"Perrian Ettis."

"Sorry for the language. But come on! What is it that he can do?"

She bites the inside of her lip and shakes her head. "I don't know."

She's lying.

"Well that's helpful, Mom," I say sarcastically. "You don't know how he can help, but you're pretty sure he can."

She mulls it over for a moment and looks toward

the kitchen. "Yes. Pretty sure." I laugh at her confusion. "Perry, you don't understand. I would do anything to protect you. Even if that means doing something that makes absolutely no sense. I don't know what else to do." My mother looks defeated.

"It's okay, Mom," I say, sighing. "We'll figure it out. What's Haines getting out of this? Maybe he knows what's going on."

"It doesn't matter," she says, looking me in the eyes. "Just as long as you're okay."

My father comes into the living room carrying a large mug for my mother. I'm pretty sure it's filled with cocoa and two shakes of cayenne pepper. "You two straighten things out?"

I feign excitement. "Not so much! But it's fine. We'll get it together."

I catch my mother and Haines looking at one another. There's something more here. Neither one of them are willing to tell me. I'll get it out of one of them.

"So," my father says interrupting my thoughts. "What are you two going to do for your honeymoon?"

"We're doing it," I say flatly. "He convinced me to take off work for a while so at least I can do whatever it is I do on days off."

I try to keep busy. Too much free time on my hands means too much time for my idle demon libido to kick in and start looking for men who are too ready to hand over their lives. The phrase 'the flesh is weak' is an understatement. Most people confuse lust with love, and people who are in love are willing to do almost anything for the person they love. Even if they know it's unhealthy for them. They crave what they lust over. Sprinkle in a bit of sex demon mojo, and they are willing to die to have that lust sated.

My father snaps his fingers as if he's remembered something. "You've always wanted to go to Ireland. Or is it Scotland? I'm sure your uncle could set that up for you."

My uncle is a travel agent. And he's not really my uncle. Just a friend of the family. "I'm good, Dad. Maybe something a little closer to home." He doesn't want to accept what Haines and I have is out of convenience. He never thought I'd get married. I think he's hoping I'll be his happily married daughter and give him grandkids. Fat chance.

Haines clears his throat. "I have a little cabin in Rolling Springs. It's about an hour from here. Perrian?"

I sigh. "Maybe. Sounds all right, I guess."

My mother finishes the rest of her cocoa and sets the mug on the living room table. "Your father and I are going to get going."

"All right," I say, shrugging.

She looks like she wants to hug me but stops herself. My mother has never been big on sappy stuff. She turns around and begins to follow my dad.

I pop her bra strap to clear the air. "This isn't over, okay?"

"Yes, I know." She smiles and pats my arm. "This isn't over. Not for a long time. We've got a lot of living to do, daughter."

Once they've left I turn to Haines and shake my head. "You should have said something."

He holds his hands up in surrender. "It wasn't my place to do so. Your mother wanted to wait until you had a little more control."

"That didn't work out."

"No," he says soberly. "I suppose it didn't." A devious smile spreads across his face. "Let us begin your lessons at once. Feel like begging?"

I grab my sneakers by the front door. "Nope, I feel like power walking. I'll be back later."

Once I've put on my shoes I bolt out of the door. I always think better while I'm walking. And I've got a lot to think about.

****

People are out all bundled up, walking their little dogs and enjoying the crisp fall morning. I'm so hot and bothered—and not in a good way—I could be walking around in short-shorts and a tank-top tee. Instead, I have on pink sweat pants and a long sleeved yellow shirt. The moisture of my breath blows out in little ringlets into the cool air as I speed walk through the neighborhood.

Two men and a child exit a semi-detached house. They laugh and hug one another. Their obvious comfort makes me feel envious. The taller of the two men—he looks like he must be the father of the little boy—kisses the other man on the lips softly and then bends to kiss the top of the child's head. The kid looks just like him or in old people terms, he looks like he spit him out. They see me, the new face, and wave as they say their goodbyes. I wave back, and my mood is slightly uplifted.

A woman in a severely neat brown and black tweed pant suit runs out of her house as if she's running late and gives me a hurried smile.

The leaves are turning their browns and reds and yellows. It's peaceful, beautiful, and completely picturesque. My insides are the opposite. I feel suppressed and stuck in a relationship that I don't want to be a part of. Haines is here to help me not get killed by an angel. How am I supposed to fight off an angel? It made me uncomfortable to listen to my mom talk about it. She looked almost tempted. Like she wanted to say yes to Samael. That alone scares me. She is far from a pushover.

And what about Haines? What is he getting out of this deal? Maybe he thought he was getting a maid? No, he can afford one of those. A fuck-buddy? No, he looks too tasty not to have women throwing their theoretical cooches at him. He's getting something. I don't know what it is, but it's something.

If I could stop myself from sexually exploding and wanting to take as many men with me as I could I'd leave the bastard. He thinks he's so…

"Oww," I hear a voice say as I ram into someone's chest. It's the tall dude. "My gawd, you're built like a linebacker, but you're so petite."

I'm still standing. He's fallen ass over coffeepot after I power walked into him. I hadn't even realized I'd made it to the end of the circle and was coming back around. With that sex demon on my mind I didn't even see this guy standing there. "Shit," I say, reaching down to help him stand. "I'm sorry. I was thinking and didn't see you there."

He dusts himself off and checks his brown and green mailbox. "Better me than the mailbox. Our son made it for us in shop class." He looks me up and down and settles in on my eyes. "You've beautiful lookers. I'm Ryan. You saw my husband Trent and our son Roman heading off to work and school."

"I'm Perry. No work this week, just speed walking,

bitching, and having devious thoughts."

"My, you're quite honest and potty-mouthed." He clasps his manicured hands in front of him. "You're the newlywed, aren't you? Your husband has been quite the talk among the single ladies. *And* the married ones, too."

I roll my eyes and pick a dead yellow leaf off his teal and gray sweater. "Yup, that's my sweetie," I say sarcastically. "I just moved in. We got married Saturday."

"Perry, is that a family name?" he asks, walking toward his house.

I think he wants me to follow him. Damn-it. "It's actually Perrian. And yes, it is a family name—Perrian Ettis."

"You didn't take his last name? I thought it was Haines?"

I start up the steps after him. Aren't you *not* supposed to go into strangers' houses? Please, with my strength, I'd rip him a brand new one and smile in the process. "I did. Ettis is my middle name."

"Well," he says, turning to look at me, trying to hide a frown. "It has character. At least you're beautiful. Now I understand why you go by Perry, if you don't mind me saying."

I eye him and smile. We walk into his foyer, and it opens up into a beautifully modern yet classic home. "I don't mind. Your house is like a mirror image of Haines'. Except it looks more…"

"Stylish? Please, I'm a gay man who's married to an interior designer. Our house changes trendily like the seasons."

It's my turn to be nosey. "Well, Ryan, you're not

on your way to work. Are you a housewife? Househusband?"

He laughs loudly and touches my shoulder. "No, I'm a computer programmer. I run my own company from home. I'd have taken Roman to school but it's on the way to Trent's job. What do you do?"

"I'm a physical therapist. Guess you could say I was born with a 'magic touch'," I say, wiggling my fingers. "It's a great job, and I only work three days a week."

The mixture of traditionalism and neoclassic lines of their home is to die for. There are unfinished borders along the middle of the earthen toned walls, but striking colors in the furniture. The wooden oak table sitting in the middle of the family room is adorned with fresh sunflowers and aged pine cones. This place rocks.

"I'll let Trent know you love our home. It gives him pride to know his hard work is appreciated. Even though I let him know I do love it, it doesn't seem to matter as much." There's a bit of sarcasm stinging in his voice.

"Dude, I know I'm easy to talk to but please don't give me a negative look at your boy-toy. I want a nice clean slate when I meet him. Are you guys happy?" Hey, I'm honest.

"Perry, don't get me wrong, I love him more than tongue can tell…"

I know that saying. "It's from a Twilight Zone episode. I love that one and know it word for word."

"That's my fav, too! We're going to get along swimmingly."

"But as you were saying—Trent."

"Yes, I love him very much, and our marriage is

awesome. But you know, nobody is perfect. I'm sure there are days you want to throttle your hubby," he says, laughing and walking toward the kitchen. Is it mandatory to have one of those glass refrigerators if you live in this neighborhood?

"You couldn't possibly imagine."

He smiles and pulls out two bottles of water. "Would you prefer wine, Perry?"

Impressed. "At eight in the morning, Ryan? Sure, why not. I don't have to work today. Why not start my honeymoon off right—with alcohol."

"Just one glass won't hurt. Besides, I'm going to cook you French toast and it pairs perfectly with a French Sauvignon Blanc. And neither one of us has to go to work." He goes to the counter, opens a drawer, and pulls out a French baguette. "Why aren't you going on a honeymoon?"

"Why are you making me breakfast? We just met and I'm pretty sure you're not interested in me." I smile and start picking grapes out of a fruit bowl.

"I don't know. You feel like…my friend. We just met ten minutes ago, but I feel at ease around you." He looks at me sideways as he begins to cut the stale bread into thick slices. "You're not treating me like a leper and most of the, um, people in this little community do."

"Oh. Well, you seem pretty cool, too. I don't care what you two do. You seemed pretty happy and your son looks happy, too." The stale bread chips away and flitters to the floor. "Why are you using stale bread? I thought that only worked in bread pudding." I spent some time in New Orleans and a chef down there taught me the many uses of stale bread. French toast wasn't one of them. If it tastes good, I'll have to call Tony and let him know.

"That's kind of heart-warming. The first part, anyway. When you use stale bread and let it soak in the sweet egg mixture it has a gentle crisp exterior with soft, fluffy insides. It's to die for. Maybe you can make it for your hubby."

Yeah, I don't think Haines wants me to cook anything for him right now. Not if he wants to be able to keep it down. "Sure. And to answer your question, we didn't honeymoon because I didn't want to. I thought I'd go back to work this week, but he talked me out of it."

"Mmm-hmm." I don't think he believes me. "Go on, settle in at the island and watch me work my magic. And pull down two wine glasses."

We share light conversation while he cooks and he tells me all about his happy family. While Trent's family is completely against him and Ryan's arrangement, Ryan's family is all for it. They used a surrogate to have Roman and plan to adopt a child next year. Ryan started his company when he was twenty-five and has a thriving business that he and his hubby could live on, but Trent loves his job.

I gloss over the relationship between me and Haines. It'd be nice if we were happy. Hell, it'd be nice if I could actually stand being in the same room with him for ten minutes and not want to savagely attack him.

"So," Ryan says as he places a plate in front of me. "How did you and your love bug meet?"

I stare down at the beautifully arranged plate. There are two lightly browned, thick slices of French toast sprinkled with cinnamon, scrambled eggs, and three thick slices of bacon. "We actually met when I was a teenager." Stick as close to the truth as you can, Perry. It's easier to remember. "Haines is um…twelve years older than me. We saw one another every once in a while, and I hated his guts." Still do. "I got older…I guess you could say we were destined to be together."

"Aww," he says, with feigned sweetness. "That would almost sound poetic if you didn't look so pissed off when you tell your fairy tale." He takes a sip of wine and sits down across from me with a plate that mirrors mine.

I cut into the French toast and look for the syrup. I see none, so either he has forgotten or it's so awesome I don't need syrup. The fork barely skims my teeth as I place the fluffy bread in my mouth. I moan and close my eyes. This has just given Haines a run for his money. "Oh. My. Goddess. This is freakin' awesome. Seriously, dude, my mouth is actually watering."

"I know right!" he says, grabbing another slice and putting it on my plate. "I use syrup in the egg mixture. Am I being too presumptuous by giving you more?"

I cut a larger piece and shove it in my mouth. "Absolutely not. This is fantastic. I almost had reservations about coming into a stranger's house, but this makes it completely worth it."

Ryan preens and begins to eat his food. "Roman has his eccentricities. He used to love syrup, but about two months ago he said it reminded him of brown glue, and he wouldn't allow it on anything. So, I tried adding it before I cooked the bread."

We finish our breakfast in silence, which makes me happy. I don't want to be interrupted while I snarf it

44

down. Someone knocks on the door while we're cleaning up. Though he wasn't expected, I can already feel that it's Haines.

Ryan goes to the door and is completely taken off guard. "Oh. Hello," he says nervously.

"Hi," Haines says with a little too much enthusiasm. "I saw my wife come in here and just…"

"Here I am," I say flatly as I walk up behind Ryan.

"Just wanted to make sure you were all right," Haines says more for Ryan's benefit than mine. I suppose he thought I was in here having sex with him. Does he even pay attention to his neighbors?

"Oh, please," Ryan begins. "We're new best friends. I wouldn't hurt a hair on her pretty little head. Would you like to come in?"

I shake my head letting Haines know not to ruin the only friend I have here. We've only just met but I think he and I are going to get along pretty well.

"Thank you, but no," Haines says, shaking his head. "Can I see you at home, please? Perrian?"

He's being nice. Too nice. He never says 'please.'

"Sure," I say carefully. "Ryan, thanks for breakfast. How about you come over later this week, and I'll make you lunch?"

Haines looks confused. "You cook?"

Ryan looks from me to Haines and back again.

I push Haines toward the steps. "Yes. I do. Bye, Ryan." We walk in silence toward his house. "What do you want? I made a friend, and no, I wasn't molesting him."

He stops walking and looks at me. "There is someone who wants to meet you." He looks strange.

"Is it your mother? Brother? Do you have any

45

family, or did you scale your way out of hell?"

He grabs my hand and starts walking again. "We need to—"

"What's with the touching?"

"I'm sorry, but he insisted on meeting you."

We walk up the steps to his house, and he enters the door before me, holding my hand tightly. I don't think I'm going to meet his family today.

"Haines, what's going on?" I ask.

He turns around and looks at me. His eyes are nervous, but his stance is protective. "He said that I would introduce you to him, or he would come to you. Alone. I'd rather be present."

I look over Haines' shoulder and see the back of a very tall man. This guy is easily almost seven feet tall, and he has on a long black coat. He's running his long fingers along the mantel of the fireplace. He spins around, too quickly, and his lavender eyes seem to zero in on me. He looks like a teenager who had an unnatural growth spurt. His faultless, pale skin seems to glow and his eyes are unnerving in their glare. A smile breaks across his face, but it looks wrong. Beautifully wrong.

"Darling!" His voice is deep, too deep for someone who looks so young and innocent.

I tighten my grip on Haines' hand so he can't pull away. "Samael, I'm guessing."

He sounds almost jovial. "You'd guess right, Lady Bug."

My father used to call me that. Until I graduated from junior high school. My insides tell me to rage against him but my good sense tells me to simmer down. This is an angel, and he looks…wrong. It seems as if a touch of insanity has taken its toll.

"You'd be correct in thinking that, Lady Bug."

Did he just read my thoughts?

Nodding, he walks toward me and Haines pulls me a little closer and I let him.

"Haines," he says, as if insulted. His eyes never leave mine. "I would never dream of hurting your sweetie. She's not even ready." His eyes finally flick to Haines. "But you are."

It's my turn to pull Haines closer to me. "Is there something I can help you with, Samael? Or did you just want to scare me out of having sex. Forever." He is freaking me out.

His smile widens and I can see his molars. "Oh, Lady Bug. I didn't know we were on a first name basis." He walks back toward the fireplace. "I just had to come meet you. I almost said hello when your mother was here earlier. But your father was present. He's really not my concern right now. Now you on the other hand…I just *had* to see what the hub-bub was about. I've been waiting for you, Lady Bug. Have another family meeting and ask your mama why. I'm sure she'd love to share."

"Doesn't sound like you know my mom too well. She's not one for sharing."

He smiles and walks back to me, leaving only a few inches in between us. "I know her better than you think, doll face." He places his hand on my cheek and moves a stray hair behind my ear. "You and I will get to know one another as well."

I want to pull away, but I can't. He seems so loving. So accepting. I feel myself leaning into his touch. Almost mesmerized. His childlike features and deep baritone are comforting.

"Perrian!" Haines yanks me back against his chest and wraps his arms around my waist. Was he yelling?

I shake my head to clear away whatever screwed up spell Samael has about him. "What the fuck was that?"

"Home, sweet girl." Samael smiles and then walks to the front door. "That's what home feels like. I'll be taking you there soon, Lady Bug."

I almost want to follow him.

He opens the door and glides out. "Tell your mother I said hello," he says as the door closes behind him without him even touching it.

Chapter Five

My face is sweaty and I'm trying hard to catch my breath. Haines is holding my hair out of the way as I finish throwing up in the large, black vase that holds umbrellas of various lengths. It felt like Cloud Nine had come to pay me a visit while Samael was here, but now I feel nauseous and I have a headache. Samael is no angel. At least not any more.

"Perrian, are you all right?" Haines lets go of my hair and starts to rub my back.

He seems sincere, and my heart is touched but my sense of logic comes first. "You son of a bitch." I swat his hand away from me. "How could you? How could you and my mother not tell me about...about that *thing*?"

He takes a handkerchief from his coat pocket and wipes it across my mouth, pausing to look at my lips. "It wasn't up to me. Your mother wanted to wait and since you are her daughter I figured she knew best."

"That's bullshit." I take one more deep breath and stand up straight. "Don't you dare tell her I said that."

"Don't be angry with me. Your mother is the one treating you like a five-year-old." He gives me a sideways glance. "Don't you dare tell her I said *that*."

I shake my head and walk toward the kitchen. Haines follows behind me, grabs two glasses from the cabinet and fills them with water as I sit down at the breakfast bar. I lay my face against the cool marble and take a deep breath.

The clink of a glass sounds in front of me as Haines gently places one on the counter. I take a long pull of the cold water. "I'm not five years old. And now you're my husband which I'm pretty sure gives you more say in my life." I laugh to myself at the thought. "So, spill it."

Haines takes a sip and gently sets the glass on the counter. "I can't tell you everything because I don't know everything."

"So! Tell me—"

"But I'll tell you what I do know." He holds his hands up in surrender. "Have a seat. I'll make you a sandwich."

"I just ate."

"Yes. And your breakfast is now coating my umbrellas."

I wince. "Dude, I'm sorry. I'll clean them up, and they'll be good as new."

"Don't bother." He shudders and then frowns. "I'll throw them away."

"Again, I'm sorry. So, spill it."

He takes the bread from the bread box on the counter behind him and then heads to the refrigerator— love that thing—to grab the lunch meat. "If you hadn't yet noticed, you are very powerful."

"Oh, pu-lease! I can't even control myself."

"Mmm-hmm," he says, putting mustard on the bread slices. "You do know your powers shouldn't even be active yet. You haven't had sex. You haven't been fed properly."

I shrug. "But I'm a succubus. I'm in my twenties

so puberty is long past where I'm concerned."

"Mmm-hum. Puberty doesn't start the change in demons like us. Sex does. Feeding from prey at the height of orgasm does." He laughs. "Your mother told you that puberty switched it on. That's cute."

I don't think it's funny. "Knock it off. It's not funny so stop laughing. And yes, that's what she told me. And yes, I believed her. I didn't think she'd lie to me."

"Eat." He finishes the sandwiches and slides a plate toward me. "So, now you know. I can't imagine what you'll be like once we've consummated our marriage. Your powers are already like fire and as time goes on you will only get stronger."

"Chips please." I take a bite of the sandwich and push my plate back to him. "There must be a good reason my mother lied to me, and I want you to tell me. You're pussyfooting around the question, and I'm only going to ask you once more. What. Isn't. My mother. Telling me. Damn-it!"

"I think you should ask your mother."

"I'm asking you."

"Perrian, it's not my place."

"Of course it is. You're my husband now and you're *the one* that's supposed to teach me how to control myself. That should start with a history lesson."

He reaches down, opens a drawer next to his leg, and pulls out a small bag of veggie chips. "Once upon a time—"

"Seriously?"

"Perrian, please." He looks annoyed and tired. I seem to have that effect on tons of people. "A long time ago there were three women and one Goddess—

Mahaleth, Naamah, Agrat Bat Mahlah, and our Goddess, Lilith."

"It already sounds like you're making this shit up." I empty the small bag of green, red, and yellow chips onto my plate.

"If you interrupt me again I will stop and will not continue until I have your mother's permission."

I hold my hands up and keep my trap shut.

He takes a sip of water and clears his throat. "The first woman Samael slept with was Lilith and after their first, and only, sexual encounter she refused to sleep with him again. No one but Lilith knows why, but we all have our theories. But now that he had his initial 'taste', so to speak, he wanted more. So, he went to a temple where people practiced sacred prostitution."

"Sacred prostitution?" I remember his warning. "Sorry to interrupt, but I have no idea what that means."

"People used to worship with their bodies and there were places you could go to *practice* religion. The first three women I mentioned were ladies of sacred prostitution. Samael went to one of these temples and bedded them. And to their dismay, they turned into succubae. These three women were the first of the sex demon blood line. This could be why Lilith refused to have sex with him again."

I chuckle. "Yeah, maybe he gave her a little more than she bargained for by turning her into one." Wait a minute. "That's why she's referred to as the Mother of incubi and succubae; she was the first! But she didn't make us on purpose?"

"Light bulb," he says sarcastically.

I want to give him the finger but I shut-up and shove some chips into my mouth.

He chews and swallows a bite of his sandwich. "The result of an angel giving in to his or her lust is to cause that object to become what it abhors the most."

My mouth forms an 'O' in realization. "Sin. What do you get when an angel gives into lust—a sex demon."

"Fast learner." He shrugs. "Moving on. From what I've been told Agrat Bat Mahlah married a man she met after she left the temple. She committed suicide after giving birth to her first child. That child was an incubus. Luckily the child's father, who was a human, didn't see things her way and protected the baby. He didn't see his son as a demon that needed to be killed, only a child that needed to be loved. My mother is a descendent of Agrat Bat Mahlah, and my father is a descendent of Mahalath. And when you count down many generations, your mother is a direct descendent of Lilith and Naamah." He takes a bite of his sandwich like he just told me what day of the week it is.

"You're too fucking calm about this, Haines. Why are you so okay with this?"

"Why shouldn't I be? I've had more time to digest everything. You're hearing it for the first time."

I shake my head and push my plate away. The half-eaten sandwich and veggie chips make me want to throw up. "I don't know. That you'd be just as freaked out about this as I am? That someone, like my fucking mother, would have told me this shit a long time ago? So she could prepare me for that sicko saying *hello*? Holy shit, I'm a member of the Line!" I get up and start pacing around the kitchen.

Lilith is the mother of all supernatural beings and her direct descendants are the ones who rule over us all.

Each species, whether they be succubae, incubi, werewolf or any other supe you can think of, have a few that can trace their lineage back to her. They are more powerful and have the ability to keep us in line. They are called the Line of Lilith. "Someone should have shared this shit."

"You should finish your food."

"You should leave me the fuck alone!" I start walking toward the door. "I need to get out of here."

Haines follows behind me. "Don't leave. You need to—"

"Wait a minute," I say, turning to face him. "What's your shtick? What are you getting out of this deal? You don't need me. And you're not doing this just to help me out. So," I say, jabbing my finger at his chest. "What do you get?"

He clears his throat and turns around.

"Bullshit! Don't you dare turn away from me." I grab his arm and spin him around to meet my gaze. "What's your perk? You get to screw someone just as powerful as you? Do you have some kind of wonder-cock that no other woman can take because you're a progeny of two of the first of our kind, and only my super-snatch can get you off?"

He scoffs and looks offended. "Deplorable. Does your mother know you talk like this?"

"I guess there's a lot of shit my mother and I don't know about each other." I step closer to him. "Nice switch, lover-boy. You almost made me forget what I asked you by trying to get me to focus on my mother. So, give it up. What do you get?"

"It's none of your business, little girl." He tries to turn around again but I step in front of him.

"What do you get, Haines? No more lies."

His ears flame red as he backs me against the wall. "Fine." He looks pissed. "You want to know what I get, Perrian?"

"Yes, just tell me the truth."

"I get to do something that makes my life and purpose complete."

"What? You get to fuck me and tame my needs?" I quote the vow that we took to one another.

"Yes, Perrian. Yes, I get to fuck you. And then I get to die."

Holy shit. I do have a super-snatch!

Chapter Six

"Having sex with me is going to kill you?" I back away from him and slam into the front door. "I could have killed you last night if we'd had sex?"

He laughs and shakes his head. "No, Perrian. It's not like that." He reaches out his hand, and I take it. He begins to draw little circles with his thumb on my knuckles as he guides me to the couch. "Come, let's sit down and I'll tell you the rest of what I know."

The simple touch of his hand on mine brings the memory of last night blazing to life. His lips on me, his tongue and teeth drawing the orgasm from my body. If I weren't scared out of my mind right now I just might drop to my knees and beg him to take me right here on the chair. The wall. The floor. Instead, I follow behind him, timidly, and sit down on the couch. Red and brown silk pillows litter the large, brown, C-shaped couch. I'm almost afraid to touch him. "Seriously, I'm going to need therapy after this. Please. Explain."

He takes off his jacket and pulls off his turtleneck revealing a black tee-shirt that hugs his contours perfectly. His nipples are small peaks and his six-pack bulges from beneath the thin fabric. *Wait a minute, that's an eight-pack!* I didn't even know they existed outside of romance novels. My breath hitches and I fight myself to keep from touching him. An image of Haines sweating, writhing against my begging body pops into my head, and I clamp my teeth down on my bottom lip to keep from moaning. He was only teasing last night. Goddess help me if we ever manage to actually have sex and he unleashes hundreds of years of his sexual experience on me.

"Cool off, cowgirl," he says jokingly. "We need to feed you properly or I think you will explode."

I shake my head. "Umm, I'm not having sex with you. I am not a killer. And I'm not an adulteress either, damn-it, which means I'll never have sex!" Woe to me!

"You won't kill me," he says with a chortle. "It's a gradual taking of power. My lineage is the reason Samael hasn't convinced me yet. My bloodline makes me so powerful he can't kill me. He can't kill you either. We're too strong. Our will to refuse him is too great. But that's what I'm getting out of our marriage."

I pull my legs under me and rest my arms on a red pillow. "I don't get it. Everything was starting to make sense and then you monkey-wrenched it."

It's never going to happen, is it? I am never having sex. It's impossible! I'll die a virgin. An angry, evil, multi-cat owning virgin who screams at Christmas carolers and kids who dress up for Halloween.

Maybe I'll join a nunnery. I'll be the mean nun who hits the hand of naughty children with a ruler, and I'll name the ruler Truth. Truth will be my only friend and…damn, he's still talking.

"Each time we have sex, I will allow you to pull power from me. It's voluntary. If I don't want to give it, I don't give it. But I want to."

"Why?"

"To make you strong. Our bloodlines were foretold, and neither one of us alone has the power to kill Samael. He's an angel. But together we're invincible. One of us, once strong enough, can lock him out of this plane of existence for good."

"Haines, seriously. I still don't follow. Why do you have to die? Why do you want to?"

His face becomes somber. "Because killing him is more important than me living. If I give you all of my power, let you feed and take it from me, I will become human."

"Ohh." Light bulb. "So I won't actually kill you. You get to—"

"Die a human death."

We sit in silence for a few moments while I process everything. And this is a lot to take in. Haines is a full-blooded demon. He can live forever. And because I'm a half-breed I'll eventually die of old age. In a few hundred years. Does he hate Samael so much that he would risk eternity? Is eternity worth it?

Too many questions. My mother is so going to get an earful when I talk to her.

"Umm…Haines?"

"Yes, Perrian?"

I clear my throat and begin to clean lint off my pants. "The first time we ahh…do the grown-up, can you not give me your life force? I'm already nervous about it and I don't want that hanging over me."

"I can agree to that. But please understand, I still need to hear you beg," he says with a smirk.

"Well I guess that settles it, I'll be virgin for a lot longer than I thought."

****

"Hey, Dad," I say, cradling the phone close to my ear. Haines has gone out to run some errands and I'm checking out every room in the house. Even though downstairs has a nice setup the rest of the house is bare and very basic. The bedrooms are white spaces with beds as the only interruptions. The bathrooms are white and plain. The hallways are long and empty. Ryan's husband needs to come decorate this place. The only room that looks lived in is Haines' bedroom. The walls are a shade of creamy beige that makes everything else in the room stand out. My toes sink into the plush white carpet and his larger than life cherry oak bed seems to erupt from the wall. Warm brown and blue hues cover every inch of the room. His phone sits on a beautiful brown bedside table that has a white porcelain circle in the middle.

"Hey, babe. Everything all right?"

I chose not to share everything I've learned today. My father has already had his fill of the 'other stuff' for at least a week. "Nope, but I'm good."

"Barb," my dad calls. "Perry is on the phone."

I hear soft talking in the background, and then my mother picks up. "Hi, Perrian. I'm a little busy right now, but—"

"I won't hold you long. Just wanted to tell you that my dearest husband has spilled his guts about why, and I am including you in this, we are so powerful."

"That son of a whore!"

"Hey! No talking about my mother-in-law that way. If I ever get to meet her then I'll let you know if she's actually a bad person."

"Why in Lilith's name would he... I'm going to shred him a new one."

"Oh, yeah. And Mother."

"That rat bastard..."

"Mother, please. I've saved the best for last."

"I told him *I* would let you know…"

"Mom, please. Can you—"

"How did you get it out of him? When I see him again—"

She's not going to let me talk here. "Samael says, 'What-up', Mother!"

Silence.

"And he called me Lady Bug. You know, as in the name dad used to call me until I was twelve years old. Freaky."

My mother is breathing hard, and I can hear the trembling in her breaths. "No. Oh, God, no."

"And, um, me and Haines haven't consummated our union yet. So, I'm not a full-on succubus, but that psycho just wanted to let me know he was around."

"Honey, I'm so sorry."

"Mom, seriously. I don't want your 'I'm sorry.' You should have shared this crap with me a *long* time ago."

"Please, don't be upset. I was trying to protect you."

I scoff. What the hell kind of protection is she offering? Ignorance is not always bliss. It's fun, but it doesn't last. "You didn't really do a good job. To keep that from me? And to not let me know that I would be taking Haines' immortality was just wrong. Can you even imagine how I feel right now?"

"Baby, I was—"

"I feel like you've betrayed me. Like I was being set up so I wouldn't even know I was turning him human and leaving him to die. Which is apparently what he wants."

"Perrian, you have to understand—"

"Mom, can I please finish?"

She stops talking but the silence is pregnant with her remorseful, ragged breaths. She's nervous.

"Mom, I'm not mad at you. I don't know how I feel. My first time hearing all this should have come from you."

"Perry, I was trying to protect you."

"That is so not a good reason. And I take back what I said, I am kinda upset with you. You hurt my feelings."

She sighs and I hear her cover the phone. She's whispering.

"Mom, please. Don't share this crap with dad. He'll have a freaking coronary."

She clears her throat. "Your dad is the one who suggested I not tell you everything."

"Aww! *Et tu,* Daddy!"

"Your dad and I wanted to ease you into this, honey."

Shit has seriously hit the fan. The fan is covered in shit! The only person in my life who I can trust is Haines. The thought makes my brain want to implode.

"Ease me, Mom?" They really need to rethink the whole 'protect Perry by lying to her' thing. "Easing me into this would have been like, 'Oh, Perrian. You're a succubus but you're more powerful than the rest of them.' Year two—'Perry, you are a descendent of Lilith.' Year three—'Hey Per, you're going to marry this douche bag and gradually take his immortality because a freaking angel is trying to annihilate our kind!' That's how you could have eased me into it, Mom and Dad!"

I'm going to start cursing in five-point-four seconds, damn-it! "Mom, I have to go," I say, staring at the beige ceiling. "I'll call you later."

My ears burn hot and a sour churning in my stomach gives way to a hollow feeling in my chest. My parents have lied to me and realizing that makes me want to cry and scream and hit.

She begins to protest and I slam the receiver down. The porcelain cracks and the brown wood splinters as the phone falls to the floor. Holy shitake mushrooms! Correction, I just slammed the phone through the base and through bedside table. That's never happened before. Note to self—getting angry makes you strong as an ape! The bond between Haines and me seems to be strengthening me even without the sex.

No, Haines! He and I were just starting to get along, a little, and this table looks really expensive. I can't let him see this!

Light bulb!

****

Chewing on my thumb, I'm crouching in the family room window behind a beige recliner waiting for Ryan's sweetie, Trent, to get home. He's an interior decorator and I need to find out where that stupid little table came from. I pray to Lilith that Trent can point me in the right direction to get a replacement. My legs are a bit stiff, and the inside of my right cheek is sore from chewing on it. So is my thumb. I've been hunkered down here for almost an hour praying that Haines won't get home before I can get my mitts on... Ohh, here he comes!

Before Trent can put his car in park I've already bounded out of the house, down the street and am standing in front of their house. I must look like a real idiot with my huge grin, strumming my fingers on Roman's mailbox.

"Hi, umm, Trent?"

"Hello?" he says tentatively, closing the gray car door and slowly walking toward me.

"I'm Perry. We waved to each other this morning? Ryan and I started talking, and he told me you were an interior designer." I still have that stupid grin plastered on my face.

Looks like I'm freaking him out. "Yes," he says, cautiously approaching me. "I am. Is everything all right? You're the woman who just married the hottie down the street?"

"Yup, that's me! Anyway, I have a little problem. Haines, my husband, had a really nice table—" Sulfur. I step a little closer and sniff him. "And you're a God damned demon!"

He shushes me. "Could you be any louder?" he says, slashing his hand in front of my face.

"Sorry." I must sound insane. "I'm a succubus. Cambion. You?"

"Chaos demon. Cambion."

He kind of smells like burning fruit. "Sorry dude. I just didn't know. You're not hurting my friend, are you?" I step closer to him and ball my hands into fists.

"Of course not! I would never hurt Ryan. Did you?" He looks pissed but doesn't come any closer.

"No! I like him."

Trent's once brown eyes begin to change to a deep green and the irises look amphibious. Ahh, yes. He thinks I'm trying to seduce his husband.

"Settle down, Trent. Yes, I'm a succubus and no I

didn't put the whammy on your husband."

I completely understand his concern. Succubae and incubi have a bad reputation in the demon community. Seduction is the key to almost anything. Amp up the power of seduction by being a demon of seduction and people, demons too, get a little uneasy.

His tongue is thinning and becoming pointed. "If you ever…"

"Calm down, cowboy." I take another step toward him. "I'm not going to hurt him. And just so you know, apparently, I'm from the Line of Lilith, and I don't know how to control myself quite yet and I'd hate to have to kick your ass out here."

His anger seems to abate once I tell him I'm from the Line. File under Mental Shelf 'Cool'—throwing around my weight as being a descendent of Lilith is awesome!

"In fact, Trent, that's why I'm here."

"Because you're from the Line?"

"No! Because I broke a table in the house and Haines is going to kill me. It's pretty and porcelain and looks expensive."

Immediately, his demon traits disappear. "You need help decorating? I can do that."

I guess that should have been the first thing I said.

Chapter Seven

"Jesus Christ! This table is three hundred fifty bucks."

Trent looks mortified. "Seriously, Perry. Lower your voice."

"Three hundred fifty fucking dollars!"

"Lower your freaking voice!" He's doing that whisper-yell thing I love to hear people do. "Just be happy I knew where we would find the table. You have a potty-mouth."

"So I've heard." I shake my head and pick up the table. "Come on. Let's get this baby home before Haines gets back. I haven't gotten a pissed off phone call or text yet so I'm still in the clear."

The aisles of the furniture store are clean and straight. No pillow out of place, no throw rug out of color order. Trent takes out a notepad and starts jotting down the prices of different items.

"So, Trent. Chaos demon. Interior designer?"

He smiles and continues to write. "Bringing order and making the most of all things messy brings me peace. It calms me down." He stops and picks up an action figure juice cup. "You can't imagine how it feels for me, a Chaos demon, to take the most disheveled, misused areas and turn them into efficient, beautiful works of art."

"Wow." I reposition the table and shrug. "That

makes sense. I'm glad for you. You're doing what makes you *not* cause anarchy. I'm trying not to kill men I have sex with."

We walk to the front of the store, and the cashier is looking at me strangely while I cradle the end table like a newborn. "Umm, Miss? We could have had someone bring that to the front for you. It's quite heavy, isn't it?" He clears his throat and takes the credit card I'm practically shoving in his face.

Dang-it, I wasn't paying attention. This thing probably weighs about seventy-five pounds. "Adrenaline," I say, shrugging. "I'm just so happy to find this thing! And we're in a hurry."

Trent looks at me, eyes wide, and puts the cup in a cart next to the register marked 'Return to Shelf.'

Cashier-guy smiles uncomfortably and hands me my receipt. Trent and I walk toward the door and when no one is around he starts his whisper-yell again.

"Oh. My. Goddess. What the heck is wrong with you? I hadn't even realized you picked it up until that guy almost had a stroke. That thing has to be at least sixty pounds. You're acting like a freaking newbie!"

I shake my head and put the table in the back of his car. "I kinda am. I haven't even had sex yet and I don't know what to do with myself! That little bit of energy I took from Haines last night is really something."

He slams the trunk after I put the table in and gives me an odd look. "You're still a virgin?"

"Umm, yeah. Not that it's any of your beeswax."

"Whoa," he says smiling. "You *must* be from the Line. Power is pretty much rolling off you *and* you're a virgin. A virgin sex demon."

"Yup. Powerful me."

"Oh my goodness." His face turns serious. "You do know that your kind is being hunted."

I turn away from him and head toward the passenger side door. "Yup. I know that, too." I slide in the car and slam the door. Guess it's time for one of those uncomfortable conversations. I've been having a lot of those lately.

Trent slips in beside me and starts the car. "Well, maybe it's better that you're a virgin. You don't have your powers yet."

Maybe life would be easier if that were the case. Unfortunately, it's not. I'm so freaking powerful I've got angels of the Lord coming to pay me a visit.

"You haven't been paying attention, have you? I'm strong. Really strong. And after me and Haines do the grown-up, I'll be super-uber strong and super-uber hunted by that super-uber creepy angel."

"But Perry, you don't have to do it."

"Are you insane? I think I'll die if I don't do it soon."

He laughs and settles in to his seatbelt. "You can't die from lack of sex. And you can't miss what you've never had."

"Says who? Let me rephrase that. I think *I'll* start killing people if I don't have sex soon."

The rest of the drive is in silence. He seems to be genuinely concerned about me dying. Since I was a teenager I never really had friends, but he and Ryan seem to be my new best buds. Well, at least Ryan is. I apprehended Trent so that kind of makes him my friend. He didn't tell me to get the hell away from him.

We pull into the neighborhood, and I don't see Haines' car. I am victorious!

"Dude, thanks for helping me with this. And thanks for your concern about me dying."

"You're welcome." He laughs and hits the button to open the back of the car. "I heard that angel is pretty scary."

"Pretty freaky is more like it. He looks like a child with the body of a really tall basketball player."

"I'd like to never meet him." He touches my hand and gives me a wary smile. "I'll help you get that in the house and then you can come sit with me and Ryan until your husband gets home. Maybe you could come with me when I go pick up Roman from school."

I get what he's saying even if he's doing me the honor of not saying it. "Thanks, but I'm okay with being alone. I'm not afraid of him. I'm not giving in."

His voice is low. "I had a friend who said that, too. He's gone now."

"I'm not going anywhere. Line of Lilith, remember?" I open the car door and head straight to the trunk for the table.

Trent gets out and helps me bring it in the house. "Well, we must keep up appearances," he says, helping me carry the table. "We don't want our neighbors to see your short self pick up that table all by your lonesome."

He helps me bring it in and we take it upstairs and put it in the place of the original.

"What are you going to do with the broken one?" He picks up the smashed pieces and heads back downstairs.

"Can you take it with you? Put it out with the trash on Friday?" It would be hard to explain the broken table in the backyard when Haines takes out the garbage.

"Sure. No problem." He still looks a little sad. He's

already mourning me, and I haven't gone anywhere.

"Trent? Why so glum?"

"You have something about you, did you know that?"

He's certainly not attracted to me so it can't be the sex-demon thing I have going on. "It must be my ladylike ways and sense of style that pulls you to me." I still have on my sweatpants from this morning's speed walk.

"Yeah, that must be it." His smile is honest. "You know, there are only about one hundred of you guys left? Like, in the whole world."

"Oh. I didn't know that."

"Yeah. There are hundreds of thousands of us half-breeds walking around this beautiful rock."

"Thanks, Trent."

We walk down the steps toward the garage. I give him a box to put the broken table pieces in. Just in case Haines sneaks up on us, Trent can smuggle the goods out of the house without them being seen.

"I didn't mean to put a damper on your day, Perry."

It's already been dampered. Crazy angels can really damper things. I shrug and sit down on the family room couch. "It's cool. You'd never know I just found out all this stuff about a murdering angel, and my bloodline all in the last"—I look down at my watchless wrist—"twelve hours. I think I'm taking it pretty good. I still don't have the whole story." I give him a sideways glance. "Wanna be part of my investigation crew? There's chocolate zucchini bread involved."

He looks thoughtful, and then a huge smile breaks across his face. "I am so in! You can keep that veggie bread crap. Ryan can help, too. He can research stuff like nobody's business."

"Ryan knows you're a demon?"

"Of course. Full disclosure. A partner is someone you can share everything with." He wrinkles his nose. "Eww. Chocolate covered veggie bread makes me want to vomit."

"You've never tasted my chocolate veggie bread. It's awesome."

"Mmm-hmm." He sits down next to me. "You know. There really is something about you. Demons have a kind of *thing,* and you don't have that *thing.*"

"Is that a good *thing*?"

Trent puts the box on the floor. "I don't know. It's some*thing*," he says, laughing.

"Says the demonic, gay, interior designer. An oxymoron wrapped in cliché."

He looks around the room and smiles tightly. "I could really work wonders with this place. It's nice but it's just so blah."

I purse my lips. "You know, since your place is so awesome, I could try to convince Haines to let you run loose in here and make it pretty. You could charge him double what you usually charge people."

Shrugging, Trent takes another look around the room and laughs. It's a genuine sound that makes me feel calmer. That look of sorrow over whether I will live or die has faded. He's looking at me like I'm a person now. Not someone to be pitied. He and I will be good friends, but I feel a better connection to his husband. With them I don't have to hide who I am or worry about getting too emotional and causing them to want me.

The sound of an approaching engine catches my attention. I jump up when I see Haines' car pull up in the driveway. "Dude, say nothing to Haines. This is just between us."

He nods his head and picks up the box.

"Oh, and Trent, Operation Investigation Crew is so on!" We can call ourselves the OIC. We'll get shirts made with an angel in a circle with a line drawn through it, and OIC will be bedazzled on the back of it. That's if I don't get murdered first.

We hear the *click* of Haines unlocking the door and Trent starts jogging in place, his coat billowing around him. "Oh my Goddess. Should I leave out of the back door?"

Crap, the broken table pieces. "No. That would really look suspicious. Just close the lid on the box and keep it short."

Trent puts the box back on the floor and sits down on the couch.

Haines walks through the door and sees Trent and me sitting uncomfortably on the couch, trying to look normal. He looks back and forth between us and then zeros in on Trent.

"Chaos demon, I suspect?"

I don't like the way he's looking at my new buddy. I stand up and walk toward Haines. "You'd suspect right. And he's my friend, so be nice."

"Perrian, why must you insist that I am not a nice person?"

"Because you're giving him the stink-eye." I make a mistake and kick the box. "He's my friend."

"Amazing," Haines says, looking at the box. "You've made two friends today. Using your feminine wiles?"

Trent starts laughing so hard he can't sit up straight.

"Yup, that's it." I smirk and point at Trent. "He and his husband, my other new buddy, are dying to get my goods."

Trent and I laugh, but the joke seems to have flown right over Haines' head. I needed this. The past few days have been so tense and stressful. Yes, I had a beautiful wedding but it was to a man I can't look at without wanting to punch him in the face, and then hop on that same face like an equestrian happily galloping away to the land of Orgasma. My parents have been lying to me my entire life, and I had to take a vacation from work without the proper notification. Yeah, that last part was my fault but I'll be damned if I will admit it.

It's all Haines' fault. Everything is.

Trent stands up and shakes Haines' hand. "Nice to meet you. I'm Trent."

"Haines," he says with a devilish smile. "All this time and I didn't know a demon was living in the neighborhood."

I interrupt before Haines starts asking questions. "Don't forget to tell Ryan I'm making brunch later this week."

"You've got it, Perry. Bye you two." Trent bends down, picks up the box and casually walks out.

Pretty good. I thought he would flinch.

I watch him walk toward his house and then close the door. I have two new friends. All in one day.

"Should I ask what was in the box, Perrian?"

"You can ask."

He takes the hint and moves on. "Have you talked to your mother?"

"Yes. It didn't go well. I'm not speaking to her right now."

"Perrian, I'm sure there is a perfectly good—"

"So, Haines. What have you been up to?" We don't need to talk about my mother right now. Any information I find out is either going to come from Haines or my Operation Investigation Crew buddies.

He walks toward the closet next to the front door. "I visited my lawyer's office."

"Ready for the annulment?" I watch the muscles ripple under his shirt as he takes off his jacket and hangs it in the closet. My eyes make their way up his body as he walks toward me, and my heart rate increases. An unsteady feeling starts in my chest and my skin begins to tingle, like gentle fingers dancing their way across my body. Good God, that man is sexy.

His wide shoulders slope down to beautifully formed arms that look strong and warm. I'm not a small woman but I bet he could pick me up, hold me tight and never break a sweat. Hold me against the shower wall while his cock slid in and out of me, and I'd never worry if I was too much for him to hold.

He smiles but doesn't say anything as he slips off his brown shoes and puts them by the unlit fireplace. "Not quite. I added you to all of my accounts. You are my wife, and you should have access to everything." He sits down across from me and chews on his bottom lip. "How are you doing that?"

A warm sensation engulfs my most sensitive areas. The fine hairs along my skin react as if Haines is caressing me, running his hands along the exposed area of my neck and arms. "I'm not doing anything." My voice is heavy. What the hell just happened? Here I am just sitting on the couch being really annoyed, and now I feel like I've had about two glasses of wine. Ardent, loose, and tingly.

"Yes, you are. You're feeding from me." He looks confused and intrigued. "May I?" he says, touching my chin and moving his face close to mine. "Do you feel satiated?"

I think it over for a moment and push my face closer to his, rubbing my cheek along his chin. "Yes. Kind of." A little more wouldn't hurt.

"You shouldn't be doing what you're doing." He takes his nose and rubs it against mine, and Lilith help me if I'm not on fire for him. "Centuries old succubae and incubi can do this. You weren't even touching me."

"Can I? Touch you?"

His pupils double in size, and his breathing increases. He looks hesitant and thrilled. "Please do."

I reach forward and run my hands up and down his arms. Little sparks of electricity buzz from him to me and back again. This came out of nowhere. I've been fighting it, but when I'm around him too long I want to touch him and have him touch me. I'd give anything to have him buried deep inside me. Hands wrapped around my shoulders as he drives himself into me, over and over. I'd welcome the pain of my first time just to have him claim me, make me scream, make me come, make me beg.

He looks at me curiously as I touch him, moving my hands from his arms to his chest, up his neck, raking my fingernails over his scalp. I pinch his hair for a bit of leverage and pull him to me, inhaling his clean scent. I bite his chin. A low *hiss* flows from his mouth and I smile, feeling his warm breath blow across my cheek.

"Perrian," he whispers, bringing his lips close to mine. "What are you doing?"

I lick his bottom lip and feel a slight surge of energy, and oh Goddess, it fills me up and urges me on. Haines said that my power must be like electricity, but the energy roiling from him and sating me is volcanic. "I don't know. It feels right, doesn't it?"

"Indeed, it does." He runs his hands up my legs, to my hips, and pulls me closer to him. "Keep feeding."

"I don't think I know how to stop." I let him pull me closer to him. Holy crap. I'm going to take the man's immortality. "This is bad. I don't want to take too much. Is this bad?"

"Not for me," he says. His hands rub soothing circles on my back as light butterfly kisses cover my face and neck, his eyes fixated on me the whole time. "A human would be sprawled out on the floor."

His lips are close to mine, and his eyelashes tickle my eyelids as he blinks.

"I don't know what I'm doing, Haines."

"Keep doing it. It's all right," he says, comforting me.

We've somehow managed our way to the floor, me sitting on top of him with my legs behind him, his legs crossed and his cock making a tent of his pants. Haines runs his nose along the side of my jaw, up to my ear. He whispers nonsensical words as his power seems to softly pour into me, filling me. If only his cock was filling me too, I'd be the best little wife he'd ever asked for. Anything he required I would give to him. If I could just feel him dancing inside me. Even now I can hear the song that would spur him along. The rapid beats of our hearts and pants of our breaths bringing us closer, making us hate each other just a little less each time we feed.

He slides his hands up my ribs and over my breasts, held close to me by the constricting bra. He kisses the small spot between my lips and my cheek. "I'd like to try something, if you don't mind." His hand dips beneath the drawstring of my sweatpants, past the elastic of my panties.

A wave of nerves hits me but my lust pushes it back. I nod my head, giving him permission, fearing the words won't come out right.

His hand moves between us and continues its descent until his thumb is on my clit. I jump as his fingers part my saturated folds. My breath catches in my throat as he begins delicate, slow circles.

"So wet for me. Only for me," he says, his voice a deep growl that resonates through me. "I could fuck you right now, here on this floor. Should I let you pass this time? Not make you beg for my cock? Hmm? I bet you would, Perry." His tongue snakes between my lips as he kisses me. I grind my hips into his hand, trying to add to the pressure that's already building.

"Keep feeding," he says, his voice heavy and raspy.

I don't think I could stop if I tried. A moan escapes my lips as I kiss him, feeling him touching me, claiming my mouth. One of his hands holds me to him, gently gripping the back of my neck as if he's trying to pull me into him.

"I won't stop," he says, almost as an apology for

last night. "Don't stop feeding. Take from me. Give me your orgasm. Feed me, wife."

"Oh, God." I sigh, breaking our kiss and wrapping my arms around his neck. I whisper his name and drag my fingers up his back and through his hair.

He pulls away from me and looks me in the eyes. "Kiss me," he says, breathing hard, a light sheen of sweat appearing across his brow.

Our lips crash into one another and I grind my hips against his hand, wishing he was inside me.

An upward climb begins as the pressure builds in my body.

"You like to fuck my hand, Perry? Will you come for me?" he says, smiling between kisses. "I can feel you coming."

I nod my head, loving the filthy words that fall from his mouth, and feel a flood begin as his power continues to fill me.

Haines pulls my shirt and bra up over my breasts and the cold air of the room contrasts so deliciously from the heat of his hands. He kneads my breasts, while his other hand continues the relentless circles. I'd like to cry. To scream. But his energy pouring into me quells my voice.

"Come now," he says, pinching my nipple and biting the column of my neck.

And I fall.

An explosion from within takes hold of me, and I throw my head back, a deep moan flowing from my lips that distort his name, feeling him fill me with a power I never knew was possible.

Upside down. All gravity seems to have left the planet and Haines is the only thing keeping me from flying away. I fall apart as he watches me, tears streaming down my face. A feeling of euphoria that surpasses any carnal craving I've ever achieved by myself. I bury my face in his neck pulling him to me as he caresses my back and whispers sweet things to me— you are beautiful, you are powerful, Perrian. My Perrian. My sweet, sweet girl.

Chapter Eight

A light snoring wakes me up as Haines and I sit here wrapped around each other.

"Perrian, you've fallen asleep."

I shake my head and burrow myself deeper into his embrace. "No, I didn't. You were snoring."

He laughs and pinches my clit. "Hey!" I pull away from him and stretch. "That was pretty awesome. I've never had an orgasm with another person before. Unless we're calling Clarence, my handy vibrator, a real person. Which we're not."

"A lover of yourself?"

I glare at him and smile. "Never had a choice, really. I didn't want to hurt anyone." I stretch again and lay my head on his shoulder. "I feel wonderful. Honestly, I've never felt like this before. Satisfied. Really, really full. Not in an 'I haven't eaten all day' way, but…"

"Really, you've never been fed. You consume food but your demon side has been starving for…Perrian?"

My skin feels like it's getting warmer and I can't catch my breath. Pin-pricks start at my toes and work their way up my body. "Something's wrong." I pull away from him and scoot back on to the couch.

He looks confused. "You're coming into your powers? We haven't had sex." A proud look blankets his face, and he grabs my hand and kisses it. "You are powerful. You…you *are* very warm."

"Get off," I tell him, moving further away and crawling back onto the couch. "Oh, God! Is this what it's like?" I grab my stomach and double over.

"No. Not at all. You shouldn't be in any pain. Quite the opposite."

A scream rips through my body as I throw my head back. "Something…it burns!" I feel like I'm being ripped in half.

Haines grabs my shoulders. "This isn't right," he whispers. "This isn't supposed to happen."

My skin burns from his touch. "Get off!" I yell, shoving him away from me.

As my hand connects with his chest, Haines flies across the room and bounces off the wall, knocking over a lamp. He looks dazed for a minute but gets up and runs toward me. He reaches out to touch me but thinks better of it.

"Haines, I'm…sorry. I didn't mean…"

"It's okay, Perry. It's all right."

I double over again, praying that whatever is going on will stop. Please, God, make it stop. Am I dying? Did I wait too long to sate my demon and now I'm unable to feed?

"Haines, please, help me." The tears that roll down my face sting my cheeks and chin. Everything hurts. It's as if my clothes should singe away from embers that should be oozing out of my pores.

"Perrian, I don't know what to do."

The ripping sensation intensifies until it feels like the top of my body will separate itself from the bottom; like my right side will tear away from the left. Like my insides are boiling. I close my eyes and wait.

Wait for it to stop. Wait to die.

Something seizes my body and yanks me upward. And the pain stops.

I don't feel anything. It's quiet. Only the sound of my breathing echoes in my head. Am I dead?

Haines' voice is soft. "Perrian? Baby, open your eyes." Though his voice sounds strong and grounded, a wavering tremble breaks though, and I can tell he's afraid for me.

My limbs are flat against a hard surface, but the pain is gone. I open my eyes and see Haines looking up at me.

And I'm looking down at him. Because I'm on the ceiling. Looking down at him. I begin to speak, but a violent cough erupts from me and frothy blood pours from my mouth, covering Haines' chin and shirt. I begin to fall, but it's not slow like in the movies. It's fast. The floor is fast approaching. The only thing I see are Haines' arms reaching out to grab me.

And then there is darkness.

Chapter Nine

"Did you call her parents?"

"No. She doesn't want to see them right now."

"Well, you'd better call someone to figure out what the hell happened to her."

My eyes are closed, and I'm lying on something. A bed? The couch?

I'm glad Haines hasn't called my mom and dad. They are the two people who have lied to me the most. Right now, I need the truth. I may not make it through another whatever the hell just happened to me.

"Who do you think we should call, Haines?"

I finally muster up enough strength to talk. "Ghostbusters?" I almost just floated through the ceiling like a ghost.

"Holy crap!" Ryan sounds relieved. "You're awake."

Haines comes and sits down next to me. On the bed in my room. His shirt is still bloody from my cough and a few flecks of red cover his cheek. "Can I get you anything?"

I try to sit up, but a deep pressure in my chest stops me. "Water. A doctor? That blood was foamy."

Haines puts his hand on my stomach to make me lie back down. "I believe you punctured a lung." He clears his throat, looks at Ryan and then back to me. "And you had internal bleeding."

Ryan grimaces. "Internal bleeding?"

"Yes," Haines says, lifting up my shirt. "Blood was pooling on the right side of her belly, but you've healed." He runs his hand up and down my side.

"I'm guessing that's not what us sex demons do?"

He smiles. "Not as fast as you did. You had your...episode about two hours ago. About twenty minutes after you passed out I *heard* your bones mend." He shakes his head and looks over at the closet where I put my clothes last night. "It would take days and a few feedings for me to heal from something like that. And I'm strong."

I think he's avoiding eye contact. Maybe he thought I was going to die in his living room while he stopped himself from calling my parents. Hell, they wouldn't have been able to do anything.

Ryan touches my hand. "What the hell happened to you?"

I shrug. "I have no idea. That's not what it's like to come into your powers, is it?"

Haines shakes his head. "No. I don't know what happened to you." A line forms between his eyes and I can see the frustration on his face.

I look at Ryan. "Where are Trent and Roman? How did you get here?"

"Trent is at home with Roman helping him with homework. He's also trying to figure out what happened to you." He looks at Haines. "Your sweetie here called me."

Haines gives me a weary smile. "I didn't know what to do. They are your friends." He uses his index finger and massages the center of his forehead. "I figured you'd want a friend near. I knew you didn't want me to call your parents. So I didn't."

Haines is being nice. Really nice. I like this Haines.

"He didn't want to upset you," Ryan chimes in. "We'll straighten this out. I did find out a few things while you were sleeping."

I try to laugh, but it hurts my chest. "You two are awesome. Not even a whole day has gone by and you're figuring stuff out."

Ryan frowns. "It may not be what you want to hear. Maybe we should—"

"Lay it on me."

"Perry, really, maybe we should wait?"

I shake my head. "Ryan, there is no better time than right now, damn-it! What is it?"

Ryan looks to Haines for help. "Neither you or Haines, or the two of you together, can kill Samael. A demon can't kill an angel. It's like impossible."

I look at Haines and he shakes his head. "We don't know for certain."

"Dude, I checked like three sources," Ryan says, rubbing my hand. "A demon can't do the job. Even if Perry takes your power, she's still a demon. And she's half human."

Haines sighs. "You are wrong."

I touch Haines' hand and look into his eyes. A desperate anger shows on his face, and I see it—a look of hopelessness. A hope for revenge, dying. Samael has taken someone close to him, and maybe me killing him is the only hope Haines has left.

I won't give up, and I won't let him give up either.

I smile at him. "We'll find a way. There has to be something." I scoot down farther in the bed. "But we'll talk about it later, okay? I'm really tired." I never did get that water.

"Of course." Haines pulls the blanket up to my chin and smiles at me. "Do you want to change your clothes first?"

I shake my head. Taking off my clothes might hurt a little too much. My goal for the next hour is to get comfortable and heal enough so I can take a shower without the fear of falling over.

Haines smiles at me and nods. He can be nice. When he's not being a dick.

****

"Haines! Something is wrong!"

I can hear Ryan yelling but I can't move. I can't open my eyes or scream out in pain. My body is shaking, and tears are running down my face. The soft bed hurts as it presses against my skin. The skin on my hand feels like it's going to blister off as Ryan holds it, trying to comfort me.

If you let go, Lady Bug, it won't hurt anymore. Samael's voice is soothing. The crazy bastard!

Bite me! I'm not letting anything go.

"Get off her," Haines says calmly to Ryan.

"I ain't gonna hurt her!" Ryan sounds wounded.

"Earlier, she said it hurt when I touched her."

Ryan drops my hand. "You have to call someone."

"Her parents haven't been that forthcoming about anything. Not to her and not to me. This shouldn't be happening."

Come on, Perry. You know you want to.

Go away! Wait, why are you in my head? Get out!

"Do you hear that?" Ryan asks.

"Yes," Haines says, almost growling. "It's her bones breaking."

"Look, you need to find someone who knows how to help her." Ryan lowers his voice. "What if she dies?"

"Ryan, please. She's not going to die."

"She's changing!" A sing-song voice sounds off in the room. It's Samael.

"Oh, dear lord!" Ryan yells.

"Help her or get out." Haines' voice is deadly.

"Nothin' I can do." Samael's voice is getting closer.

"Please."

I wish I could open my eyes. Not being able to see scares me. I don't know if Samael will try to hurt one of them, or me. I'll focus on their voices. It's better than trying to ignore or breathe through the pain that racks my body.

"You know, Haines, she really does like you." Samael is standing next to me. I can feel the crazy pouring off him. "Lady Bug may curse and look at you like she wants to stab you in the face, but you're starting to grow on her. All fungus-like."

"Please." To listen to Haines is heartbreaking. His voice is usually so casual and strong and sure. But now he's pleading for me. "Make this stop."

"Especially with what y'all did this afternoon." He sounds disgusted. "Woo-doggie. She's stronger than any of us thought she'd be. Wait till you tell her mommy and daddy. They. Will. Freak!" I hear him clapping.

"Get out!" Haines and Ryan say in unison.

"Oh, lookie-lookie! She's gonna do it again."

"Do wha—" Ryan starts.

My body is yanked upward, and I hit the ceiling, hard. The initial shock is painful, but the cool feel of the paint is almost comforting.

"If you can hear me, Lady Bug, and I'm pretty sure can, you come to me when your parents lie to you. Again. And *I'll* tell you the truth. The whole truth and nothing but it, baby. Then you'll know exactly what you got yourself in to, Haines."

A scream finally explodes from my mouth when I feel and hear a grinding noise. My bones are mending. Grinding all my teeth against a chalkboard everyday once an hour would be better than this.

All at once the pain is gone. And I'm falling.

Strong arms catch me before I hit the bed.

****

I open my eyes to a white ceiling stained with bloody handprints. My bloody handprints. There's a splatter in the middle where blood must have oozed out of my mouth. Or my ear.

Soft breathing catches my attention. I glance over and see Haines. He looks tired as he sits across from me. He must have brought a chair upstairs from the kitchen.

"You know," I say, "you should really get Trent to decorate this place. Then you wouldn't have to bring a kitchen chair upstairs just to have a place to sit."

A light smile crosses his face. "You and Trent can work on decorating the house when you get better." He comes and sits on the bed. "How are you feeling?"

My voice wavers. "I'm fine." Tears begin to fall, and I thank Lilith it doesn't hurt my face. "But I'm afraid. I can't do that again. I don't think I'll make it."

"You'll be fine."

"I don't know if I can hold on if it happens again. Maybe something is wrong with me. Maybe I should just let—"

Haines touches my lips with his fingers. "Never think that again. You'll be fine."

I shake my head. Maybe Samael did something to me to make my change go all wonky. This is terrible. I don't think my body can take that again. I don't think my sanity can take it again. "We have to find someone to help me."

He bites his bottom lip. "I called your mother."

"I was just starting to like you, Haines." I know he wants to help but I don't want any more lies. "Why would you call her?"

"Because I don't know what to do." He moves a stray hair from my face. "I can't listen to your bones break and heal or watch you turn blue because blood is pooling beneath your skin."

I laugh. "You wuss."

"Call me what you will."

It's dark outside. "What time is it?"

"About five."

I haven't been asleep that long.

"In the evening. On Tuesday. You've been unconscious for almost twenty-four hours."

Wow. "What time should my mom get here?" I look down at my clothes. They should be covered in blood. I haven't changed them since… "My clothes?"

"Yes, I ahh…bathed you last night and changed your clothes." He almost looks bashful.

"So, you got to see my goods, eh?"

He clears his throat. "Your parents should be here soon. Barbara said she would call the witch that led her to me. It's a start."

"Can you get me some water? I'm kind of afraid to

move."

"I did have water and a sandwich waiting for you that Ryan made before he left, but I ate it. I didn't want to leave you."

Less than twenty-four hours and Ryan and Trent are our new besties. I hate that word—besties.

Haines stands up quickly. "Yes. I'll be right back."

He walks out of the room, and I can hear him running down the hallway. I guess he wants to be here if I go all ouchy and floaty again.

I don't want to be here if I go ouchy and floaty again. I can't go through it another time. It may sound like a bad move, but if this is the norm, Samael will have one more of us to add to his list.

"Lilith," I say to an empty room. "If you can hear me, please help me. Tell me to keep going or tell me to let go. Tell me something."

"You may not let go."

"Lilith?"

"No, you dolt, it's me."

"Aunt Rita!" God no! "Are you Lilith?" Her round face peeks from behind the door.

"No, you silly girl. I'm just a witch who knows a little too much."

My mother and father trail in behind her, followed by Haines who looks completely murderous.

I sit up in bed as Haines hands me a glass of water. "You know, I didn't want my dearest husband to call either of you. But you," I say, shaking my finger at Aunt Rita. I look at Haines. "Why didn't you tell me the witch was my Aunt Rita? Or should I just call you Rita?"

He looks confused. "I didn't know it was your

Aunt Rita. She looks different."

Different. That's one word we could use. She looks less like the round hag with eerily glowing eyes and too many teeth than my slightly plump aunt. Great cover.

Rita huffs and takes off her jacket. "I've lost weight. Two hundred and eighty pounds really changes the way people look at you." She winks at me. "Your mom brought you to me to do a reading when you were sixteen, when your mom was ready to admit to herself that you were different. Before that I was just your homebound, weird aunt that you barely came to visit." She sits on my bed and puts her palm to my forehead. "And you can't blame Haines, dear. I always change my appearance when I'm in my 'lair.' It's to protect all who come to seek my advice. Though I may not be your blood relative I am still your aunt and you may not call me 'Rita.' I've been around since before you were born."

My father sits down next to *Aunt* Rita. "Your aunt has helped to keep you safe. Our other brothers and sisters don't speak to me anymore."

I smile at him. "Because you're a liar? Because you married a liar? People usually don't like to be lied to, Dad."

My mother comes to stand next to my dad. "Don't talk to your father like that, Perrian."

"Do you know what she's been through the past few days?" Haines' voice is low and his hands are shaking. He must really like me! "You weren't here to listen to her bones break, to see blood pour out of her ears and nose—"

"It did!" I interrupt.

"—to watch her limbs contort while she slept as

her bones healed! I listened to her breathing slow to the point where I thought she was going to die."

My mother stands up and points at Haines. "Who do you think you are? You two don't even like one another."

"In some way I've cared about her since we met. We may not get along perfectly, but…"

I shrug. "He's all right. I don't hate him." I look at Haines and smile. "I kinda like him now."

My mother steps closer to him. "She's *our* daughter so you can—"

"And now she's my wife. Either tell us what you know or get the hell out of our house."

Wow. Our house. Haines does like me. A lot.

Everyone is silent while auntie and I stare between my mother and Haines. Looks like they may wrestle it out. Haines may be bigger but my money is on my mom.

I tug on Haines' shirt to get him to back off. "Should we clear the floor so you two can scrap?"

"Well," Aunt Rita says. "That was uncomfortable. Back to Perry. What did you two tell her?"

"Nothing," Haines and I answer.

"She's a succubus and human mix," Haines says. "*I* told her about Lilith and the three women who are our ancestors, and that they are the reason we are so strong."

"And that's all we know." I think it over for a minute. "Oh, and that I'll be taking Haines' immortality and killing Samael."

"Oh, boy!" Aunt Rita laughs and points at my parents. "That's…that's wh-what you told her?" She's laughing so hard she can barely speak.

"Harty-frickin har, Auntie."

Once she's finished laughing she sits up and wipes the tears from her eyes. "You two!" she says, pointing at my parents. "That is horrible. Shall I do the honor or would you like to do it?" In their silence she takes her queue. "Let me start." She turns to me and takes my hand. "Let me clear one thing up, darling. You are not human. Not one bit."

I glare at my father.

Aunt Rita understands my look. "Oh, Perry. He is your father. And yes, he is human. But he wasn't always human."

I look back to my dad. "Take it away, Dad. I want the truth. And if I don't think you're being completely honest with me, I'll ask Samael."

My father looks horrified. "Stay away from him, Perry."

"Then start talking because I'm done with the bullshit."

He takes off his hat and rubs his bald head.

"Now, Dad."

Chapter Ten

My father sits down on the bed beside my mother and gazes at her as if she's the most beautiful thing he's ever seen in his life. I never noticed until just now that he's always looked at her like that. When I was growing up even if they were arguing, which they rarely did, his eyes never lost the look of reverence for her. How am I just realizing that he loves her more than the air he breathes? Will I ever have that with Haines?

"I met your mom a long time ago, Perry. She was beautiful and lively." He rubs his thumb along her cheekbone and smiles. "I knew from the moment I saw her that I would give up everything to be with her. If she'd have me."

"I was completely afraid." My mother glances at him and grins like a schoolgirl with a brand new crush. "No one had ever done what we did."

"Eww," I say, with a look of disgust. If this is where we're going then they can keep this story to themselves. I've had enough pain and suffering this week.

My father touches my mother's hand. "Not like that, Lady Bug."

I feel a shudder ripple through my body as visions of Samael begin to dance in my head. "Let's pause this for a moment." I put my hands up. "Samael's new nickname for me is Lady Bug. So, Daddy, I'd like you to never call me that again. But please, continue."

He frowns and shakes his head. His look is almost sentimental. "Your mother can trace her lineage back to Lilith and Naamah, the first two succubae turned by Samael. I knew it was forbidden to be with her, to be with a demon. I tried to blame it on her powers, but that wasn't it. I was immune to her call."

"Barbara," says Haines. "Why were you afraid of him?"

"Because our kind aren't supposed to mix. It was unheard of." She looks at my father. "I met your dad in 1712 in Italy. I'd seen him through the years, but we'd never actually talked."

I close my eyes to clear my thoughts. "Let's pause this again. What?"

"I'd been around for millennia, Perry," my father says. "And your mother was the one thing that made me want time to stand still. The one thing that made me want to give it all up."

Haines comes and sits next to my pillow. "Give up what?"

"Grace," my father says, pulling my mother's hand to his lips and kissing her palm. "She was the only thing anywhere, in any dimension or plane of existence that made me want to forsake my grace."

Bells, whistles, and light bulbs go off. They met over three hundred years ago. He'd been around for millennia. Grace. Grace is the kicker. "Dad, you were an angel?"

"Yes."

"Holy fuck."

My mother's voice is stern. "Watch your mouth, Perrian Ettis."

"Jesus, you two." Aunt Rita stands up and goes to sit in the kitchen chair in the corner of my bedroom. "You never told her anything?"

"Keep talking," I tell my dad.

He laughs. "Do I need to continue?"

"Keep Goddamned talking!" How could he laugh? This isn't funny. I'm half angel and half demon, and no one thought to share this with me? To hear his empty laugh hurts more than the changes my body has been going through. Almost.

My father excuses my tone and continues. "Your mother and I had trysts, tried to keep our relationship a secret. And then twenty-six years ago, we found out she was pregnant. With you."

He tries to touch my hand but I pull away from him.

He stares down at the vacant space where my hand once was and frowns. "I knew I wanted to be with you and your mother but we couldn't simply live as a demon and an angel. So, I made the plunge. I loved her so much. And to know she was carrying my child made me love her even more. So, I stood on a cliff in Heaven, looked down at your mother, and jumped. I gave up my grace, but I gained so much more."

"What was Heaven like?" I ask.

My father winces. "I don't remember. I try sometimes, but I can't. After I woke up in your mother's arms the memories of Heaven started disappearing."

Haines hands me a handkerchief from his pocket. I hadn't even realized I was crying. "This is how you tell me? By having me threaten to talk to Samael? How could you do this to me? How could you lie to me like this?"

"Perrian," my mother says. "We didn't even know how to begin. There has never been anyone like you before."

I want to hate them right now. Hate them for lying to me. Hate them for not preparing me for Samael. "So if I'm half angel, why is Samael trying to kill me? I'm like him."

"Oh, no dear," Aunt Rita says. "You are not like him. And you're not like your mother or Haines. To Samael, you are an abomination that needs to be done away with. But your demon and angel sides make you immortal, so your essence would live on. He can't simply kill you. He probably wouldn't even know how to."

My father nods. "There is a great chance you'd be reborn as an angel."

"And that, my dear niece, is why Samael is itching to get his hands on you," Rita says, rubbing her arms as if a chill has set in. "An angel-demon hybrid reincarnated as an angel? Only God knows what would come of that."

Haines strokes my hair. "That's why he needs you to give in to him, like the other succubae and incubi have done. And that's why you have to kill him. If he absorbs your essence he won't need demons to give in to him. He'd be able to kill them without any thought at all."

A huge weight descends upon me. I'm supposed to get rid of Samael, an angel, so that he'll stop annihilating our kind. Me. The 'me' who just found out who she was and what she was supposed to do.

I sneak a look at my mother and instantly feel like

crap. She's proud of me; proud of what she thinks I can do. Yesterday, I could see it on her face. Hear it in her voice. She's frightened of Samael. I've never known her to be frightened of anything. Why should she be? She's a badass succubus who can kick butts, take names, and look hot in the process. Her life is up for grabs.

I look up at Haines. "You heard Ryan. I can't kill him."

Aunt Rita laughs. "Yes, you can, honey. If anyone can, it's you. You are part angel. And only an angel can kill another angel. God can kill Samael, but He can kill anything."

"What's happening to her body?" Haines asks.

Oh, yeah. I forgot about the hot, searing, praying-for-death pain I've been in. Hearing your father was an angel will do that to you.

"You poor girl." Aunt Rita comes and rubs my arm. "Your body is changing into something else. You'll still look like you, but you'll be stronger. Faster. Your bones will be denser. You will truly be immortal." She looks from me to Haines. "Did you ah…consummate your marriage?"

I look at my parents. "Not that it's any of your business, but no. We did um, something, but for all intents and purposes I'm still a virgin."

Her eyes become slits. "Haines, you demon, how did you feed her?"

He looks at my parents and frowns. "It was unlike anything I've ever experienced." Haines looks proud, but once he realizes my parents are giving him the evil eye he calms down. "And that's all we'll say about that. More importantly, how long will it last?"

She frowns. "Perry, how many times have you changed?"

"Twice. Please tell me two is the magic number."

Rita shakes her head. "No darling. It will never stop."

"No! I can't do that for the rest of ever."

"I'm just kidding," she says. "It's three times. That sounds better than 'ever,' doesn't it?"

I think it over. "I suppose it does. That was not funny."

"But it made you feel better, right?" she asks.

This is not the time to crack jokes! One more time and it's done. Or I'm done. I don't think I can survive that torture again. Looks like I don't have much of a choice.

Haines massages his temples. "Is there anything we can do to make it less painful?"

"Feed her while it's happening. Her strength comes from both her angel and demon sides." She shrugs. "That's the best I've got."

I touch her arm. "So, you're not completely sure?"

"I'm pretty sure."

Haines rubs my shoulder, silently letting me know that he'll do all he can to help me through this. The fact that he's still here with me even though the poo has hit the fan comforts me. The people that I've held dear and trusted my entire life have put me in a very precarious position.

"So," I say, reaching for my glass of water, "I guess I don't need to take Haines' immortality. Unless you want me to?" I take a sip of the cool water and breathe a sigh of satisfaction. I've been so busy trying to ignore how terrible all the pain has been and I didn't even realize my throat was raw. Probably from all the screaming.

He takes my glass from me and sets it on the night stand. "That's a bit of a relief. I was willing to—"

"Take one for the home team?" I say, giving Haines a huge smile.

"—what you said." He gives me a devious grin and a wink. "And I suppose living life as a human would have been interesting, but I'd rather pass."

Wow. He was willing to let go of everything, his life included, to stop Samael. It's rather peculiar. Haines was ready to die to get rid of Samael. More than anything I want to live, but if I let go and forfeit my life, Samael goes away. My life never meant so much to me until forking it over could save an entire species. Of demons.

"Hey!" I yell as an idea slams into my brain. How could I have forgotten? "What's with me being pinned to the ceiling? Right before all the pain ends I'm usually stuck to the ceiling. It's weird."

Aunt Rita smiles a knowing smile. She must be really happy today. "It's your wings, dear. You are sprouting wings."

I fight the urge to rub my back. That's awesome, in a completely non-awesome way. What am I going to do with wings? The image of me walking around in a huge trench coat pops into my head. I don't think Samael has wings. Maybe the more insane an angel gets the smaller their wings become.

Aunt Rita seems to have read my mind. "You won't be able to see them in this dimension, Perry. This earthly plane hides your angel wings. Shift to another dimension and there they'll be—big, colorful, beautiful."

My father smiles and a sentimental look covers his face. Poor Dad. He says he doesn't regret giving up his grace, but I bet he'd give anything to remember.

"Aunt Rita, how do you know all this stuff?"

She smiles. "I've been around for some time. I used to be an angel, too. But I knew it was time to give it up when I became envious of humans."

I let go of her hand. "Seriously? What a way to drop the 'I used to be an angel' bomb. Doesn't being an angel trump being human?"

Aunt Rita and my father laugh. They exchange a look and then reach for one another, holding hands and smiling.

"Dear girl, you have no idea. Your father found love. I found…peace. A real peace I never knew existed." She reaches out and caresses my face. "God gave me a vision of you when I was still an angel. He knew you were coming. He knows everything. I think I was charged with keeping you safe."

"Bang-up job, Auntie!" I say, pointing at my parents. "You couldn't even keep me safe from them."

"Yes, I should have been around to guide you, but your parents wanted to raise you with no help from anyone. What do you get when you mix an angel and a demon?"

I look at my parents. "A confused, pissed-off kid."

"Oh, Perrian." My mother shakes her head and then stands up. "It can't be that bad, can it?"

Has she not seen the bloody handprints on the ceiling? "Are you insane? Haines wouldn't have called you if he didn't think I was about to die." I would have a few choice words for my mother if I didn't respect her. "Besides the emotional turmoil I haven't even had a chance to deal with, my body is being torn apart." My eyes are burning from unshed tears. I've cried enough. "Mom, come here for a minute. Let me break your hand. Then imagine it's your whole body!"

She puts her hands up. "Perrian, I didn't mean it like that."

"And then let me toss you down the steps of Chechen Itza a few times so you can sustain some internal damage."

"Perry, I just meant that…"

"But here's the kicker, Mom. Let me turn back time and lie to you for your entire life. Let's see how that feels."

My father gets up and stands next to my mother. "Honey, we tried to do what we thought was best."

"She's right, you two." Aunt Rita shakes her head and looks between me and my parents. "You should have done this differently. You should have told her something."

I bring my hands to my face and hold them there, thinking of what to do next. What can I do? I peek through my fingers and look to Haines for an answer. I know he doesn't have one, but maybe he can beat them up.

Haines clears his throat. "Thank you all for coming, but Perrian needs her rest."

My mother looks like he just slapped her in the face.

She begins to protest, but Aunt Rita chimes in. "Come on Barbara. Kevin. Let's give her some space."

I can tell my parents want to stay with me, but they get up and walk toward the door anyway.

101

"Good night, Perry." My father kisses me on the forehead and then leaves.

My mom touches my hand and then follows behind him.

"If you need anything," Aunt Rita whispers, "anything at all, just call me. I'll do what I can." She smiles and gives me a hard kiss on the cheek. "We humans are limited, but we have our ways."

Haines looks back at me before he walks out the door. A gentle smile breaks across his face. Sweet bastard.

A tree branch dances across the bedroom window as a strong gust of wind hums by. I smile in spite of everything I've learned. We've only been married a few days and have loathed each other from the start, but the thought of him helping me through this makes me blush.

When did he and I start liking each other?

"About ten seconds after he thought you were going to die, Lady Bug."

"Gnahh!" I almost fall on the floor once I realize Samael is sitting right next to me. "You are fucking creepy!"

He buffs his nails on his black jacket and preens. "And I don't even try. Must be a God given talent."

I hear the wood of the headboard creak as I lean against it, trying to get as far away from him as I can without actually getting off the bed. I'm still sore.

"Ohh!" he says sympathetically, tsk-ing and covering his mouth like a fucking fool. "Poor Lady Bug. It must really hurt."

"You have no idea." I pull my knees to my chest. "What do you want?"

"To talk."

"About?"

"Us."

"There is no us."

"Lover, you have no idea." He gets up and goes to look out of the window. "So, what do you think?"

I mull it over for a few seconds and let go of a breath I didn't know I was holding. "I think that this is stupid. I think you should stop killing your offspring and leave me alone."

Samael pulls out a can of soda and pops it open. The *click* and *fizzle* from the can startle me. Where the hell did he get that from?

He takes long pull and breathes a sigh of satisfaction. "Go on."

"Okay," I say slowly, weighing my words. "If you stop killing us I won't pony-up and try to kill you. And leave my mother alone."

"Sweetie, you don't have the cojones to kill me." He chuckles. "I'm an angel of the Lord, and you're a goddamned mutt."

Ouch. That really hurt my feelings. "That's a bit harsh."

"Lady Bug, that was me putting it nicely."

"What's with you calling me Lady Bug? It freaks me out."

He looks wounded. "You don't like it?"

"Not so much now."

He shakes his head. "What do you want me to call you?"

I shrug. "My name."

If I hadn't been looking at him I wouldn't have noticed the change. A kind of ripple starts at his head, working its way down his body, to his shoes. Even his clothes look different. Less wrinkled, more fresh. What the hell was that?

"I don't like your name. Perrian. PerryAnne. Peerian." He rolls my name around on his tongue a few times, putting emphasis on different syllables. "Sounds like an alcoholic beverage or one of those stupid dolls that grow hair when you pull it."

"Then call me Perry."

He shrugs. "I'll think about it."

I stare at him and frown. "Why do you hate me? Why do you hate my kind?"

Samael looks thoughtful for a moment. "Because, *Perry*, your *kind* are my punishment. And now I have to clean house."

"How are we your punishment?"

He doesn't speak. He looks as if he's praying. When he comes back to the present time and opens his eyes, he looks like the epitome of what an angel should be. His features are soft and his cheeks seem full. His lavender eyes are strong, and he looks to be in full control of his sanity.

"My weakest moment was made manifest." Samael scratches the side of his head and then pushes his blond hair back into place. "I wanted to know what sex was like. What made people go crazy over it. And borne from that moment was an abomination that draws on the power of sex itself."

"I'm sorry you feel that way."

"But you." The crazy look comes back, and he sniffs the air. "You are just…uncalled for. Repugnance made into flesh. The child of an angel and a demon."

"Are you trying to hurt my feelings?"

"You just have to die, and you don't even know why." He smiles a freakish, toothy smile that shows all of his teeth. "I'm a poet."

"And you didn't even know it." I feel sorry for him. All this hatred directed at me and all of his offspring for the simple reason that he feels guilty.

"I know, right!" He comes back and sits on the foot of the bed. "You just gotta die, *Perry*. And you don't even know why."

A shiver runs down my spine, and I feel goose bumps cover my body. "Don't tell me—abomination, repugnance. I'm uncalled for."

"Oh, no. There's a secret, Lady Bug. And no one knows what it is." He leans toward me, almost sizing me up. "Your parents don't know. Your auntie doesn't know. Why, only a few beings on the face of anywhere know it."

My throat is suddenly dry and my breath catches in my chest. "Sure, I'll bite. What is it?"

He leans back and puts his feet up on the bed. "*You*, you terrible girl, will bring death to all those around you. That is your gift. That is your curse. And that's why you, Perry-Lady Bug-girlie, have got to die." He pulls away from me and walks toward the window. "And I'm going to take you before you implode on everyone around you. So, you're welcome." He opens the window and begins to climb out.

I want to run to watch the bastard fall, but his face still hovers above the windowsill as if he's standing on solid ground. We're on the second floor.

"Was that cryptic enough?" His head bobs out of sight and when I see his face again, he is sideways. "I'm actually doing you a favor."

"You...you're lying." No matter how calm I try to sound I stammer and begin to shake.

"Were that I was, Perry-girl. Were that I was."

Samael's face drifts upward as he disappears from my sight.

Chapter Eleven

It's been thirteen hours and my body is still the same. Haines has been next to me, waiting for something to happen. He promised that he'd do all he could to make the transition less painful.

Ryan and Trent brought over a few casseroles and keep calling to check on me, but I don't think either of them wants to be here. Ryan doesn't want another run in with Samael, and Trent doesn't want the pleasure of meeting him. I don't blame them.

"Perrian," Haines says. "You've been staring at the wall for ten minutes. What are you thinking about?" The newspaper he holds ruffles as he folds it, placing it on the bedside table. He turns to look at me.

"Who did Samael take from you?" I didn't tell him about Samael's surprise visit. Bringing death to those around me isn't a conversation I want to have. "You want me to kill him so badly. There has to be something fueling that hatred."

He rubs his chin and grabs his glass of red wine sitting on the bedside table I just replaced. Haines brought me into his room a few hours ago. He said the bed in my room wasn't big enough.

The brown and blue pillows on his bed are soft and smell of soap, fabric softener, and ylang ylang oil. Just like Haines. The striped beige and blue bedspread feels velvety, and my body sinks into the mattress.

He sips the dark red liquid and gently places it back on the table. "My father."

"I'm sorry."

He smiles. "He was wonderful. With all the women he could have seduced, his eyes were solely for my mother. He loved us. We were his heart and soul."

"What made him choose to let Samael take him?" I begin to wonder how a father would choose to leave his family but then it dawns on me.

Taking a sudden interest his abdomen, Haines sighs and shrugs. "My mother. My brother. Me." This is the most vulnerable I've ever seen him. He lifts the bottom of his tee-shirt up and pokes and pulls his navel, then he settles on rubbing his abs.

I'd love to rub them for him. Lick them. Kiss them. Biting them is out of the question. He has like zero percent body fat.

"It was a deal to keep you safe, wasn't it?" I ask, turning my attention away from his muscles. I would never hear a word he said if I didn't. "If your dad gave himself up Samael promised he would leave you guys alone."

Haines picks up his glass and eyes the table, brushing it off and then looks at me. "Yes, Perrian. That's why he leaves me alone. He's an angel of his word."

"How honorable," I say sarcastically. "Where is your family?"

He turns toward me and crosses his ankles. "Wondering why they didn't come to the wedding?"

I shrug and begin to chew on my lower lip. "That, too. But really I'm just being nosey."

He runs his hand through his hair and then rubs his

108

right ear. He fidgets when he's nervous. "My mother is holed up in Alaska, waiting for something. Maybe to die. Maybe waiting for Samael to die. I don't know. I visit her a few times a year. She and my dad were together for centuries. She still doesn't know how to live without him. My brother, Daniel, and his wife are expecting a baby any day. She can't fly and he didn't want to leave her. They live in Arizona."

Wow. A family makes Haines seem more normal. All these years and he has just been an entity to me. Nothing real. Just a guy I needed to help me out. A guy who thought he could boss me around if he tried hard enough. But now, he seems like an actual person.

"Haines?"

"Yes, Perrian?"

"Why were you such a douche when we met?" I pull the covers off my feet and pull my legs under me. "What made you treat me that way?"

He sighs and looks at the wall. "I really don't know, Perrian."

"Well, think about it because I'd like to know."

He rubs his hand across my forehead, and I lean into his touch. "I will do that. I believe I owe you that much."

His small show of affection makes me blush. "Thank you. I believe you and I are capable of getting along." I clear my throat, pull the covers back over my legs, and grab for my glass of water. "Haines?"

"Mmm-hmm," he says, reaching for the television remote.

"Just so there'll be no hold up when it comes down to it, I'd like you to have sex with me." I turn my body toward him and nervously fondle the glass in my hand.

"Please, oh please, have sex with me you manly-man. This, oh sir, I beg."

A laugh reverberates through his chest and his smile is genuine. "I will accept that as you begging me for sex."

We both laugh, and the mood lightens. I hadn't even known there was tension hanging over us. Must be all this talk of death and angels. Is there anyone else on the face of the planet who has these conversations? Probably not. We're the weird ones walking around going through this crap.

"Perrian?"

"Yep?"

"What made you do that?"

"I didn't want to do it while I was writhing in pain and praying for death."

"Ahh," he says, changing channels on the television. "I see. That makes perfect sense."

I flip through books on my e-reader while Haines flips through channels, neither of us saying that we are waiting for my body to begin its last change.

I'm terrified this time will be worse, and I think Haines is just as afraid. Afraid he won't be able to help me through it.

"Perrian, I have an idea."

"Is it you running to the market to buy me more ice cream?" I say hopefully, but I'm almost sure of what he's going to say. I've been thinking the same thing myself.

"With your permission, I would like to try to induce your change."

Yep, that's exactly what I was thinking.

"That way," he continues. "We can try to keep you

from feeling the pain. I imagine it's dreadful."

"Haines, you have no fucking idea how *dreadful* it is."

He cracks his knuckles and bites his bottom lip. "If your aunt thinks it'll help you, I'm willing to give it a try."

I take a deep breath and lay my e-reader on the table. "I'd like that. What do you propose?"

He turns the television off and faces me. My mouth is suddenly dry and I am beyond nervous. We're going to do it!

In one sudden and graceful move Haines pulls his tee-shirt over his head and climbs up on his knees, pulling the blanket and sheets off my legs. It tickles its way down my legs, exposing me to the cool air. I want to pull them back and bring the blanket up to my neck to cover myself. Even though I'm wearing pajama pants and a shirt, I feel completely naked. I finally get a chance to really look at his beautiful body but I can't move my eyes from his.

Haines' pupils are dilated, and a knowing smile plays across his eyes. I look down and see his full lips, soft and wet. He licks his teeth and smiles, and my body is instantly set aflame to be taken by him. Memories remind me to rage against our joining, but every other part of me overlooks those thoughts. Haines knew what he was getting into when he agreed to marry me, kind of, but he did it anyway. There is something there that flickers in his eyes that shows me he cares. It's not the obvious lust that we both feel right now. It's something more.

He could have left me to be alone with Samael. He could have called my parents when that first spasm of pain overtook me, left me to be cared for by anyone else but him. But he didn't. Haines cared enough to try to comfort me, to bathe me while I was rendered unconscious, healing from the physical torture my body has to go through. Even right now, he could leave me to bleed my way through another episode. But he's here, with me. Ready to help me become the best version of myself that I can be. Ready to help me defeat a rogue angel that has his hopes set on killing every single sex demon on the face of this planet. This beautiful man is here with me.

"You're the most magnificent man I've ever seen," I say.

His chest is sleek and the color of honey. Each fluid movement causes a ripple of muscle beneath his skin and I can only imagine what he will feel like against my body. He reaches for the drawstring of his pants and slowly unties it. He crawls closer and moves between my legs. "I'm going to taste you." His expression is volatile.

"Okay," I tell him, sounding like an idiot. Don't I have a sexy voice?

"May I?" he says, gently pulling at my shirt.

"Ohh." Clumsily, I yank my shirt over my head. "Look, before we go any further let me just say that I am nervous and you're going to have to tell me what to do 'cause I've never done this before, and I've never even had a guy get to second base before all sleepy hell broke loose and the poor bastard passed out and I just sat there like a freaking moron hoping I didn't kill the poor guy…"

"You have lovely breasts."

I guess that was a whole lot nicer than him saying,

Perry, shut the hell up!

"Thanks."

His eyes are raw, hungry. Just for me. He leans forward and kisses my forehead, my nose, my lips, and then my chin. I feel cherished.

"Kiss me," he says faintly, rubbing his lips against mine.

I lean and fall into the kiss, breath hitching in my throat as his arms surround me. His mouth claims me, pulls from me. His hand lightly touches the small of my back, pulling me toward him as he draws me forward and guides me back down on to the bed. For a moment, his touch becomes possessive, and he grabs my ass and pulls me against his hard erection. I moan into his mouth as his kiss deepens and his teeth knock against mine. I revel in his loss of control and smile into our kiss.

His thigh pushes my legs farther apart as he makes room for himself, pulling me down farther on the bed so I won't hit my head on the headboard. I tighten my arms around his neck, loving the sensation of his hands shamelessly touching every part of me as if he owns the only map in existence to my body.

"Should I cut the light off?" I ask, looking at the lamp.

"No," he says, a sexy smile playing across his lips. "I want you to watch me."

"Oh," I say, feeling anxious. We're gonna do it! I'm gonna do it with someone!

"Perrian, calm down."

"Oh, okay." Easier said than done.

He pulls away from me and hooks his thumbs on either side of my pajama pants, slowly drawing them down my hips. His hands are warm and they make my body sing to be touched by him.

Goosebumps erupt as his fingers lightly graze my legs. He folds my pants and lays them next to him, pausing only to slide off his own. From a smattering of dark hair, his cock bounces free—long, thick, slightly curving upward.

"I want you inside me," I admit, almost ashamed to let the truth leave my lips. I've wanted him for so long, and now he's here.

He is beautiful. Our kind were made to be beautiful, to be desired. And I am not immune to his prowess.

Haines leans over and kisses my left knee and then my right, pulling them apart as his kisses make their way up my thighs. Forcefully, he grabs me by each knee and yanks my bottom to the edge of the bed and kneels before me.

Dear Lilith, thank you. You're the best. This was so worth the wait.

"You are exquisite, Perrian." His lips and tongue tease their way higher. "Are you watching?" he says, without looking up at me.

My voice is barely audible as my eyes are trained on his lips. "Yes."

He smiles and kisses the lips between my legs once, and then again, hands kneading into my thighs.

The air is heavy with lust. I tilt my head back and close my eyes.

"Perrian. Eyes on me."

I snap my head up.

"This may be the only time I get to tell you what to do," he says, hands massaging their way to my center while he pulls my left knee over his shoulder.

"This may be the only time I'll listen."

He takes his left hand and rests it on my belly, using his thumb and forefinger to pull back the hood, giving him clear access to my clit. His tongue strokes it over and over as I hold on to the bed for all I'm worth, trying to keep my hands from shaking as the heavy ache between my legs continues to build.

He hums and my vision blurs. I feel the vibration through my entire body. "Hmmyeah," and other babble manages to escape my mouth. I clamp my teeth together and fight to keep my eyes on him. I sit up on my elbows and watch his mouth slide over me, his hand caressing its way up my ribs.

His lips are voracious as he tastes me, demanding my pleasure as a feast for his demon. I give it to him. All of what I'm feeling I imagine flowing into him, making him stronger, making *us* closer. I grab the back of his head and pull him toward me as my hips thrust toward his hungry mouth. His fingers dig into my flesh, painful almost, but oh God, how I love it.

I begin to feel a pulling sensation. He's feeding off of my lust. Haines should have more than enough energy to feed on. My skin tingles and power floods the room.

And then it starts.

My body begins to overheat and a sense of boiling fills my stomach.

"Haines," I say, whimpering.

"Start feeding," he says, without taking his lips off me, tongue still stroking, fingers reaching up to knead my breasts and pinch my hardened nipples.

I'm afraid. I'm terrified. Everything rubs my skin

the wrong way—the sheets, the air, even the sweat that beads across my brow.

But his mouth feels magnificent.

"Haines," I say again, holding tighter to the sheets, afraid that if I touch him I'll hurt him.

"Feed," he says forcefully, this time enclosing my clit with his lips. He begins to suck and bite and flick his tongue. His fingers make their way through my slick folds and he thrusts two fingers into my empty channel, stretching me, filling me.

Throwing my head back against the soft pillows I cry out and begin to spiral as he tastes me.

His mouth on me is the only thing in the world worth feeling. And here it is. That magnetism of me drawing energy from him. Feeding off of him. Of him filling me up. Of him taking energy from me.

He winces as bones begin breaking in my body. I silently thank Lilith that it only feels like a knuckle cracking, but the sound is clear and Haines' discomfort is unmistakable. But a quick glance from him shows me his relief that I'm not screaming in pain.

Instead, I'm laughing. So happy there is no ache, no hurt. Only warmth from his mouth, a nibble from his teeth.

"Please keep doin' that—" I say, the words almost a song I sing in praise of Haines.

He hums again and the burn in my belly disappears, turning into the most pleasurable, aching warmth that radiates to every part of my body.

"Haines—Oh, Haines—" My legs begin to shake, and I grind my hips toward his face.

I stop breathing as the orgasm hits me, and I throw my head back, calling his name. "Oh, God.

ThankyouHaines." One big word that plays over and over in my head. The fear of burning and ripping are nonexistent and I am grateful that Haines is the reason. "ThankyouthankyouHainesthankyou. It doesn't hurt," I whisper to the top of his head, breathing hard, hips still rocking forward.

His head snaps up, and a wily look is in his demon-red colored eyes. The carnal glare is almost frightening as he bites his bottom lip and roughly pulls my legs apart, pushing me farther up on to the bed.

"Haines?" I say, whispering. "Are you—"

He quickly crawls up my body, bringing my knees high near my armpits. "I'm sorry," he says, kissing me hard.

His lips are on mine. My scent and taste on his tongue, warm and salty. His proud cock is near the apex of my thighs and he apologizes again. He slides his hands under my ass and pulls my pussy toward his waiting cock. He rams his full length into me.

I try to scream but his kiss drowns out the sound. He is large. He stretches me, forcing my aching pussy to accept every inch of him, and I welcome him. "Haines," I say over and over, my voice sounding like an erotic soundtrack that plays along with the slapping of flesh, the whisper of sheets.

Pumping into me, he apologizes again and again. "I'm so sorry. I don't think I can stop. I'll be gentle next time," he says, biting my shoulder. "So sorry."

"It's all right," I say moaning, getting used to the feeling of him filling me to the point of pain. Breathing hard and holding on to him I shake my head, letting him know that it's okay.

He feels wonderful. The friction rubs all the right

places and I feel like I'm flying as he slides in and out, as his hips piston against mine.

I shiver and run my hands up his back, exploring the silky skin over his body. I relish the feel of his hot skin. "Please," I whisper, not knowing what I'm asking for. Please don't stop? Please take me higher? It doesn't matter. Just as long as he keeps moving.

He traces his tongue along my sensitive earlobe. "This is how I've dreamed of us. My cock deep inside you. You begging me for more." He kisses me again and bites my bottom lip. "You're so wet. So mine. *Fuck*, Perry."

The discomfort recedes and a warm ache replaces it. Heat rushes through my body as his possessive hunger claims me. His mouth glides along the skin of my shoulders. He feels so good touching me, biting me, kissing me, fucking me. The feel of his sweat slicked body writhing against mine makes me fly. With each thrust of his hips and kiss from his lips I am taken higher.

"I've got you," he says, holding on to either side of the bed but still thrusting into me.

I open my eyes and realize my body is starting to lift off the bed as I begin to float to the ceiling. But Haines has me.

He snakes his head down and pulls my nipple into his mouth. He laves and sucks, and good God, he bites. "Come for me," he says, moving one of his hands between us and rubbing tiny circles around my clit.

A rumble sounds in his chest as he pushes my legs further apart. "Perrian," he whispers.

And with the sound of my name on his lips the orgasm rips through me, a wave crashing over me again and again. I dissolve into him as he pushes deeper and comes for me. Comes into me.

My body is still; no sounds of bones moving. I rest on the bed and smile in spite of the soreness that is already setting in.

Haines is panting, his large frame draped over me. "I'm sorry," he says. "I don't know what happened. Did I hurt you?"

He pulls away and I look in his eyes. "A little. But trust me, I'm completely fine with it."

He laughs. "I guess your super-snatch took over and compelled me."

I giggle, pinch the hair in the middle of his head, and pull back. "Shut-it."

We lay there for a few moments looking at each other.

"Haines?"

"Yes, dearest."

"Thank you. Besides my first time being absolutely amazing, thank you for helping me."

He kisses my neck. "You are very welcome. For a moment I thought the both of us were going to go hurtling toward the ceiling." He smiles and rubs my hair out of my eyes.

"But you saved me. Thank you."

"Well," he says, rubbing his nose against mine. "That's what I'm here for."

I don't know if it's the post coitus euphoria talking, but I feel happy with Haines. We could be happy. I've been a bitch to him, and he's probably wanted to throttle me at times, but it led us here. Over the past few days I've learned to enjoy our relationship. I don't want a guy I can push around, because I know I can be bossy, and Haines gives me what I give him. And I don't think he would have respected me if I had let him be in charge. That's not how we work. And that seems to work just fine.

He begins to pull himself up, and I wince.

"Am I hurting you?" A line forms between his eyes on his forehead.

"You can't stay in there forever, so…"

Slowly, he pulls himself away and then lies on his back. "Can I get you anything?" he asks, covering our legs with the blanket.

"Unless you can help me fall asleep, which I'm pretty sure you just did your best at doing, I'm fine." I stretch and feel his weight between my thighs. It's almost as if my body misses the feel of him already.

He reaches across me and turns out the lamp. "Perrian?"

I feel like liquid. Warm, soft, comfortable. My eyelids slide closed, and I already feel exhaustion taking me under. "Yes, Haines?"

"Rest well. You've been through a lot."

I smile and roll over onto my side. He slides up behind me, wraps his arm around my waist, and intertwines his legs with mine.

"Oh, and Perrian?" he says, kissing the back of my neck. "I am fully aware that this is not my bedside table."

My eyes pop open and I begin to stutter. "Look— I umm…"

"But thank you for caring enough to try to replace it. Or were you just being sneaky?"

"Haines, we were just starting to get along, and I didn't want to ruin it by admitting I put my fist through your table. My mother drives me insane."

He clears his throat and moves closer to me. "I'll accept that."

"Goodnight, Haines."

"Goodnight, Perrian."

****

I glance at the clock. It's two thirty-eight a.m.

Haines and I both needed rest after the shenanigans—love that word—of the past few days. I wiggle out of his grasp and tip-toe to the connecting bathroom.

Washing my hands, I look in the mirror to see if I notice any differences.

No cherub-like features.

No wings.

Just me. The progeny of an angel and a demon.

Standing here in a beige and blue bathroom. Those must be Haines' favorite colors.

I cut off the light, open the door and walk toward the bed, only to notice Samael sitting in the chair in the corner.

"Get the fuck out!" I whisper-yell.

He stands up, unfolding his long body from the chair, and walks toward me. "Put on some clothes and come with me."

Damn-it! I'm naked. I bend down, grab my pajamas, and shove myself into them as fast as I can. "I'm not going anywhere with you."

He walks toward me and shoves his finger in my face. "Do as I say or I will rip his heart from his chest."

My eyes cut to Haines. His breaths are gentle. He's still sleeping. A delicate, white rose with black squiggly lines on it lies on my pillow. Did Haines get that for me? "You promised his father you would leave Haines and his family alone."

He shrugs and his eyes are deadpan. "Haines no longer belongs to his father's family. You're married."

A verse from the Bible pops into my head about a man leaving his family. Once he's married he pretty much has a new family. His wife.

Samael's smile is terrible, and his eyes are vicious. "And I don't owe you anything, Perry-girl."

He steps closer to me, and I have to lift my head to look at his face. "Where are you taking me?"

Samael backs up and pulls my sneakers from behind his back. "You and I have business to attend to."

I look at Haines' sleeping form and wonder why he hasn't woken up. "Is he all right?" I ask.

"Oh, yes," he says happily. "Just a bit of angel mojo to keep him asleep. He's fine. But he won't be for long if you don't hurry up." He looks at the bed. "I made that rose especially for you. You've been deflowered, so…"

I scoff and shove my shoes onto my feet. Freaking perv. "Where are you taking me?" I ask again.

"To show you how it ends, baby-girl. To show you how you become the Bringer of Death." He dances toward the bedroom door, twirling once before he grabs the knob. "And that would be your official title."

"What?" I say, wrapping my arms around my stomach. "You're lying."

"Oh, no baby. It is very much the truth. Grab your rose."

I walk toward the bed and look down at Haines. His lips are parted, and his face is serene. I carefully grab the rose. Is this thing going to explode?

After closer inspection, I notice that the black lines on the petals are music notes. It's beautiful. I'm pretty sure some kind of crazy is attached to it.

The phone rings and I glance at the clock again. It's almost three in the morning. Who would be calling at this hour?

"Come on, Perry-girl. Focus!"

I follow him down the hallway and down the steps. The phone is blaring, and I can't concentrate.

I'm not going to kill anyone. Bringer of Death is probably some crap he pulled out his ass to scare me. Maybe he saw it on television and thought it would be a fun way to creep me out.

Samael is insane. He's lying.

"Lying? Why would I lie?"

I shake my head and stop walking. He's not going to string me along, making me feel terrible about myself so I'll give in. "I'm not coming with you and you won't hurt Haines. And stop reading my Goddamned thoughts!"

He throws his head back and laughs. "My, my, my. You are correct. I am indeed an angel of my word. All of us are. Except one."

I turn around and start walking back toward the bedroom. "Get out, Samael."

"You think you've got me, huh?"

"Goodnight," I say over my shoulder.

He's fast and I don't even get a chance to turn around. "Let's try something else."

Samael grabs me by my hand and yanks. Everything starts spinning and flashing and when it all stops I fall to my knees.

"Jesus Christ," I yell, looking down at his brown

and black shoes.

"I don't think He wants to talk to you."

Samael grabs me by my arm and pulls me to a standing position.

Once my head clears the familiarity sets in. I know this room. The wood paneled walls and modern art. The queen sized, four poster bed I used to sneak into after bad dreams. The scent is clean, like mint and lemon.

My parents' house.

I look at their bed and see them sleeping. It's dark but I can make out their shapes. My dad sleeps closest to the bedroom door.

A lamp light pops on and I see my mother blinking rapidly. "Kevin. Wake up." She looks like a teenager in her long, lavender night gown. Her eyes are sleepy but the fear shows true once she realizes Samael is in the room.

"Why are we here?" I walk toward the bed but Samael grabs my arm and throws me behind him. I slam into the wall, and with a loud *thud* my head bounces off the paneling and a few pictures fall down. The rose rolls across the floor toward my parents' bed. I had forgotten that I'd been holding it.

"Because I'm not going to play games with you, Perry-girl."

Ringing. My ears are ringing, and my vision is blurry. "I'm not going to give in to you and neither is my mother."

My head clears a bit and I look up to see my father with his arm draped protectively across my mother's chest. "You cannot have her, Samael. She's made her choice." His eyes cut to me. "Come over here to me and your mom, Perry."

I try to get up, but Samael's large hand palms my face and shoves me back down, slamming my head against the wall again. Harder this time.

"You will give in to me, Perrian." Samael walks toward the bed.

"Leave her alone!" I say, trying to get up. My balance is still off from the brain-rattling he just gave me.

Samael rolls his eyes and breaks a post off their bed. "This'll hold you 'til I get my point across."

He's instantly next to me, pushing me backward. Samael's hands are quick, and it all happens so fast. He shoves the wooden post through my belly, impaling me to the wall.

"Perry!" my parents yell.

There is pressure and a dull ache. My breaths are ragged, and I feel like I'm losing consciousness. I pull at the post but I can't get it out. The pain has weakened me, and my blood begins to pour down my pants and pool on to the floor. "Mom," I whimper. I don't think this can kill me, but it sure as hell feels like it should.

"You see, Perry-girl," Samael says, pointing at my parents. "I'm not going to let you become who you're *gonna* become. I started this *happening* all those years ago, and I'm *gonna* finish it. The only reason you are exactly what you are is because of your demon blood. Your succubus powers. So, you're *gonna* give into me or I'm *going* to start killing people!" His eyes are wild, the dainty lavender now the color of a purple and red sky that signals a quick and vicious storm.

My mother runs toward me and puts her hands on the bedpost holding me to the wall. "It's all right, baby. I'm not going anywhere."

Samael laughs and starts hopping up and down. "You silly, stupid woman. I didn't come here for you. I came here for the easy, human pickings." He looks at my father and then back to me. "You need a little convincing."

My mom yanks the wooden post from my belly, grabbing hold of me before I fall to the floor. "Kevin!" she shouts, realizing my father is the only one in the room who is vulnerable. Who is mortal.

She's still next to me as Samael grabs my father, his delicate, long-fingered hands wrapped fully around my father's head. "I send you safely home, dear brother. God-speed," he whispers, kissing my father on the cheek.

There is no fear in my father's eyes. Only sorrow.

A sickly crunch echoes through the room as Samael twists my father's head around. Chopin's Funeral March begins to croon from somewhere close. My father's body falls back to the bed, and my mother screams. Flashes. It all seems like flashes of images. My father was alive. And now he isn't. My mother was happy, and now she's incomplete.

"Daddy," I sob, grabbing my belly as waves of pain radiate from the wound.

My mother is silent now. Her grip on me tightens. I look at her and see tears running down her face. She mouths my father's name over and over. No sound comes out. She's not breathing. This is the pain people talk about when they say their heart hurts so bad that they can't breathe, and they don't know if they'll live through another second.

Samael frowns and shakes his head. "If you don't give up the ghost, so to speak, I will kill Trent, Ryan and their little firecracker of a son. And then I'll kill Haines' sister-in-law, who happens to be human. And their newborn baby. Oh! And your auntie, too."

"Why?" I whisper. "Why are you doing this?"

He shrugs. "Abomination, remember? You shouldn't be here. You are the Bringer of Death. Don't you want to die?"

Right now, I do want to die. And I want to take Samael with me.

Samael winks. "Well, Perry-girl. That's a start. If you die then you'll pretty much take me with you. I give you my word that if you let go and come quietly, I'll leave your family alone. No one else will die." He reaches down and rubs my father's face, closing his eyes.

"Don't you touch him," I mutter.

"One week, Perry-girl. Get your business in order or I start killing."

There is a bright, blinding flash. And then he's gone.

If it weren't for the gentle playing of the Funeral March, the room would be quiet.

No more screaming or sounds of crying.

My mother's face is buried in my neck. Her body is wracked with sobs as she clings to me, and I still can't hear her breathe.

Maybe she's trying to breathe. Trying to remember how to draw in air and let it out.

I look around and try to find the sound; to find where the music is coming from.

Next to the bed where the rose fell, it is standing firm on its stem, spinning as soft music pours from it. Playing a melody for my father. For the people who will die if I don't give in to Samael. When the song stops, the music notes fade, and the petals begin to fall from the rose. And to think, I'd hoped it was a gift from Haines.

I glance up at my father, waiting for him to wake up. Hoping that by some miracle his grace will return to him and he'll open his eyes; hoping that maybe once the music stops the spell will be broken and my father will wake up. But I know he's not going to.

My mother finds her voice, and she screams. She screams as she clings to me, trying to pull me closer. And I hug her tighter and remember that I'm bleeding. All over my mother's pretty nightgown.

Somewhere distant, behind her screams, I hear a phone ring.

A part of me that's looking for normalcy speaks. A part of me that wants to undo and forget everything that's happened. That voice is so calm.

Who is that calling at this hour?

Chapter Twelve

"Perrian, you need to eat."

"Haines, please go away."

The door to my bedroom opens wider and I turn my face away from the light of the hallway. I've been lying in my bed for the past day or so, only getting up to use the bathroom. They've brought me food, but I can't eat. Part of me hopes that if I lay here long enough maybe I'll wither away. "Please, Haines. Just go. I don't want to talk."

"You need to feed." The bed dips as he sits down behind me. "It's been two days. I think you're still bleeding."

I shift and bury my face deeper into the soft, damp pillows. Damp with tears and sweat. Pain makes you sweat. Up until this morning, I think, they smelled of fresh dryer sheets. "I can't feed. I keep thinking about my dad. Anything sexual just…"

"You need to be strong. The funeral is tomorrow and you can't go with a hole through your body."

After Samael killed my father Haines brought me and my mom back to our home. Our home? Aunt Rita took care of the body.

My father's body.

Aunt Rita is taking care of everything. She put a ward around the house so that Samael can't come in to do any more damage. She'd figured it out the night my dad was murdered. She was so excited that she finally managed to angel-proof the house that she called at three in the morning to let us know.

I lift my head and look at Haines. "Did Aunt Rita ward Ryan and Trent's house? Your brother's house?"

He lifts my shirt to look at my stomach. I'm pretty sure there is still a bedpost sized hole in my belly.

"Yes," he says, frowning. "Rita sent the instructions to a local coven near my brother's home. She's also working on a way to keep everyone safe when they're not at home. Especially for Roman, and my new niece." He smiles. "Her name is Riley. Riley Marie. She was born a few hours ago." His face lights up.

A ghost of a smile teases my lips. "That's beautiful." I flinch as he pulls the bandage off my wound.

"My God." He gently returns the bandage and goes to the one on my back. "You are healing. I've never—"

"Demonic angel, remember?" I say, pulling my shirt down so he can stop gawking at me. "Or would that be angelic demon?"

The full weight of what I am finally seems to fall on me. My mother is a full-blooded demon and my father was an angel. He wasn't an angel when he died. He wouldn't be dead if he was. I'm what you get when an angel and a demon procreate. The Bringer of Death.

"You are amazing, Perrian."

"I am useless, Haines. I can't do anything." As I lay back, a sharp pain shoots through my body where the wooden post once was. "Samael is going to start killing people in less than a week if I don't give in to him."

Haines kicks off his slippers and lies down behind me, spooning me. When did we get so comfortable with each other?

"You can kill him."

"How? With my bare hands? Maybe I'll seduce him and see if that'll do it. Drink him dry."

He shakes his head. "I don't know. Your aunt says there are ways."

"Maybe he'll stay still long enough for me to do it," I say sarcastically.

I have no idea how to kill an angel. A batshit crazy angel. Maybe I should pray for God to take him. Is that even allowed? *Dear God, kill this crazy angel to make him stop terrorizing me and my family because he thinks I am an abomination. And I pray for world peace. Amen.*

"I'm sorry. We can talk about it later." He scoots up closer behind me. "You have to feed, Perrian."

I sigh and wince. It hurts to be awake, and I wish everyone would leave me alone. There is no amount of discussing or thinking or brainstorming that's going to fix this. I can't fix this. If I could I would have done it back at my parents' house.

That son of a bitch just comes and goes as he pleases. Will the wards keep him out forever or are we just buying time?

"Does it hurt to breathe?"

"Yes. Hurts to talk, too," I say, pushing him away. "Leave me alone."

"No." He moves closer to me. "I'm not going to leave you alone."

I pull my legs up to my chest. "No! I haven't taken a bath. And I'm pretty sure being impaled and having your blood ooze out of your body doesn't smell nice. I just want to lay here and be sad!"

"Perrian—"

Why won't he give it a rest? I've been listening to him and my mother and my aunt tell me how I need to be strong and keep my chin up, and it all sounds stupid. They're trying to encourage me but it just makes me feel even worse. Even more powerless. I don't know what to do, and having them tell me that I am strong enough makes me feel even less so.

"I'm supposed to save my family and friends and the only way I know how to do that is to die!" I sweep away my tears. "And I'm not ready to die."

"You're not going to die," my mother says from the bedroom door. "We don't have time for this." She comes in and kneels in front of me. Her hair is a beautiful brown, curly mess and her eyes are hollow, empty. She's still absolutely beautiful, but there's something missing. "I'm sad, too, Perry. But we've got to figure out how to get rid of that crazy bastard, so let your husband feed you so you can be ready."

Dear God, please make them shut-up and go away. Is that a mean prayer?

She uses her sleeve to wipe away the tears and snot—only a mother—that are about to ruin my already ruined pillow. "Tomorrow morning, we're going to have a home going service for your father. Your aunt and I are going to the Wiccan shop to get whatever she needs to finish the satchels that will protect us from Samael. And then we're going to collect kindling for your father's funeral pyre."

I look her in the eyes and shake my head, silently pleading with her to stop trying to make this better. "I can't kill him. I don't even know how. It's not like I can cut off his head or shoot him. Maybe I'll impale *him*."

She smiles. "We'll figure it out. Rita will figure it out." She sighs. "Your father—"

"Is dead. So please don't tell me what he would want me to do. Auntie came in with that crap last night."

"Perrian!" Haines says. "Don't talk to your mother like that."

I gather as much strength as I can and push myself up off the bed. "Just get out! Both of you." I wrap my arms around my belly and double over as I try to stand. "Don't bother. I'm leaving. I'm going to take a shower to get this blood off me and pick out the shards of wood that I can feel rattling around in my belly. And then I'm going back to sleep."

Pushing against the wall for support, I look up and see bloody hand prints next to me.

Yup, I'm still bleeding.

"I could have been prepared for this," I say, looking at my mother as I open the door. "You and Dad lied to me." I can hear the venom in my voice. This is their fault. My mother and father tried to protect me and did nothing but set me up for failure. My nose begins to tickle, and I start panicking. What the hell is that smell? Rita and her fucking potion spices!

Dear God, please don't let me sneeze. The first time I sneezed a few hours after my father was killed I almost passed out. The pain radiated out from my wound, and I thought I would die. I wished I had died.

"Damn-it." I sneeze, and everything looks fuzzy. I fall to my knees and sneeze again. "Jesus," I whisper, the pain spiraling around me like the confusion and hopelessness inside me.

Haines jumps up and starts toward me. "Perrian. You can't stay like this."

"Don't you touch me!" My vision is hazy from the pain and the tears.

I deserve to be in pain. To feel like I'm being ripped in half. This is what I deserve for letting my father die. There's nothing I can do to help them. It's not their fault. It's mine. It's my fault my dad is dead. Not my mother's.

I sneeze again and see black spots as I begin to lose consciousness.

God or Lilith, please, just let me die.

Chapter Thirteen

"I'd like you to stop bathing me while I sleep."

"If you'd stop allowing yourself to be covered in your own blood, I wouldn't have to."

I wake up lying in Haines' bed with clean clothes on. His bed smells like dryer sheets. And of him. Haines always smells nice. He always looks nice. I wonder if he can buy the ingredients so I can teach him how to make my homemade butter pecan ice cream? I bet he'd be really good at it. I could spread it on his chest, watch his nipples harden and pebble beneath my tongue. Smile as he shivered from the… Damn-it, he's putting the whammy on me so I'll want him. "Haines, I don't want to have sex."

"Well, Perrian. I don't want to have sex with you either."

I'm a little disappointed. I shrug and look at his bare chest. "Then why are you straddling me with no shirt on and making me want to eat ice cream?"

"Because you need to feed."

"Haines. No."

I try to push him but he slaps my hand away and cups my face with his palm. He looks at me with distress and understanding in his eyes. His father was taken from him. He feels sorry for me. He wants to help but feels just as helpless as I do.

Everyone feels helpless, and I've been treating

them like crap. Samael is a cross that all of us have to bear. I'm just the one who has to kill him. But we all have to deal with him.

"Perrian," he says indignantly, "I know what you're doing." He makes himself more comfortable by pulling my knees up and settling between my legs. "You think you deserve to suffer. I think you're acting like a child."

I roll my eyes and cross my arms. "Shut up."

"There's only one way to make me shut up."

"Damn-it, Haines! I'm in mourning."

"Perrian—" His voice is condescending.

"Stop saying my name like that!"

"I'm going to kiss you. You're going to pull energy from me. And then we'll get to work."

"Fine," I say, grabbing him by his ears and pulling him into a kiss.

It's an angry kiss. An emotionless kiss.

I wait to feel a pull of energy or at least a tingle of power. But there is nothing. No healing. No energy. Just anger. Have I lost my mojo? Am I so weak from not feeding that I can't even feed anymore? That would make things easier. Then I'd have an excuse. Nothing is that simple.

"This shit isn't working," I say, pulling him away from me by his ears.

His eyes are slits and his lips are thin. A look of annoyance covers his face. His stupid, smug, handsome face. "Get off my ears, Perrian."

"Well then leave me alone, Haines!"

I know I'm being a brat and that using my physical pain as an excuse is a cop-out. Part of me knows that once I'm healed I'll have to do something constructive with my time, which probably means killing Samael. Which no one knows how to do. Especially me.

God, please. Just take Samael. I know you like to help us and want us to be happy, so killing him would do us a whole world of good. You'll be saving so many of your wonderful people. Do my prayers fall on deaf ears because I'm part demon? That's bullshit. I've asked for forgiveness and know that I'm saved. Why aren't my prayers working?

"Perrian, you are forcing my hand."

"What the hell are you talking about?" I know what the hell he's talking about. He wants to do his demon thing and make me want him. Want him more than anything. "Haines, don't do it," I warn. If he ignites the lust inside me to make me have sex with him I will never let him live this down. We would never get back to this happy place in our relationship. I wouldn't allow it.

"You need to feed."

Welp, time to hit him where it hurts. "You know, dearest husband. Forcing me to have sex when I don't want to is frowned upon in many cultures, and punishable by jail time."

His lips thin out and his ears begin to redden. Low? Yes, it was low. And after the stupid words shoot out of my lips, I feel terrible.

"Haines, I'm sorry. And you're right. I am trying to make myself suffer. But that isn't helping, is it?" Rhetorical question.

Just a few days ago I couldn't care less about what Haines thought of me. About anything. Now, we snuggle and kiss and spoon. I love it. But I hate it. I hate it because death seems like the only way to ensure everyone's safety. Being happy with Haines, if even for a little while, makes it all seem like a loss. My loss. And Samael doesn't give a rat's ass about me as a person. He only cares that my existence makes him look bad.

And I'm being a real shit to Haines.

"You don't have to do anything," he says, running his lips along the side of my neck. "I'm going to take care of you. I'll make you stronger and then we'll figure this out. You're not going to sacrifice yourself. I won't allow it."

I laugh at his arrogance. "Well, just because you said so…"

He pulls away from me and takes his pajama bottoms off. How cute. I have on the top, and he has on the bottoms. His cock springs free and points in my direction. I've heard people say that sex makes you stupid. The thought of having sex with Haines allows me to stupidly want to forget that anything is wrong.

My stomach contracts from the memory of our first time, and I recoil in pain. Everything involves your stomach muscles—moving, talking, breathing. And apparently the sight of Haines' manly parts letting me know it's coming for me involves my stomach muscles, too.

A concerned look flashes in his eyes and then disappears.

I reach up and begin to unbutton my pajama top. "You know, this is probably going to be pretty painful for me."

"We don't have a choice. You're healing fast but not fast enough. We're working with time restrictions and I won't allow you to hinder yourself."

I start to sit up to take off the shirt but he gently pushes me back down. "You couldn't put a bra and panties on me after you bathed me in my unconscious state?"

"Why would I?" he growls. "I was going to make you feed one way or the other." He traces a line with his tongue from my chin to the middle of my breasts. "Besides, you told me a few days ago that you went 'commando' at night." He frowns and shakes his head. "My God, that is such an un-ladylike phrase."

I begin to laugh and then slap my hands over my face, feeling the tears I've been holding back rush to the surface. My father used to say things like that to me. *Be exactly who you are, Perry. Screw being ladylike. You're a wonderful woman.* Around my mother, I tried to be appropriate and watched my mouth. My father never cared. He always told me to be exactly who I was. Potty-mouth and all.

"Haines, I can't do this."

"Just close your eyes, Perrian. You don't have to do anything. I'm going to make you stronger," he says, crawling backward and lifting my leg, hooking my knee over his shoulder. "And then we will figure out a way to dispose of Samael." He lightly kisses the inside of my knee. "I don't want to hear of you giving up. I know you don't know what to do. You're beginning to sound like a broken record. I love this part of your thigh," he says, kissing the inside of my knee again. "No matter how many times I kiss you there you shiver. For me."

White-hot bolts of heat race through my core as I watch his tongue snake through his lips as he places wet, sucking kisses up my inner thigh. My cheeks burn and a wetness begins to pool between my thighs. His warm breath on my most sensitive flesh feels like a promise. He grabs my ass and pulls my heated flesh against his mouth, forcefully parting my folds with his tongue. He zeros in on my sensitive bud, and dear Lord, every stroke of his tongue is a healing balm all by itself. Each lick, each suck, each bite makes me more and more desperate to have him inside me. Have him feed me. Have him fuck me until nothing else matters.

"When you are ready," he says, looking up at me, "start feeding. Feed as long as you need. As long as you like. I was rough the first time, and I plan to take my time with you tonight, little girl."

I love it when he calls me that. Protesting seems like the thing to do, but instead I settle into the bed and put my hand on the side of his face. "Okay. I—thank you so much for being here with me. For me."

He smiles and goes back to placing feather kisses on my slit and thighs. Slowly, he licks the full length of my opening, stopping just shy of my clit. He does it again and then settles in closer to me, his five o'clock shadow abrading the delicate skin at the bend of my thigh. He's teasing me, torturing me. Every time he gets too close to my sensitive bundle of flesh, he stops and starts again while his fingers roam up and down my legs.

When he floats toward my clit again I dip my hips down, push myself toward his mouth, and it hits home. With a small flick of his relentless tongue, my entire midsection contracts and I protectively wrap my arms around my abdomen. It hurts like hell, but Haines doesn't stop. And I don't want him to.

His left arm snakes around my leg, and he uses his index finger and thumb to pull back the hood, making the small nub readily available for him to taste. To bite. I look down in time to see his lips close around my clit as he uses his free hand to finger me, hitting the perfect spot with the perfect amount of pressure. Watching him suck and finger drives me over the edge. The ardor starts in my belly and a beautiful ache overtakes my pussy as he continues to give me all of him. I throw my head back and hear myself make a deep, throaty moan as Haines continues sucking. The pain in my stomach hits a pinnacle as I feel muscle and skin stretch and heal, coming together as the shards of wood from the bed post come to the surface. But it's no match for the pleasure that I feel radiating through my entire body, originating with Haines.

"Again," he says, his mouth full of me as he tenderly uses his teeth to skim the delicate flesh. His lips close around me, and he inserts another finger, pumping in and out of me.

My nails dig into his shoulders as my body quivers, as he takes me higher; feeding me, feeding from me. Nothing else in the world exists right now but us. Who we are and what we will mean to each other. He hums deep in his chest. The feel of the vibrations pulsate through his mouth and take the dying throb from my first orgasm, turning it into a raging inferno of pleasure. I grab his head and scream as another rips through my body. This time there is no pain. Only bliss and warmth and Haines.

My Haines. My husband. That thought alone almost makes me come again, but Haines stops his assault and kisses his way up my body, paying close attention to the healed skin of my abdomen.

"I love your taste. Your smell. The feel of your

tight pussy around my cock." He rubs my belly and smiles. "Amazing, my sweet girl. Simply amazing."

Haines climbs up my body, forcing my legs further apart with his knee, and settles himself between my legs, pulling them up around his waist. He kisses me, and I can taste my lust on him. "Are you ready for me, Perry?"

I nod and smile into his lips, ready to feel him fill me. Inch by inch he enters me, gentler this time. We both let out a cry of relief as he seats himself inside me, balls deep, his beautifully muscular body covering mine. Our first sexual encounter, the loss of my virginity, was so primal that he couldn't help himself. I was left sore and satiated, and I loved every second of it. But he takes his time now, kissing me and palming my breasts, fingers dancing along my skin as he claims me in so many ways.

"Oh, God, you feel so good." I sigh into his mouth and feel the warmth of his breath against my lips.

He pulls back, and his eyes glow red. "So warm. So tight. So mine and no one else's."

"No one," I tell him, shaking my head and lifting my hips to meet his.

I moan as he pinches and rolls each nipple between his skilled fingers. He takes his time and explores every inch of me with his loving hands. Our sweat slicked bodies slowly writhe against one another as his hands steadily roam my body, getting to know every curve and bend. He slides his hand around my neck and kisses me. His tongue mimics his cock, sliding in and out, claiming my mouth.

He pulls almost entirely out and I growl, missing the feel of him.

"You like the feel of my cock inside you?" he says, his voice light and teasing.

"Yes," I plead, pushing my hips toward his to enjoy the fullness of him.

"Take me," he says, pumping into me, filling the hollow space that now belongs to him.

The building pressure starts its ascent as he pulls my right leg up and over his shoulder. This new angle gives him deeper access, and I moan and mumble as Haines whispers sweet, filthy words in my ear, telling me I'm strong and warm and his. Telling me he can't wait until *his* pussy milks his cock.

"My Perrian. I've loved you since I saw you at your twenty-second birthday party. You didn't know I was there. I didn't want you to." His words are strained and strong. "That's why I've been so terrible to you."

Umm, okay. Where the heck did that come from? Love? "Haines…"

"Don't," he says, pulling back to look into my eyes. "I don't want to know how long you've loved me or if you even love me. You will. Right now, part of you does."

I nod my head, mostly to myself, admitting the truth. I have fallen for him.

His strokes become longer and deeper. Grabbing the back of his head, I pull him down for a kiss and my body reacts to him.

"I love you, Perrian." So much emotion in his voice.

He whispers it again and I come, the orgasm rising and bubbling this time. The others felt like they were pulled from my body, forced by Haines' cock or fingers or tongue and lips. This one lasts longer and rolls over my body, making me quiver and pull him closer as his movements become shorter and deeper.

Thrusting harder, he pulls my legs farther apart, going deeper as his cock slams into me. "Fuck…Perry," he moans, grasping my ass and pulling me closer against his body as my pussy is flooded with his warm seed. His ragged breaths tickle my neck. "I love you, Perrian. I'll keep telling you to make up for the way I've treated you."

I catch my breath and kiss his chin. "We don't have to talk about it. I forgive you." I'd forgive him of anything right now.

"I was like a child, a little boy with a crush on his classmate who tormented her during recess." He laughs and tucks my hair behind my ear. "When I first met you I thought of this as a task. Your aunt invited me to your birthday party a few years after we'd first met and when I saw you I realized that I could love you. All the years I've been alive and I had never felt that way; never felt a spark as I did that day. I followed you like a puppy."

My twenty-second birthday was the first time I got drunk. I never even noticed him.

His eyes darken and he smirks. "I followed you as you *talked* to your friend's boyfriend."

Ah, yes. I remember that talk I had with Gavin. He was dating my coworker Donna, and I'd watched him push her and talk to her like she was nothing. He was ready to leave, and she wanted to stay. He tried to force her to leave, and I followed them to the parking lot. Gavin had grabbed her by the hair and called her a stupid bitch. In my inebriated state I didn't care who saw how strong I was. I gripped his arm and spun him around to face me. He tried to slap me but I caught his hand, breaking his fingers while I wrapped my other hand around his throat. Pulling him close to me and threatening to kill him, I pulled energy from him, making him too weak to stand, and threw him into a wall a few meters away.

That was the first time I realized I could pull energy from someone who wasn't sexually aroused. It's also the first time I realized how powerful I was. The sensible part of me tried to rationalize what happened, but in the end I put it on the back-burner and didn't think about it. There were more serious problems to worry about; like how I wanted to have sex and couldn't.

I smile up at Haines. "Donna never questioned what happened. She jumped out of the car, kicked him in the ribs, and dragged me back inside. She moved in with me after that. She and her boyfriend had an apartment and she needed a place to stay until she got herself together. Donna has a nice boyfriend now. They live in California."

Real friends are far and few and after I hit puberty I stayed away from people. To protect them? To protect myself? I don't have many friends but the few I do have can ask me for anything. I just met Trent and Ryan but they've been here for me and I will rip Samael a new asshole if he hurts them. Or my family. He took my father away from me. I won't let him do it to anyone else.

"Perrian, you're making a terrible face. What are you thinking about?"

"I'm thinking of how I have to get rid of that fuckwad before he hurts any of you guys. My family, new or old."

He smiles triumphantly and then allows stoicism to cover his face again. Sweet bastard. He's rooting for me. Whether it's because he owes Samael pain or because he doesn't want to see me die, I appreciate the support.

"So, you've decided not to die?" he asks smugly.

I look down and clench his cock with my vaginal muscles. "I've decided it's time for you to come on out of there. And I've decided that the next time you and I have sex there will be no pain or suffering involved. No healing. The sole purpose of our lovemaking will be to make one another happy." Of course, I've decided not to die!

He bends down, pushes my breasts together, and sucks both nipples into his mouth. "Well, I've determined to make you come again." He grinds his hips into mine and grins. "And look at that, I'm hard again."

Well, look at that.

Chapter Fourteen

"You look refreshed, Perry," Aunt Rita says, walking into the kitchen to find me and Haines eating cereal. "And you're no longer bleeding. That's a plus."

I swallow my cereal and give her a sarcastic smile. "Did you move in?"

She swats my butt as she passes and grabs a bowl out of the cabinet. It's nice having Aunt Rita and my mother here with us. Makes for a great distraction. None of us really talk about what's going on. We don't have a solution. Besides, there is strength in numbers and I want to keep an eye on them. Not that I can do much.

"Just for the next day or two." She shrugs and starts going through the cabinets. "Maybe a week or so. I want to make sure those satchels work just as well as the wards around the houses do." She grabs three boxes of cereal and begins to mix them all in a large green bowl. "Do you have lactose free milk?"

"Bottom shelf," Haines says, giving me a sideways smile.

It's nice to get along with him. And have mind-blowing, awesome sex in the process. Up until a few weeks ago if Haines would've smiled at me I would have anticipated nothing but nefarious intentions. Now, it makes me feel nice to have him smile at me.

Aunt Rita puts her hand over her heart and

stumbles away from us. "My God, Perry. What the hell did you do to him? He looks happy." She seems to be in a good mood. She's teasing Haines.

Or maybe she's just trying to lighten the mood. My father's funeral is in a few hours. We're going to drive to a secluded area in the nearby woods and cremate him. Part of me wants to stay here and let them tell me how everything went. I don't want to watch them burn his body. It's just a shell for who he really was, but it's *his* shell.

A knock at the front door pulls me from my thoughts. It's four in the freaking morning. I look at Haines and his face is unreadable, but I know what he's thinking.

I touch his hand. "It's not Samael. He can't get past the wards. Besides, I don't think he'd knock." I stand, but he grabs my waist and sits me back down. "Haines…"

"No," he says. "If he did manage to get through I don't want you anywhere near him." He disappears through the kitchen door.

Aunt Rita is a kick ass witch, and I have no doubt that Samael would be in flames right now if he tried to get in here. In fact, I wish he would try. The wards extend a few meters beyond the porch and watching that son of a bitch burn would make me happy. But according to auntie it wouldn't matter too much. He'd be healed within minutes. The wards are just a deterrent. Not a solution.

Hushed whispers from the hallway get closer as Ryan and Haines come through the kitchen door.

I'm out of my chair so fast it tips over and hits the counter. "Ryan? What happened? What's wrong?"

"Oh, sweetie," he says, hugging me tightly. "I saw the light on and wanted to come check on you. Trent and Roman are asleep. Are you all right?" He grabs my hand and leads me back to the breakfast bar, taking off his coat and draping it across the chair. "Your dad's funeral is in a few hours. I want to come. Plus, I couldn't sleep."

Ryan is sweet. A great friend. We haven't known one another very long, but he and Trent are awesome.

"I'm good, Ryan. Thanks for coming to check on me. And no," I say, patting his hand, "you can't come to the funeral. You won't be safe."

He reaches his hand under his orange night shirt, pulls out a gray satchel and wiggles it in front of me. "Umm, yes. I'll be fine. Besides, you need a friend around. Family and friends help in times of need. You've got the family here already. I'm your friend."

Rubbing his shoulder, I pull him in for another hug. He's off his rocker if he thinks I'll let him come. He's mortal, and he has a kid. "Thanks. And no. Things go wrong."

He looks at me stubbornly. "You can't stop me."

Before I get a chance to threaten him a light tapping at the back door catches my attention. Is there an 'Open for Business' sign glowing in the window?

"Did you guys hear that?" I ask.

"Yes," Haines says, standing to walk toward the door.

I walk past him, yank open the door, and am hit with a small rock right above my left breast. "Oww. What the fuck?" I say, looking at two people standing about three feet from the fence surrounding the backyard. Whoever they are, they can't get too close to the house. "Fucking angels! What? Come to stone me to death?"

There are two people, angels, standing just outside the barrier of the ward. They are tall and thin and they both have a tender look about them, but the woman looks soft. She's tall with dark brown hair and olive skin. That angelic look is absolute bullshit.

I begin to walk toward them, and Haines grabs my arm. "Really, Perrian? You're going out there?"

"I'm not going outside of the ward. I just want to know what they want."

"We've come to talk to Perrian," the woman says. Her voice is regal with an Indian accent.

"I'm sorry, I don't believe I asked you a question," Haines says, giving the woman a vicious look.

That kinda turned me on. A few weeks ago, he probably would have shoved me past the ward just to get rid of me. "Haines. I can talk to them."

"*We* can talk to them," he says, entwining his fingers with mine.

Aunt Rita brushes past us. "I hope that *we* includes me, too," she mumbles, walking toward the angels.

As Haines and I walk closer to them I see that the woman's eyes are a rich brown with gold flecks around the iris. Her long, dark, bone-straight hair reflects the light of the moon. She has on a blue and gray petticoat with brown pants and gray flats. She looks sweet, normal. Like Samael, but not. I can't put my finger on it.

"Ari-el," Auntie says, nodding to the woman. "And Adkiel. What do you want?"

The guy, Adkiel, nods toward her and smiles. His college frat boy look makes him seem harmless. Wavy brown hair and a delicate chin are almost a distraction from the strong arms and wide shoulders. "It's been too long, sister."

"Well, you don't come to visit me. None of you do. But now you want my niece. Come to tell her she's an abomination? Have you taken the side of Samael? He is mad, and you two joining forces—"

"No, sister, "Adkiel says. "We've not joined him. We've come to pay tribute to our fallen brother. And to give Perrian information."

I walk closer to them. No one wanted to give anyone information a few days ago. Maybe this crap could have been avoided if information was given. Part of me wants to tell them to go kick rocks. "What kind of information?"

Ari-el's smile is wicked. "The kind that will help you stop Samael."

Yeah! That sounds like the kind of information we need. Why don't I trust them? "I don't trust you. I don't know you. Why would you help?"

The two angels look at one another and then back to me. They don't look like they want to share, but why else would they be here? Oh yes. They could want to hand me over to Samael.

Adkiel reaches out to touch me, but thinks better of it. "Because, sister, you are not the atrocity Samael gives you credit for. Much the opposite. You were foretold by the prophets of the Lord and being evil, though you are half demon, is not what or who you are."

He doesn't think I'm evil?

I don't know what to think. "So, I'm not the Bringer of Death? That's comforting."

Ari-el looks at Aunt Rita and then to me. The sides of her mouth draw up and she wrinkles her nose. "No, Perrian, you are the Bringer of Death."

Holy shit. That can't be good. That's just not a good title to have.

"I'm the reason my dad is dead? Because I bring death to those around me? That crazy bastard was right?"

Ari-el shakes her head and begins to walk toward me. "No, you have it—"

With a bright flash, she hits the ward and looks like she's caught in a slingshot. Her body floats forward into the barrier and then she is shot backward, smoke rolling from her body as she hits a large tree. A sickly crunch echoes and makes me cringe.

"Jesus!" I try to run toward her but Haines grabs my arm and pulls me back into the yard. Silly me, one step off the property and I'm Samael fodder. Where's my satchel?

Aunt Rita and Adkiel run toward her. There is smoke coming from her mouth and some of her hair is missing. She groans and tries to stand up but falls back to the ground.

Ryan runs up behind me and whispers in my ear, "I swear to God, if that wasn't so violent and painful looking I would say it was awesome. Your aunt made a kick-ass ward! Someone has a new pupil."

I snicker, but stop myself. That did look really painful. "Is she going to be all right?" I yell. "I think we should bring her in the house. Haines, your neighbors aren't going to appreciate a fried angel unconscious on your property."

"Perrian," he says, never taking his eyes off my

aunt and the angels, "I don't think it safe. Your aunt would have to lower the ward to let them in."

I understand his hesitation, but if they know something that will help me I'm all for it.

Adkiel picks Ari-el up and cradles her like a baby. He whispers in her ear and looks around the neighborhood, making sure no one is watching us. Werewolves may be out of the closet, but even they don't do anything weird like trying to magically cook someone who gets too close to their house.

Aunt Rita walks them toward the backyard and puts her hand up. "*Quiesco.*"

My ears pop and the wards lower as they walk past us.

"Rita?" Haines warns.

"Haines, just calm down. If either of them attacks I'll do what the ward just did. Except there won't be any singed angel left over. Well, at least for a minute or two." She turns around and puts her hand up again. "*Sine carmine reditum.*"

Again, my ears pop, and goose bumps cover my skin. The ward is back in place. I turn to Ryan and point toward his house. He doesn't need to be here.

He starts to argue but sees a light turn on in his house. "You are so lucky Trent's awake." Ryan stalks through the backyard and heads toward his house.

I wonder if she can teach me to do that to Samael. Frying him would be a good way to incapacitate him long enough for me to kill him. But how the crap do I kill him? Gun? Knife? Bedpost?

Haines hooks my arm through his and turns us around, guiding us to the backdoor. We walk into the kitchen and are met with the putrid smell of burning flesh.

"You should probably open the windows," I tell Haines.

He wrinkles his nose. "Yes, that sounds wise."

The smell gets stronger as we walk toward the living room and see the angels on the couch with auntie. She looks at Haines and timidly smiles. "I know a spell to get rid of the smell. But not the stains on your couch."

He shakes his head and pulls me to stand behind him. If I'm as powerful as they say I am and all hell breaks loose, I want him behind me.

Ari-el opens her eyes and it looks as if every blood vessel in her once white orbs have erupted. Her lips flutter and she looks at Adkiel. "Tell...her," she says, pointing at me.

She looks terrible, pained. I look at Adkiel and shake my head. "No, stay with her. You both can talk to me later."

Okay, that was the grown-up thing to say. But the part of me that is itching to find out what the hell they have to tell me wants to haul Adkiel's ass out of there and make him talk. But I'm an adult. I pay taxes and all that crap.

Aunt Rita stands up and walks toward us. "Close your eyes, dears." She bites her bottom lip and frowns. "Better yet, Haines, go upstairs and tell your mother-in-law to stay up there, too. Perry, get behind the couch."

Haines' eyes widen and he looks as if he wants to say something. A look of panic spreads across his face as he looks to auntie and the angels. "I must insist that you do not destroy my house, Rita."

She shrugs. "Here's the thing, I'm about to help her

evoke the Light of Heaven. She'll heal instantly and we can find out what they know."

"The light!" Ari-el says. "Tell her about the…" Her eyes close and her breathing quickens.

Holy shit, she's dying. This may be completely selfish but if she bites the big one her buddy over there may feel too much like crap to tell me whatever the hell they came here to tell me.

I lean into Aunt Rita and whisper, "Can you tell her not to go into the light, please?"

Aunt Rita looks torn. She wants to tell us what the hell is going on, but she wants to help her friend. And I'm being a complete and total shit.

I shake my head. "Never mind. Just help her. She looks like she's in a lot of pain."

"Dear, Lord," Auntie says as if tired of being interrupted, "please let me finish. I'm going to evoke the Light of Heaven. Haines is a full-blooded demon so it would probably incinerate him. You, Perry, are half angel. It won't kill you. I'm not really sure what it will do to you, but you won't die."

Umm, that is not too comforting. I won't die, but I could end up fried or worse. Upstairs seems mighty appealing.

Epiphany—so therein lies the problem. I'm half angel, half demon, and no one knows what to make of me. Well, Samael wants to kill me so he seems like the only one who has a definite plan for me.

I was happily oblivious a few days ago. Now, I don't know anything that can help any of us, but I know just enough to make me wish I didn't know anything.

Haines grabs my arm. "We're going upstairs, Perrian."

I shake my head and look at Ari-el on the couch. Time to woman up and makes things happen, see what I am capable of. Glimmer of hope sparking inside me? I just pray it doesn't lead to my bursting into flames. "No, Haines. I'll be fine. If the healing Light of Heaven—"

"—the light, brother please, tell her…"

"—does something terrible to me then we know not to ever use the stuff around me again. Remember, dearest husband, I'm a bad-ass half-breed. Or at least that's what I hear."

Trying to lighten the mood I smile to reassure him that I'll be fine. *God, please let me be fine.*

He grabs the back of my neck, pulls me closer to him, and looks into my eyes. His expression is unreadable. "Rita," he says, still looking at me, "I leave Perrian in your care. Please do not disappoint me. I've come to care for her well-being more than I do my own."

Giving him a sideways smile, I touch his hand that's resting on my neck. "Don't worry. I'll see you in a few minutes."

He rubs the back of my neck and walks away, heading toward the stairs to tell my mother to stay put.

This should be interesting. A half angel, half demon being surrounded by the Light of Heaven. I don't know much about it, but it doesn't sound warm and fuzzy for a demon. Just a few days ago every bone in my body was broken, mended, and my skin felt like it was going to splinter off. After that kind of torture pain doesn't sound all that scary anymore. I should be fine.

Adkiel comes and stands next to me. "Perrian,

would you like for me to hold your hand?" he says, smiling sweetly.

Is he coming on to me? "Nope. I'm good." I take a step back and start focusing way too much on my shirt-lint.

"You seem uneasy," he says. "I have the gift to comfort those who need it. That is where my gift lies. I help the dying cross over. I'm sorry if I made you uncomfortable."

Well now I feel pretty bad. He just wanted to make me feel better.

"Thanks, Adkiel. I appreciate the offer, but I'm good." I give him a sincere smile and look back to Aunt Rita.

She's whispering to Ari-el and making the sign of the cross over different parts of her body—her forehead, heart, wrists, and feet. Ari-el lies there staring at me and trying to smile. I wish she'd knock it off. It looks like it hurts her face to make the subtle movements. And she's missing half of her front tooth.

Before I realize what he's doing, Adkiel reaches over and makes of the sign of the cross on my forehead.

"Thanks?" I say, leaning away from him.

"Perrian—" he begins.

"Call me Perry."

"—Perry, I know the only angel you've known is Samael but not all of us wish you harm. Samael has lost a bit of his mind, and his grace. It's his own doing. He decided a long time ago not to ask for forgiveness, but to try to earn it. He should have known better. No one, not even angels, can earn forgiveness. It's already there for you to receive. You just have to ask for it."

I never thought of it that way. Samael pulled this

whole 'wipe-out-my-offspring-and-God-will-forgive-me' thing out of his ass. Even if he does succeed he's still screwed. And so are we.

When I was younger and found out I was part demon I never tried to make things right between God and me. I hadn't done anything wrong. No one is perfect and I'm not claiming to be, but I knew there was nothing I could possibly do to make things right. I just kept doing what I'd always done—prayed. The Big Man hears me. Of that I have no doubt.

Adkiel clears his throat and looks at me. "There is something we needed to talk to you about. I'm sorry for forgetting, but things took an unexpected turn, did they not?"

Thank cheesy bread he's the one who brought it up. I was trying to be the bigger person here. "Yeah, things did get a little weird. I completely understand if you want to wait."

"No," Adkiel says, taking me by the elbow and leading me toward the love seat. "There is no need to wait, Perry. In fact, this will help us see if you can use the weapon."

That sounds super promising. And super scary. What if I can't use it? What is *it*?

"The weapon," he continues, "is the Light of Heaven. There are very few things that can kill an angel, and the Light of Heaven combined with Hell's Fire is one of them. Angels cannot wield this weapon. We cannot touch Hell's Fire. Just as demons cannot use the weapon either. The Light of Heaven is lethal to them. This is why we believe you are the one to do it."

Words? I don't have any. Did he just give me the key to killing Samael and stopping this whole crazy situation? Did he just fill me with the hope that had been slowly slipping away from me, no matter how badass I tried to be? Or did he just snatch it all away? What if one side is stronger than the other and I can't use the weapon? This just brings up a whole new list of shit I don't know.

I scoot a little closer to him, trying to be quiet. "Well, thank you for sharing. It's good to know but it also scares the crap out of me. There's nothing I can do about it right now, so I have a question for you. Bringer of Death. Why am I the Bringer of Death? That doesn't have a nice ring to it."

He shakes his head and smiles. "Oh, no, Perrian. Quite the opposite. You are one who will bring peace to those who need it."

"I don't understand."

"Sister," he says, touching my folded hands, "you will take the place of—"

"Come now, you two," Aunt Rita says as she comes to stand in front of us. "Let's get this done. That way we can cremate Kevin at dawn. It is the best time to do it."

Damn-it! "Aunt Rita, we just need a minute more."

"Then you'll have it later," she says, brushing it off. "It's the morning of the third day, and dawn will ensure we will be surrounded by our brethren. It's what he would have wanted."

Okay. I can do this. I can keep my yap shut and not tell my aunt to shut the hell up. Whatever these two came to tell me sounds like the game-changer. I can wait five fucking minutes.

Looking at Ari-el I see she's reaching for me. The tips of her fingers are burnt and there is a patch of singed skin on her hand.

I stoop down and take her hand. "Yes? Do you need something?"

She shakes her head, takes her other hand, and rests it upon mine. If she didn't look like she was in God-awful pain I'd say she looked peaceful. "Everything happens…for a reason…sister. I knew not to touch it. But I did. I…I didn't mean to touch it. The barrier. But now…we will see if you are really the Peace…Bringer."

Peace Bringer. That sounds a lot more awesome than the Bringer of Death.

I shrug and start to stand. "Well, I hope I don't let you down."

As I try to pull away she holds tight to my hand. "Stay…please. Hold my hand."

Holding her hand seems like the nice thing to do, but getting fried by the Light of Heaven is not on my agenda for the ever. "Umm, shouldn't I be behind the couch?"

I look at my aunt. Her eyes are wide, and I can see her nostrils flaring from her increased breaths. Holy fuck, she's afraid.

"Ari-el," she says, "we need to keep her safe. I don't want her getting hurt. She's suffered enough these last few days. We don't know what will happen."

Adkiel comes and puts his hand on my shoulder. "Have faith, sisters. Perry will be fine."

Aunt Rita shakes her head and crosses her arms over her chest. "I will not allow it. Perry, get up and get behind the couch." She looks between Adkiel and Ari-el. "You should be glad I'm allowing her to stay in the room. Do not test me for it will not go over well. She is mine to protect."

I'm pretty sure a wrestling match is about to go down, and no matter how high and mighty these two may be Aunt Rita is going to be victorious.

I try to stand but it feels as if a weight has settled in to my legs. All the bells and whistles that are supposed to go off when you're in trouble begin to float through my head, but another more pleasant feeling begins to steal in. This is where I'm supposed to be and moving from this spot will prove me a coward. It doesn't sound like my idea, but it feels better than trying to hide.

"No, Aunt Rita. I'll stay right here."

She harrumphs and begins to argue, but I cut her off.

"You said you had a vision about me, right?"

She shakes her head but still doesn't seem to want to give in.

"You're here for a reason. So am I. Maybe I am more than some half-breed mutt Samael keeps claiming me to be. And before you interrupted me and my buddy Adkiel here, he was going to tell me what I was."

"Bringer of Death," he says in a matter of fact voice.

I glare at him. "Thanks, Adkiel. That helps." I turn back to my aunt. "I'll be fine. Let's start answering some of our questions. Help me to stop being confused about me and my purpose. This may not be the solution, but it may help us find it."

She inhales deeply and begins to chew on her bottom lip. "I'm supposed to protect you. I haven't been all that great at it."

I smile at her. "Hey, you've done pretty well. Let's point the 'you're wrong' finger at my parents for right now. You and I are good."

Without going into it any further Aunt Rita closes her eyes and begins to chant. I look at Ari-el and see a proud look in her eyes. Thank Christ she's not trying to smile anymore.

Aunt Rita's voice gets louder with each passing word. It sounds like music; the most beautiful music I've ever heard. It's melodic and soft and powerful. It's the most beautiful language I've ever heard.

Looking at Ari-el as she closes her eyes, I pat her hand and close my eyes too. My aunt's voice begins to climb, a crescendo nearing, and a subtle cool wind begins to blow through the room. I know a few of the windows are opened, but the tranquil drift doesn't seem to come from outside. The air outside of our house is crisp, the smell of changing leaves and new fallen rain. This breeze that floats through the living room is sweet and smells of flowers. Like roses and orchids and new born baby skin. And it's suddenly so bright in here!

Oh, God, it's so bright. Through my closed eyes a blinding, beautiful, warm light pulses through the room. I need to open my eyes, but I'm afraid the light—if you could call the most pure of all lights that—will hurt me. But I will. I will open them.

As my eyelids peel back from my eyes and Aunt Rita's voice becomes farther and farther away, the wind I feel fluttering against my face pulses. The radiance is so brilliant and so lovely. I can't focus. It's a sensory overload. The light is like a field of freshly fallen snow. It hurts my eyes, but I dare not close them.

"Look at me, sister," Ari-el says as she stands in front of me.

I'm still kneeling. "What's going on? Where

is…the house?"

Her hair is once again soft and long, and her olive skin seems to glow from the inside. Her magnificent brown eyes are clear again. And she has wings! Big freaking wings! They are so white they are almost clear. They stand at least twelve inches above her head and come down below her knees. Her gown is the most stunning shade of blue; like the ocean or the sky. I don't think I've ever seen a bluer color in all my life.

"Be not afraid, Perrian. This is what I wanted, to bring you here to this plane."

It doesn't matter what she meant to do. I'm so happy. Happy? That's not the right word. God help me, I don't know the word!

"This is the Heavenly Plane, Perrian. This is how our kind heal, by coming home."

Tears are falling from my eyes. I'm so…delighted. I've never been so fucking happy in my fucking life. *God, please let me stay.* I don't want to leave. Since I have demon blood coursing through my veins, will I be made to leave? "Is this Heaven?" I ask her, tightening my grip on her hand.

"Not quite," she says, pulling me to stand. "If we were going to enter that marvelous place, this would be where we would find the Gates. Adkiel and I were going to take this slowly, but since you and I are here we can do this now."

Here. I should be looking around, trying to take in what I can only imagine is the most beautiful scenery I could ever lay eyes on. But something stops me. Something within me is so afraid to look around, and I keep my eyes glued on Ari-el's face. Why?

"Perrian. We must complete our task. You must do

what you've been chosen to do."

What? "Do what?"

"Have you claim your part of Heaven's Flame. The Light of Heaven which is part of the weapon that will defeat Samael. My brother told you of this, yes?"

I shake my head and put my hands on my hips, only to have my elbows brush against something soft. Looking to either side of me, and catching a glimpse of the lush green grass, I try to grab the fabric of my— Heavenly?—gown that seems to puff out on all sides. I pull at the soft fabric and feel a tug at my back. Yanking harder, I yell out as a sharp pain radiates up my back and to my shoulder.

Turning around, it seems as if the material moves with me. It's not... "Oh my...is this...what is this?" I don't think I like it! It feels wrong to have these on me. "When did I get wings? Jesus Christ, they are huge!" And dark silver, almost gray.

Even after yanking on them the cashmere soft feathers align effortlessly with one another. The edges of my wings are thicker and look more plush than the middle. Though I love the feel of them, the darkness of my wings contrasts so severely with the light that surrounds us.

"They are beautiful, Perrian. I've never seen wings such as yours," Ari-el says as she reaches for me.

But I back away from her and keep turning, trying to get a better look at them. They keep fucking moving! "This is too much! Too much too soon."

I'm frightened. I don't know why, but this seems wrong. Her wings are beautiful and well, angelic. Mine look ominous.

Her wings seem to glow, but mine seem to reflect

the light. Or are they absorbing it?

Demon. That's what I am and knowing it makes me feel guilty, like I don't belong here. When I first found out I was part demon, I flipped. Started apologizing to God about it. After a day or so of crying my mother asked me if I felt the love of God before I knew what I was, and if I did then why was I doubting it now? He always knew what I was.

She grabs my face and pulls me close to her. "Calm down." Her eyes are stern, but kind. "I can't claim to know how you feel because I've had mine since my creation. But you must calm yourself. The more emotion you feel, the more forgotten memories will begin to surface. This place is a remembrance of your life. It serves so that you will leave it all here and go in to experience the wonders of Heaven. Are you listening to me?"

Freaking out. I'm still freaking out. This is off. I'm in the Heavenly Plane with silver, menacing looking wings. I want to calm myself, but this is too much.

"Perrian, close your eyes and just listen to me, okay?"

I shake my head but don't close my eyes. The wings are distracting. Hell, I haven't even bothered to take a look at the rest of the scenery. Fear won't allow me. When I try, Ari-el tightens her grip and pulls my focus back to her.

"Sister, close your eyes and listen to my voice. Now."

Fighting the urge to slap her hands away and shove her, I close my eyes and grab her elbows.

"That's it," she says. "Just listen. You are safe here. More safe than you have ever been. Remember that blinding light? Pull that into your mind and concentrate on that. Can you do that?" Her voice is calming.

"I can do that. I'm doing that." Center on that light, Perry. It was wonderful. You would look at it every day, all day if you could.

"Good," she says, smoothing out my eyebrows. "Reach out your dominant hand and imagine that light coming toward you."

Instantly I feel white hot heat in my right hand. The heat sates me and makes me feel whole. But it also scares the shit out of me. I begin to panic. Will it hurt me? Will Heaven's Flame cast me out because I don't belong here?

"Perrian, it can't hurt you. You are of this place. The Light of Heaven didn't hurt you and neither will the Flame you shall invoke. Do you understand?"

I nod my head. "If you say so." Fuck. This feels off. A part of me wants to flee, to somehow make it back home with Aunt Rita chanting over Ari-el's burnt body. But the other part wants to dance. Wants to sing and run free.

"I do. Now, pull that light, that heat toward your hand and mold it into something you can hold. A sword, a thunderbolt. Anything you can wield."

What if I let it in and it destroys me? "Ari-el, why am I scared? I should feel good, shouldn't I? I did at first but now I'm scared."

She kisses my forehead and keeps a steady grip on my cheeks. "It's your demon half. It's rebelling against this place, but you must fight it. There is a part of you that wants to escape because you feel like you don't belong."

Tears fall down my face. They rain. Are my tears falling to earth? I don't like this. "I don't belong here, do I? That's why I feel so bad."

"Listen to me. If you weren't supposed to be here then you wouldn't have been able to shift here. It's all right. Remember what I told you to do? Focus that energy? Do it now. Turn the Flame into something you feel comfortable handling."

Fencing. I took fencing lessons when I was in high school and was pretty good at it. I had to quit the team my junior year of high school. At the last fencing match of the season I lost to that slutbag, Melony Porter. When she dealt the winning blow and I got extremely pissed off, everyone within ten feet of me either experienced the best orgasm in their life, or a killer headache for the rest of the day.

How did I forget that? How did I forget that that was the day I realized I could affect people when I wasn't sexually aroused? I thought it was at my birthday party, but it wasn't. That's important. I think?

"Perrian!" Still holding my face, Ari-el jolts me back to the present. "Do it. Stop thinking about the past. That's what this place does. It brings back memories of extreme emotion. Focus on your weapon."

Quieting myself, I think about the sword; gently gripping the handle. Feeling it conform to my hand. I look at the vibrating light now coming toward my hand and imagine it forming into a fencing sword. I was always partial to the epee. It's a little heavier than a foil, but it made me feel like a musketeer. The handle fits perfectly in my hand. The blade and the hilt are of perfect balance.

"Good girl, Perrian. You are a quick learner. I

thought we would have to practice this for weeks before I even brought you here. See, this is who you are. This is who you are becoming. The Peace Bringer. Don't forget that."

I quiet myself as I look at my sword. Its light shines so true and hot. And mine. It is mine through and through.

"You feel it, don't you?" she says, letting go of my face.

I don't know what 'it' is but I feel something. "What is *it*? And what am I supposed to do with this?"

She backs away and clasps her hands in front of her. "You feel your power. Who you are becoming. And you can put that where ever you want."

"Umm, like my pocket?" It suddenly disappears, but I can still feel its presence.

"Now that you have claimed it, it is yours to call when you see fit. Come, your aunt is almost complete."

No! I didn't get a chance to check this place out. I was too afraid, but now I—

As if someone just took a picture, a bright light flashes and we're back in the living room. We were there and now we're here. I don't want to be here. I want to go back. I want to go home. No, it didn't feel like home, not at first. But it is. No matter how hard my demon side rages against Heaven, it will always be my home.

"Holy shit!" I yell. Still kneeling next to Ari-el, I hear Aunt Rita's voice begin to fade away as she completes her ritual. It's as if no time has passed here at all.

Ari-el is lying on the couch just as she was before, but where she was once burned and pained, she is whole and healed. Falling back on my butt, I pull my legs up to my chest and roll on my side.

It's gone. That wonderful, beautiful, frightening feeling is gone. *Please come back. Please don't make me come back here.* This place is different. It's dark and full of sorrow and pain. That place, where I just was, was perfect. Perfection.

I rock back and forth on the floor, pushing my face into the plush carpet to blot out the darkness. So empty. I feel so empty here. How do the angels bear it?

How could my father and aunt choose to be here rather than there?

Aunt Rita comes and starts to smooth the hair from my face. "What the hell just happened to her?"

"She was at The Gates," Ari-el says. "I helped her claim her part of the Light. Her part of the Flame. I hadn't planned on doing it this quickly, but she shifted with me as I healed. I didn't think she'd be able to. Not so soon."

"Perry," Aunt Rita says. "Perrian, honey, open your eyes. What's wrong, dear?"

I cover my face with my hands and sob, sucking in short breaths of stained air. It tastes different here. Contaminated. The darkness in this world is almost corporeal, entering me through the air I breathe, being filtered through my body. "There's no light here, but it's too bright. I don't understand. Why would you want to be here?"

God, please, help me. I...I don't know. I just don't know.

I feel the slight hand of Ari-el touch mine. "It's how angels feel when they leave the Heavenly Plane. She feels the loss of it."

169

"I never felt like this," my aunt says. "What did you do to her?"

Adkiel picks me up and sits me on the couch. "You wanted to come here, Rita. It was your choice. She has never known such peace, and amid all the turmoil in her life right now the Heavenly Plane made her feel the way it was designed to make everyone feel—like it was time to go home and be at peace. Time to leave all the emotional baggage behind and move on."

Get your shit together, Perry. You're freaking out and you know it. Breathe. Just breathe. You're here with your family and you have what you need to defend yourself.

Out of a great feeling of loss and distress I feel heat. Heat and love and lust. I look up to see Haines standing at the door, watching me.

"Why is she crying?" he asks my aunt. His ears are red. Is he upset?

Sitting next to me, Aunt Rita begins to rub large circles on my back. "This may sound odd, but for all intents and purposes she was in Heaven. And now she's here. Back to a place where the sole responsibility of saving us falls on her shoulders."

For a moment he looks dejected. Crossing his arms across his wide chest, his gaze lowers and he worries his bottom lip. He thinks I'm going to reject him again.

We've made such progress in the past few days, and him feeling rejected could throw us backward. I won't let it.

I clear my throat. "Auntie, please let Haines and me know when things are ready for the funeral." I look at the angels. "Thank you for coming and thank you, Ari-el, for showing me how to... I don't know, claim my part of the light?"

She smiles. "*The Light*. And you are welcome. But we still have much to tell you."

I nod. "After the funeral, please? Or tomorrow evening. Is that all right?"

"Yes," Adkiel says. "We will attend the funeral and then take our leave. We will return at dusk to tell you what we know."

I think he understands what I feel, to a certain degree. He misses the Heavenly Plane—or Heaven—probably more than I do. He knows what Heaven is like. I only got a small taste of the front door. But unlike me he doesn't feel torn. He can return there and have nothing here to miss. I have my mother.

And my husband, whose stoic face shows flashes of pain. He doesn't know what to do for me, watching me sit here with tears still running down my face as I constantly rub my arms.

"Thank you all," I say, standing up and walking toward Haines. I wrap myself around his body, almost climbing him as if he were a tree. I bring my lips to his ear and lock my arms around his neck. "Take me upstairs, please."

Wrapping his arms around my waist, he quickly turns around and walks toward the stairs.

"Where is my mother?"

Haines hikes me up higher on his body and wraps his arms around me, bringing me closer. "Resting in the downstairs guest suite. She told me to keep an eye on you while she prepared herself before the cremation. I think she just wanted a bit of quiet before we left."

I understand. She and my father have been together for centuries. They sacrificed so much to be together.

And now he's gone. And she's still here.

"What happened, Perrian? Were you really in Heaven?" He carefully walks up the steps, taking his time so he won't juggle me back and forth as I cling to him.

I shake my head. "Not Heaven. I think it was the passage way to Heaven. Ari-el called it the Heavenly Plane." I feel fresh tears fall down my cheeks. "Can we talk about it later?"

Haines pushes our bedroom door open with his foot and sits me on the bed. He tries to walk away from me, but I won't let go of his hand. I need something to hold on to here. All I want to do is go back there to that beautiful place, but I can't. Can I?

"I'm just going to lock the door, all right?" Before letting go of my hand he looks at me for approval, brows knitted together and lips drawn in an attempted reassuring smile. "All right?"

Nodding my head, I let go of his hand and crawl back on the bed. I've got to pull it together before we leave in a few hours. I've never felt stronger and at the same time more weak than I do right now.

Even though I can't see it I know my sword is still here with me. I feel its presence; its light. It makes me feel powerful and in control. But I've never been more emotionally unstable than I am right now. I still want to cry. Because I'm happy and because I'm miserable.

Haines takes off my shoes and socks and pulls the blanket over my legs. Resting his back against the headboard, he pulls me into his arms and rests his chin on top of my head. "Shall I have your aunt bring you something?"

"No," I whisper, taking a deep breath and pushing

my face into his chest. "You smell nice. What cologne do you wear?"

The rumbling of his laugh echoes through his chest. "I don't wear any. It might be my deodorant."

I put my face close to his armpit, inhale deeply and rub my foot up and down his shin. "Will you make love to me?" I need to feel grounded and the only thing that makes me feel *here* is Haines. His arms. His deodorant?

Holding my chin, he tips my head up. "Do you need to feed?"

Is that what he thinks? He couldn't possibly believe that's the only reason I would want him. "No feeding. Just touch me, please." I unbutton my pants and pull them off, along with my panties. I crawl up and straddle him.

"Perrian, I don't want to take advantage of you. You just had a very trying experience."

I unhook my bra and then pull his tee-shirt over his head. "I'll beg if that's what you want." I feel completely naked in every single way. My heart is on my sleeve and my emotions are raw.

Haines pulls me in, holding on to the back of my neck. "No. Please don't," he says, his breath tickling my neck.

I back away from him and grab the band of his pants, pulling them down just enough to free his cock. On my knees with my ass in the air, I wrap my hand around his velvety hardness and feel how heavy he is. I look up at him and say, "I won't be any good at this."

"You're already perfect, Perry," he says, eyes glued to my lips.

His cock throbs and I use my tongue to trace the mushroom-shaped bulge, a drop of his seed sitting there just waiting for me to taste. I suck his cock lightly into my mouth and use one hand to massage his balls. A quiet *hiss* escapes his lips as his fingers reverently move around my jaw, and I feel victorious. He grabs a handful of my hair and starts to guide my movements, pulling closer, deepening his hardness into the back of my throat.

As I bob my mouth up and down on him, swirling my tongue and tenderly scraping his shaft with my teeth, I look up at him and see his eyes half closed as he looks down at me. He whispers my name and thrusts his hips forward over and over, his cock swelling in my mouth. I gag and fight the urge to pull away from him.

Haines pulls me away and pants, "No. Not yet," he says, his stomach contracting as he takes deep breaths. "I don't want to come in that beautiful mouth of yours tonight. Come here," he says, holding the sides of my face and pulling me toward him for a kiss.

Hungry kisses cover my lips, my neck, and my breasts. His hands cup my ass, stroking the rounded flesh. He lifts up so I can free him of his sweat pants. At this level, my thighs are on either side of his, and my breasts fall right in his face. He pulls one nipple into his mouth while gently pinching the other. One hand slips between my thighs, and he slides a teasing finger through my wetness. I arch toward him, pushing my breasts further into his mouth, and feel a soft shiver race up my spine. I wrap my arms around his neck as his gifted tongue laves my nipples, his large hands tease me as they run along the planes of my body.

His teeth surround my nipple and he bites, hard enough to make me cry out. Pain and pleasure come together, and without any hesitation he places his long, full member at my entrance and pulls me down. Though my body is the one absorbing the shock, Haines cries out and holds on to me. Sheathing his entire length with my body, I pause for a moment and feel my muscles stretching as he fills me.

"You are always so tight," he says, teeth gritting as he takes deep breaths. "You fit me, and I fill you."

Getting up the courage to move as his body fills mine, I lift up and slowly come down as I coat his cock with my juices. "You always feel so good," I tell him as I slowly ride him, the delicious friction already causing a massive frenzy deep inside me.

He grabs my ass and spreads my cheeks as he thrusts upward again and again. The muscles in his shoulders flex as he lifts his hips and pulls me down on to his hard shaft, going deeper and deeper with each plunge. I gasp but he kisses me, harder this time, and softly bites my bottom lip. "Feed if you need to. Take what you want. But not my immortality. I don't offer it to you. Not anymore." His voice is strangled, raspy.

I break our kiss and sit back to look at him. Did I hurt his feelings downstairs? Does he think I don't want him anymore?

His gaze holds mine as everything falls away, and he tightens his embrace to keep me still against his body. "Now that I know you don't need it to defeat Samael, I will not give it to you. I want to live as long as I can and be near you. And when you've decided you've had enough of me I will fawn for you, begging you to come back to me."

He takes his hands and grips my hips, urging me to move again. Haines runs his palms up my ribs and cups my breasts. His fingers squeeze my hardened nipples and it feels like a direct line to the orgasm already brewing deep inside me. I rock back and forth as he releases my tender buds, and he strokes his hands along the column of my spine.

For the next hour we disappear into one another. If there was nothing holding me to this world before, I believe on this night I have found my anchor.

Chapter Fifteen

The funeral was lovely, if you could call it that. Why do people say things like that? *The ceremony was beautiful.* What makes a funeral ceremony beautiful? The flames that reached to the early morning sky as his body was incinerated? The way my mother fought back the tears so hard that I thought her midsection would cave in because she held herself so tight? Or was it the way my palms bled as my nails dug into my own flesh?

My anger at Samael far outweighed the sorrow that seeped through my skin. Knowing that my father had been murdered and that I now held half of a weapon that would end this brought a dichotomy of hatred and relief. The sword itself seemed to call to me to be manifested. I don't know why. Maybe because I was pissed off and wanted to hurt something.

Not sure whether the sword would appear if I lost control I walked away and told my mother and Haines to stay with Aunt Rita, Adkiel and Ari-el. The sword was made from the Light of Heaven. Would it harm my mother and husband because they were demons, even though we're on the Earthly Plane? We're not going to find out.

As I walked through the heavily wooded area I would catch glimpses of people, angels, standing in the distance. I can only guess it was because Haines, my mother, my aunt, and I wore the protective satchels that kept the angels at bay. The only reason Ari-el and Adkiel could be so close to us was because of a spell that allowed them to be present. At the fucking funeral of my dead father.

Stalking through the woods, I could hear the occasional whisper of *'I'm sorry'* or *'Solace to your heart, Peace Bringer.'* My personal favorite was, *'Peace upon you, Bringer of Death.'* Angels sure know how to make you feel special.

If they actually felt bad for me why don't they band together and kill Samael? Imprison him? Do something to help. I can only imagine it's because he's killing demons and my father, the angel who decided that becoming a human was better.

When we came home from the funeral I crawled into bed with my mother. I used to do it when I was a child; crawl in to my parent's bed and wait until I felt better. That's not going to happen now. We both lay here in silence, drifting off and waking up to more silence.

Haines and Aunt Rita have left us so that we could find comfort in one another. I suppose auntie should be here with us. She has lost someone, too.

"Mom," I whisper, wondering if her slow breaths means she's asleep or just pretending.

She shifts a little closer to me and opens her eyes. They are red-rimmed and puffy. "Yes, Perrian."

"Mom, I'm sorry. If—"

"Do not finish that sentence. I know where you're going with this and it is not your fault. Never think that. Do you understand?"

We're so close to one another that when I nod my head I bump her forehead with my own.

"Perrian," she says, rubbing her hand through my wild hair and pushing it behind my ear. "I wonder why we're considered demons."

I shake my head and settle closer to her.

"Demons are of hell," she says. "Succubae and incubi are born of humans and an angel. Granted we were created when Lilith was going through a particularly confusing time, but we are not of hell." She laughs. "I take it back. She was made a demon long before she bore us. But at her core she was human."

I never thought of it that way. Lilith technically was human, but by the time we were created she'd become something more. Something a little less human.

"Perrian, you are powerful not because you are evil, but because you are of the Line of Lilith and an angel. No matter what kinds of terrible names Samael calls you, you are not evil. You are not bad. I believe he's afraid of you. Do you understand?"

I understand just fine.

"Mom, why did you and Dad decide to keep everything from me? Did you honestly think it would help? Or was it like the 'sex' conversation that parents don't want to have with their kids?"

She shrugs. "By the time you were old enough we kept thinking that telling you later was better. And then later came and it didn't seem like the right time. You were so powerful, and we thought upsetting you would... I don't know. Your powers are tied with your emotions. We thought that if someone could first teach you..."

"—I wouldn't go ape-shit on everyone? Sorry for the language."

She laughs and then holds her breath. When she

179

lets it out, it sounds shaky and labored. "I'm so sorry your father and I didn't do this better. We should have told you sooner, no matter how uncomfortable it made us." Her voice is almost a whisper.

Thank you. Finally, some admission to this madness. I've been so upset and confused that pointing the finger just made me feel better. But now that it's out there, blaming someone just seems so pointless.

"Do you forgive me, Perrian?"

"Of course, Mom. I forgive you. I know I gave you crap about this, but I never held a grudge. Never. We'll figure this out."

She smiles at me, and I feel a tiny bit better.

My mother pulls my head to her chest and begins to stroke my hair. "The angels will be here soon. We can get this sorted and move on with our lives."

I look over at the clock. They should be here in an hour.

"Mom?"

She hugs me and then starts rubbing my head again. "Yes, Perrian?"

"I'm a badass. I can pull the Light of Heaven out of my pocket. And once I get Hell's Fire I am going to rip Samael a new one."

****

My mother and I walk down the stairs hand-in-hand, laughing. Seems as though she thinks the sword is pretty freaking awesome. She'd love to see it, but neither of us want to see her burst in to flames.

She sees Aunt Rita and walks toward her. "Rita, I'm sorry Perrian and I have been locked upstairs all day. You've lost someone too, and we shouldn't have acted as if you didn't."

Aunt Rita pulls my mom in for a hug. "Think nothing of it, Barbara. You were the one sleeping with him."

I wince and close my eyes. "I don't mean to be *that* guy, but please let's not talk about this around me."

They exchange a look and start laughing. It's good to see my mom smile again. Aunt Rita never lost her smile. Even when the tears threatened to betray her she kept smiling.

It's funny. I never paid much attention to my aunt before all of this happened. I would see her and she would make a comment about me being single for the rest of my life, and I would roll my eyes and ignore her. Why did she pretend?

"Aunt Rita?"

"Yes, dear?" She puts the tea pot on the stove and then reaches over to start the coffee maker.

Do angels drink coffee? Tea? "Why did you act as if you didn't know what I was? As if you didn't know why I was single?"

She laughs and begins making watercress sandwiches. "It was more a jab at your parents than at you, Perry. They were always around when I made those comments. Watercress?"

Disgusting "Eww. That's grass. And not the good kind." I reach in to the refrigerator and grab the lunch meat and cheese. "Thanks for trying to get them to spill the beans. I still can't believe I didn't know you were the Seer we came to see when I was a teenager."

I begin rolling the lunch meat slices, setting them against one another so they won't unravel. Busy work. Maybe that's why she's making this spread for the angels. Keeping busy takes your mind off of why they are actually coming.

Aunt Rita pulls out a box of toothpicks and slides them toward me. "I told you. It was a good cover. What would you have done if you'd known it was me? You would have pestered me, asking questions and I would have eventually caved. Besides, no one knew who I was. They still don't."

Good points. It doesn't matter now. It's all out on the table.

"Where's my sweetie?" I ask, taking out the stovetop espresso maker to make *azuquita*; stuff that makes Colombian style coffee awesome. "And why are we making snacks?"

Aunt Rita takes the espresso maker from me and puts it back in the cabinet. "Angels like finger foods. And they need to be comforted."

Okay. "Why do they like finger foods and why do they need to be comforted? And please don't tell me they're mourning my dad. They never bothered to stop in and say hello before he was killed, and I would hate to *hate* them for being assholes." I look at my mother. "Sorry for the language."

My aunt shrugs. "Lower level angels, though wise, are childlike and children like little things. And they are now on the outs with Samael. They chose to help you and if he gets his hands on them…let's just say it won't be pretty."

They risked their safety to help me? And now that bag of douche wants to hurt them? Can he? "Can he kill them?"

"No," Haines says, walking into the kitchen. "But he can make them suffer. He's an archangel, and they are messenger angels. He's much more powerful."

Why the hell does everyone but me know this stuff? Maybe there's a manual or book called *All the Things Perry Doesn't Know About her Life*. Can I get a copy?

I reach for the espresso maker again and Aunt Rita slaps my hand.

"Auntie, do you have something against me making my coffee stuff?"

She turns me around and points on top of the microwave. "Your husband already made it for you. I'm amazed your poor teeth and gums couldn't sense the amount of sugar you plan on ingesting already present in the room." She scoffs and goes back to the snack making.

I turn to look at Haines, instantly turned on by his thoughtfulness.

"Please," my mother says flatly, "for the love of all things holy don't do that while I'm in the room."

My lust must have ballooned out for a moment, and my mother's words immediately put a stop to it. Going to have to work on that. No sex-demon powers activated while anyone is in the room.

Haines smiles and hands me the container, along with a coffee mug full of fresh coffee. He kisses my forehead. "Is there anything I can do for you?"

"I'm good, thanks. Where've you been?" I mix a tiny bit of *azuquita* in my coffee and bring the cup to my nose. Smells like I'm going to be awake for a few hours.

Haines takes out the container of half-and-half and hands it to me. "Talking to my brother."

It's nice to see a routine develop between Haines and me. It'll be interesting to see what this will turn into once my beef with Samael ends. And I've made it out alive. Which I am totally going to do.

"How are mommy and baby?" my mother asks as she pours herself a cup of coffee.

Haines sighs and grins. "They're doing wonderfully. Molly is recovering nicely from the long labor and Riley is very loud." He rubs his hand through his short hair and sits at the breakfast bar. "My brother wants to know if we've made any progress. They are both concerned."

My snark wants to kick in but I take a deep breath and look at it from their perspective. People's lives are on hold, waiting for me to get rid of Samael. We've just added three more people to the mix.

"Everyone, I'm sorry. I know it's not my fault that Samael is insane, but nonetheless, I feel responsible."

The three of them begin talking at the same time, telling me that I have no control; that it's out of my hands. I put my hands up to quiet them. "I know, I know. I just had to say it. So there. It's out." I hear a faint humming and look toward the door. "The angels are here," I say a little too quickly.

They look at one another and then back to me. I shrug and point to the back door. For a few moments there is only silence, and then a tap on the door heralds the throwing of pebbles.

Aunt Rita smiles. "How did you know? Did you hear it?"

I nod. "What was *it*? And why is this the first time I'm hearing *it*?"

She walks toward the door and opens it. "Angels can sense one another. You're getting stronger." She lowers the shields and beckons them inside. She tells them about me sensing their presence, and Adkiel grins like a fool.

He looks me up and down and then frowns. What the hell was that about?

"The vibration?" Ari-el asks.

This is a bit disturbing. "Yes. It was more like a hum."

She waves it off and comes to stand beside me. "You are Peace Bringer. Your power is immeasurable. May I have one?" she asks, motioning toward the tiny sandwiches.

Aunt Rita pulls out a tray of mini-desserts. "Have as much of whatever you like. The both of you. Please."

Adkiel and Ari-el light up like Christmas tree angels—ha!—and begin making little plates of everything. I smile and think of how innocent they truly seem to be. When they first came here and Ari-el was crispy-fied, they both seemed wide-eyed and nervous, as if they were telling some secret that would earn them a spanking from a parent.

I suppose it is kind of like that. Samael is the crappy big brother who wants to make them suffer simply because he can. These two are risking their safety to make things right for us.

"So," I say, looking between Adkiel and Ari-el. "How does me becoming the Peace Bringer/Bringer of Death benefit you two? Or are you seriously doing this out of the kindness of your hearts?"

Adkiel shoves a mini-éclair into his mouth and chews slowly. He looks around and then starts paying way too much attention to the coaster rack. He's stalling. Why do I get the feeling he doesn't like me anymore? It almost hurts my feelings.

I clear my throat and look at Ari-el. She seems to mean more business than he does. "Spill it, girlie."

She wrinkles her face and wipes her mouth with a white linen cloth. "You know my name is Ari-el. And we are going to help you fulfil the prophesy." She pats Adkiel on his arm and smiles. "He's afraid that you'll get upset once you know why we're doing this and what the outcome will be."

Aunt Rita walks over and sits next to Adkiel. "I knew there was a reason I was sent to help Perry. I just didn't know why. When the Father puts it in your mind that you're to do something it's really not a suggestion. So, what's special about her? Not that you're not special, Perry."

Here we go. The history lesson is about to start and I'm more anxious than I thought I'd be. I've wanted to know what all this mess was about, and I've been afraid that it'll turn out that I truly am a bad person.

Shifting in my chair, I look around the room and see that Haines has managed to come stand behind me. I look over my shoulder and meet his reassuring eyes.

Ari-el, always the gung-ho one, stands up. "In many sacred texts Samael is said to be the Angel of Death, and that *is* who he is. But he has been the reason of his downfall that has taken centuries to complete. He used to delegate how things would run among the Reaper Angels and their Messenger Angels, but his insanity has left us with no one to tell us what to do. In his role he was supposed to be neutral, being neither good nor evil. But he can't perform his function anymore. And that's where you come in, Perry."

Holy shit, I know exactly where this is going. I stand up and go for the dessert trays, piling a tiny plate with mini-éclairs and cheesecakes. Comfort food. I'm going to need every bit of it.

"I told you she would get angry," Adkiel says, whispering in Ari-el's ear.

He blanches when I look at him. "Dude, I can hear you."

He sinks back in the chair and shoves more food into his mouth.

Ari-el rolls her eyes and continues. "He's an angel and is almost incapable of partiality. Samael has turned what he thought was good into his own twisted version of right and wrong. He committed a sin and that sin became flesh and bone; the birth of the sex demon. If he would have gone to Father and admitted he made a mistake this would be over with and he would no longer carry the burden. But he's allowed it to eat away at him, and it has made him what he is now.

"But you, Perry, you are both good and evil. It lives within you making you exactly who you are. You are angel and demon. You are duality in its most natural form, and Samael knows that. He's threatened by you. The ancient texts of Heaven say that he is supposed to bow-out as the Angel of Death and hand the Rite of Death over to you. Then he would take his place in Fifth Heaven and continue there forever.

"Since he has chosen not to step down you must make that choice for him. But he has become far too dangerous. You must use the key, your sword of light and dark, to lock him away and take your rightful place as the Angel of Death, bringing peace to those whose time is over on this plane, whether they be human or supernatural. Only you can wield the Sword of Duality. It can't hurt you, for it is an extension of you. Even if someone were to manage to take it from you it would be useless in their hands. You have to stop him, take the Rite, and end this."

Freak out? Say a prayer of thanks now that I know what my role is in everything? I don't know what to do. I can't be the Angel of Death. I have a bad attitude and like to be left alone. They have to be wrong.

"Bringer of Death," Aunt Rita whispers. "Peace Bringer. My god, you are the Grim Reaper."

Lies. They are lying to me. Grim Reaper my ass. I start laughing until my cheeks hurt and the tears run. This can't be right. It sounds crazy.

I chew my top lip and worry my fingers as Aunt Rita looks at me like I'm the most horribly beautiful thing she's ever seen.

Her eyes are wide, full of fear and adoration. My mother has been silent this whole time, but her expression is loud and clear. She has the same look in her eyes as Aunt Rita.

But not Haines. I don't know when he moved, but he's made his way back to the trays and is making a little plate. He has that same proud look as when he first found out I was healing from being impaled. After he found out I was part angel and part demon.

"Haines," Ari-el says. "I'm sure you've been wondering what your part is in Perry's life?"

Confusion flashes in his eyes. "After learning that I don't have to give Perrian my immortality what more can I do?"

The angels look at one another. Adkiel finally speaks up. "No, your interpretation is wrong. You will not give Perry your immortality and become human. You *are* her humanity. Her love for you is what will anchor her to this world. You are her tether that will keep her neutral."

He's right. I don't know how, but I see it. I've had an extreme love-hate relationship with Haines from the moment we met. The angel in me rebels against our union and the demon in me adores him and wants to please him, recognizing his incubus as the mate of my succubus. And the love I now feel for him keeps that grip on humanity that the other halves know nothing about.

Instantly, I feel better when I look at Haines. I still want to cry and scream and ball up in a corner until I can completely process what's going on. But I don't have that luxury. We are running out of time.

Haines' eyes are trained on me, and I feel stuck. He nods his head slightly, and I close my eyes. In my mind I can still see him looking at me, feel his eyes on me. That nod was permission for me to freak out or hold it together, or maybe do both at the same time, and not be ashamed of either decision. I decided earlier this evening that he would be my anchor, keeping me sane amidst all the chaos, and I do everything I can to hold on to that. Hold on to him. How in the hell did he and I get here?

I open my eyes to look at him and see a devious, vengeful grin playing at the corners of his mouth. "So," I say, staring at Haines but talking to the angels. "How do I get the other part of this key so I can kick the dog-shit out of Samael, and lock his crazy ass away for good?"

Chapter Sixteen

"They don't know how to get the other half of the fucking sword!" I yell at Haines as I pace back and forth in our bedroom. "They come here and tell me this awesome story and make me feel like, 'Hell, yeah! I can do this shit!' and then they drop the fucking ball." I completely blame this shit on Adkiel. Why? 'Cause I don't like his face!

Haines sits quietly on the bed, slightly reclining on the pillows with his legs crossed at the ankles. He yawns and stretches, his chest filling with air making his muscles roll along his torso. He reaches to the bedside table and grabs a bottle of water, and my eyes are drawn to the building tent in his pants. He looks at me and his erection jumps.

"Why are you hard?" I ask.

He reaches down and adjusts himself. "Because you're pacing around the room with no bra on. I'd love to have your breasts in my face right now. But we don't have time." His lips curve into a smile. "As you were saying."

I look at his erection again and feel lust pool between my thighs. That looks like so much fun. I snatch his robe from the chair in the corner of the room. "Haines, can you please put a shirt on or something?" I ask, handing him his robe. "You are completely making me not want to be angry right now, but I wanna be!

Damn-it."

Adkiel's suggestion was to find a demon to help me get Hell's Flame, but my mother and husband who are demons and technically have no ties to Hell can't help me. I am so screwed. And we've only got two days left. I feel like I'm back at square one—give myself over to Samael to save the lives of the people around me. Well fuck that! I am enjoying life. I'm all for taking one for the home team, but I need to come up with another plan.

Haines takes the robe and folds it up, using it as a cushion for his lower back. "We'll get this all sorted. You've already learned so much in such a short period of time. There are ancient texts written about you. You will not die."

I scoff. "I'm not worrying about me dying. It's everyone else I'm worried about. Your niece is only a few days old. She was born into an impending shit-storm. I don't even know the little cutie pie, but she will not live in hiding for the rest of her life. Ryan and Trent are keeping Roman home from school until this dies down. He keeps taking off his satchel because apparently it smells like syrup." I shake my head and smile. "His dads are afraid he'll take it off at school and then he'll be easy pickings for Samael. I am so going to kill that bastard."

How dare he threaten children? Anyone who hurts a kid should be tortured and killed. I'll fix Samael before he even gets the chance to do anything to them.

Light bulb!

"Perrian, I believe I may know someone who—"

"Screw that," I say, bending down to pull on my socks. "I know a guy. I wonder if he's home from work?"

****

It took a few minutes to convince Haines to let me leave the house by myself. I've got the satchel safely around my neck, and I'm not going too far. Ryan and Roman should be home, but Trent may still be at work. I still can't believe it took me almost seven hours to remember that right down the street from me lives a Hell-borne demon. Or at least a half breed.

Ryan snatches open the door before I get a chance to knock. "Your husband called to tell me you were on your way and to open the door. He wanted you safely within the borders of the ward. How are you?"

The worry in his eyes is genuine, but the wariness hiding behind his smile makes me nervous. "I'm good. You got your hair cut."

Ryan shrugs and helps me take off my coat. Shaking his head, he takes a big unsteady breath. "Roman and I went to the barber shop. He was getting a little antsy being cooped up in here."

I want to comfort him and say that it'll all be over soon, but I don't know how long soon is. If Trent can't help me, we could all be in hiding for the next few weeks. Months?

"Look, Perry," Ryan says, hanging up my coat and pointing me in the direction of the kitchen. "Trent told me not to worry you, but I thought you should know." He gently grabs my arm and pulls me closer to him. "Samael was at the barber shop. It's like he knew we were there, like he could sense us, but he couldn't see us. It's hard to explain."

Holy crap. This is bad. Really, really bad. He sniffed them out. He's trying to prove a point and it's coming through loud and clear. Time for Samael to move on to that big padded room in the sky. "Ryan, I am so sorry. This is my—"

"Stop it. The satchels do their job and you're going to figure this out. No worries." He starts moving toward the kitchen again. "I trust you."

Roman and Trent are sitting at the kitchen table making a picture using different shapes of pasta noodles. The picturesque scene makes my heart clench and brings a misty tear to my eye. I am running out of time. We all are. I have a feeling that Roman is going to slip that stupid satchel off when no one is looking, and he's not going to be within the safety of the wards. I hope it doesn't happen, but something tells me it will if I don't end this.

"Hey, guys," I say, pasting on the sweetest smile I can plaster on my face for Roman. I'm worried Trent won't be able to help me, but Roman gets the happy face.

"Hey-hey, hi-hi!" Roman sings. "You came over because you want Daddy to make French toast, didn't you?"

I nod and grab a banana off the counter. "Yup. That's exactly why I'm here, kid. You've got a taste for breakfast for dinner?"

He nods his head and sticks a pre-glued veggie pasta string on his picture. "Uh-huh. And since you and me both like breakfast for dinner we're gonna get it. Aren't we, Dad?" He looks at Ryan and smiles.

Why the heck not. I'm in. "Yeah, Ryan. Aren't you gonna make it for us? Please?" I sing.

Ryan frowns at me, and then reaches his hand out for Roman. "Sure," he says, as Roman puts his hand in

Ryan's. "You've got it. But let's finish your picture upstairs while Perry and Dad have some grown-up time."

They both gather up the noodles, paper, and glue and head upstairs. Life must be awesome for a kid—no worries, no bills, and danger is cool. *God, please let me keep his life this simple.*

I turn around and see Trent grabbing a bottle of white whiskey from a child-proofed cabinet along with two shot glasses. He twists off the top and fills the tiny glasses, shoving one toward me and picking up the other.

"Drink it, Perry." He downs the first shot and pours another. "We're going to need some courage juice. Haines already told me what you needed my help with."

His words are clipped, almost cold. He's probably pissed off about Samael sniffing out his husband and son. I'd be raging mad if I were him, too.

Trent pushes the glass toward me. Usually, whiskey isn't my thing but the thought of going to Hell, or a dimension that leads to it, makes me down it in one giant swallow and then fight the urge to strap Bible pages all over my body. "Jesus," I whisper. "Did you actually get this *from* Hell?" I choke out. I can feel it burning its way through my chest and into the pit of my stomach.

He pours another shot for me. "Two for the show," he says, downing his second shot. "If we manage to get this done I'll take off my satchel and be crazy-angel bait. That's the only way I've been able to come up with to lure him to us. That cattle rapist killed your father, is trying to kill you, and is hunting my family. At the damned barber shop! The only thing standing between us and him are the satchels. And you."

Nodding my head, I fight the urge to throw-up and down the next shot. "Oh. My. Goddess. I can't breathe." I slam the glass on the counter and grab my chest. "It's...fucking...boiling." Is this corn liquor? Can't a bad batch of moonshine kill you?

He's out of his fucking mind if he thinks I'll let him be bait. How could he even think of risking it? What the hell was in that liquor? Does the body of the male praying mantis really keep pounding away during sex while the female eats him, starting with the head? Why is Roman in the room? Why the hell am I thinking in questions?

"Dad? Can you hand me the bowtie pasta?" He's looking at me strange.

Come on, Perry. Keep it cool while Roman is in the room. "Hey, kid," I cough out, slapping my hand over my mouth so that I don't throw up on his colorful pasta.

Smiling, Roman pats my hand, soothing me, and then takes off running into the other room and up the stairs.

Once I hear his little footsteps in the rooms upstairs I give myself permission to let go and stop pretending I don't feel like I'm dying. A pain-filled tightness grabs hold of my chest, and I can't take a deep breath. Sound and light seem to get sucked into a wormhole, and it takes me along with it. Sliding out of the chair I back up and clutch the counter, feeling the cool marble as my fingers fight to find something to hold on to.

Trent is standing there just looking at me, shaking his head and twisting the cap back on the bottle of liquor.

"Trent, what did you do?" I ask, attempting to pull myself to a standing position.

My head spins, my eyes flutter, and everything goes black. It's quiet, and dark. And it smells terrible. Did Trent just poison me? Did he make a deal to save his family? As much as it pains me, I wouldn't blame him. Not one bit.

****

"Holy shit!" I scream out. "What the—" Trent grabs my arm and tries to help me up off the floor. I slap his hand away. "What just—"

"It's a potion that shifts us to the Gates. Thought we'd jump right into it."

Gates. This isn't Heaven or the Gates that lead to it. This place sucks. It makes me feel like hitting. And crying.

Trent steps away from me, and I finally notice that he has purple pointed horns on either side of his head and his eyes are yellow. His shoulders are broader and his bronze skin has a weird yellow tint to it. I guess his demon form shows through in Hell.

"Trent, you're a scary looking mama-jama while you're all demon-ed up."

He's looking at me with his mouth hanging open, and his eyes are wide. What the hell does a sex demon look like in this place? Am I a sexy beast or just a beast-beast?

That dueling feeling starts inside me again. But unlike being at the Heavenly Gates I feel poised and...powerful. My demon half is rejoicing and thinking of all the men I could seduce if I'd just let go. But my angel half is quiet. Like she's waiting to see what happens.

196

"Perry," he whispers. "You've got big, silver wings and…your skin. It's almost glowing."

I look down at my body and notice a long, silver, flowing gown that cinches at the waist and billows out all the way down to my feet. Picking up the gown so that I don't trip over it, I notice that my hand is glowing. Not like a light bulb; more like someone put a towel over a lamp, but the light still manages to shine through. I turn my head to check out my wings and notice they are luminescent too.

"It's the darkness here," I say more to myself than to Trent. "It wasn't as noticeable in Heaven because it was so bright. But this place is so…"

Empty. It's so empty and void of everything. I look around and see nothing. No shapes. No trees, no walls, no anything. It's just me and Trent standing in a vast empty place that seems to go on forever. It's maddening, and I want to go home. Not to the house I live in, but back to the Gates that lead to Heaven.

"Come on, Trent. Let's do our thing so we can get the hell out of here." I don't want to stay here any longer than I have to.

Trent is still staring at me, but the once friendly look has turned predatory. His stance is firm and balanced, like he's ready to pounce on me—broad shoulders squared, one foot in front of the other as if he'll run toward me, and his hands are balled into fists.

Take a bite of you, a voice says. *Consume that beautiful light so that it will shine through me and make me less of what I am. A demon.*

I take a few steps back and then mimic his stance. If he attacks me I'll be ready. "Trent, are you thinking of eating me 'cause I'm sure things like that are frowned upon. Especially by your sweet husband and that awesome son of yours. You know, Ryan and Roman?" He shakes his head as though the names of his loved ones brings him a little closer to reality. "Besides, I'd hate to have to kick your ass, and I don't know how to get home."

He seems to think it over and then takes another step toward me. I put my hand to my waist, ready to pull out my sword.

This place seems to bring out the worst in you. I want to cry, kill, and abandon my duties to my family.

Trent seems to want to eat me.

"Come on, Trent. Get your shit together. Ryan and Roman need you." I say their names again to get him to reconsider. "And right now I need you. Help me get Hell's Flame so I can stop Samael from killing your family."

That seems to do it. His eyes squint and he bares his teeth. "Touch the Gate, Perry." His voice is low and thick, like he's trying to stop himself from throwing up.

Gate? What the hell is he talking about? There's nothing here but me, Trent, and a huge fucking gate that appears out of nowhere. It's so large, and eerily close, that I have to take a few steps backward to see the entire thing. It's made of shadows and despair. The top of the large gate isn't visible. If there were clouds hanging in the gray, muted sky, the top of the Gate would rise high above them.

"How?" I whisper.

"It's going to open soon," he says, instantly getting nervous. "Claim your fire and let's go. Souls are about to be ushered in."

What? How does he know? I don't want to see this.

"How do I claim it?"

The Gates seems to groan, like a person in tremendous pain and ecstasy, and the whole thing shudders. Trent grabs my arm and pulls me backward.

"Hold your hand out, but don't touch it, and let it flow into you." His words are rushed and his eyes begin to dart back and forth. "Perry, I don't want to be around to see this when it happens. I saw it once before and I've been wishing for years that I could scrub it from my brain."

Take it into me? I don't want to take it into me. Whatever this thing is made of, whatever is in this place, I don't want it inside of me. I took the Light of Heaven into me and felt whole. Goddess knows what taking a piece of Hell into me would do.

"Hurry the fuck up, Perry."

Nope. Can't do it. Won't do it. This place is tainted and I refuse to have it be a part of me. But it already is a part of me, isn't it? I am half demon.

Screw that. "Dude, I can't do—"

"Get *your* shit together, Perry! You've got people to protect and one of them is my son."

I look at him, and then back to the Gate. The sound of something unlocking echoes and the entire structure convulses. Everything stills as the Gates begin to open.

"God damn-it, Perry!"

God help me. Lilith help me. I don't want to do this. My upper back trembles, making my wings flutter like a butterfly caught up in a sudden gust of wind. Nervous angelic tick?

With my right hand I manifest the hilt of my sword, keeping it hidden so that I don't hurt Trent, and with my left I reach out toward the Gate. My angel half begins to stir, lifting her head and finally taking notice of everything that's happening. She gives me strength. I close my eyes and imagine the shadows and darkness that make up the rungs and simple pattern of the Gate are coming toward me. Opening my eyes, I see that it's not my imagination. It's actually happening. My first instinct is to snatch my hand away, but I fight through it as the angel in me pushes us to keep going. The shadows touch the fingers of my left hand and begin to disappear into my palm.

"Trent," I say in a low voice. His name sounds more like a question. "Get out of here. Go back home. I'll meet you there."

I can't see his face, but I hear the terror in his voice. "I'm not leaving you here! You don't know how to get home."

In Heaven the demon part of me rebelled and tried to claw her way out, afraid of being surrounded by such peace. But the angel feels no fear. Only victory. "Please leave," I tell Trent, gripping the hilt of my sword tighter. A quiet calm takes over and I feel like I am capable of anything. Even taming my demon half. "I have to pull out my sword. It'll kill you. Just go." I know I can make it home. I don't know how I know that, but I do.

"Look, Perry, I'm sorry I thought of eating you. I would never hurt you. You're safe with me." *God, you are beautiful.*

A strong wind starts to build, and I feel my hair and dress begin to flow as whispers and soft cries fill the empty space. I close my eyes again, focusing on the energy flowing into me. A bright light flashes, and it's so brilliant I can see it through closed eyes. It's coming from me. The pulsating light that shines through me lights this space up like a disco hall.

"Trent, you have to go. I don't know what I'm doing, but that doesn't mean I'm not going to do it." That sounded absolutely stupid, but I know what it means. My body, my spirit, my sword made of Heaven's Flame knows what to do, even if my brain is still unsure. All of this seems to be ingrained in my body. "Demon!" I say in a voice that doesn't seem to be my own. "Leave this place before you never get the chance."

"Please," he pleads. His voice trembles, and I can hear his words become heavy with threatening tears. "You can't... I didn't mean to..."

I turn my head to look at him and see his whole body shaking. "I will not tell you again." My voice is hard and cold. Every fiber in my body wants to leave now, with him. But something greater than my will keeps me here.

He lowers his head and disappears with a barely audible 'pop.'

The soft cries and pull of the wind gets stronger, and a feeling of dread settles in to me as the Gate begins to open. I pull out my sword and hold it close to my chest.

With the light of the sword and the light of my body beginning to build within me, shining so brilliantly, I begin to see things hidden in this dark place—disfigured forms rising from the ground; horned figures slinking out of the darkness. They are drawn to my light and want to consume me.

These bitches don't stand a chance.

I raise my sword in the air and see the magnificent

light gleam through the blade. The darkness of the Gate that entered my body dances through my right hand and curls its way around the light of the sword. The light and dark coil around one another and join at the end, making the tip of the sword blunt, but thin. As the light and dark mingle everything becomes clear. I know the answers to all the questions I never even thought to ask when it comes to Heaven and Hell and how everything in this world started. The hilt wraps itself around my hand and wrist and holds tight as I look around and see these frightening monsters surround me. These are demons. Not like my mother or Haines or Trent. These are full-blooded, Hell-borne demons that know nothing but destruction and death. One of them reaches out and wraps its talon-ed hand around my arm. I've never seen anything more evil, more destitute, more hellish in my life.

I've done what I came here to do. Home. I want to go home!

A blinding explosion erupts through the darkness, and I slash out with the sword aiming for the claws and hands that reach out for me. I swing so hard I knock myself off balance, and when I hit the ground it's the floor in Ryan and Trent's kitchen.

"Oh my God," Trent screams. "She's here, Haines. She just appeared in the kitchen." He hangs up the phone and slams it on the counter.

He walks over to me and reaches out his hand to help me up.

"Get the fuck away from me!" God, I feel terrible. That place. That thing. *This* place. "I need…air. I need…" Haines. I need Haines. But I need to be by myself.

It's so hot. Or is it just me? I scramble up off the floor and tear my sweater over my head as I run for the back door. Haines will probably be coming through the front, but I need to get away.

Somewhere behind me I hear Trent yelling, telling me to come back. His voice is shaky. Is he embarrassed? Does he feel guilty for thinking of taking a freaking bite out of me? Why would he think that? Why did I hear him think that?

I stand just outside of the fence that encloses Trent and Ryan's house. My breath forms ringlets in the cold air as it rushes from my lips. All I have on is a tee-shirt and sweatpants, but I don't feel the cold. I should. Last I checked it was only supposed to reach a high of twenty-eight degrees. Why don't I feel cold? I usually feel the cold.

"She's out back," I hear Trent say. He's probably talking to Haines.

With one hand as leverage I jump over the fence and take off running toward the wooded area. It's only half a mile away, and I need space. Space to think. To cry. Just space.

Maybe it'll help bring peace back into my life. Deep inside I know that that won't happen. Not for a long time. Even if I manage to defeat Samael, peace won't be any closer. Because this isn't Heaven. And that's where I want to be. That's where I don't belong.

"Perrian!" Haines screams.

I turn around and look at him, putting one hand up in a 'stop' motion. He can't help me. Do I need help? I don't know.

He looks vulnerable as he stands there in the yard, the corners of his lips turned down and his eyes wide with…fear. His hands are balled into fists and the warm fog of his breath shoots out quickly, over and over. He looks like he's measuring how long it would take him to get to me. I can see he's struggling to let me go. If he tries to come closer I'll run, and I have the feeling that I could outrun him. Maybe not before, but I can now.

"Let me…" His voice trails off and he lowers his eyes.

I shake my head. "No, Haines. Let me go."

His eyes meet mine, and he nods his head. And I love him for it. I turn around and begin to run.

In the past week I've been to Heaven and Hell, and I honestly don't know which one was worse. Hell was terrible, and I know that I never want to go back there again. But Heaven was… It was almost just as bad. It was beautiful and full of light and love. I want to go back there and never come back here, to this place. To my family. To my friends. They can keep this life and all the shit that goes along with it. Maybe they'd be better off without me. What makes this so difficult and makes Heaven just as bad is the thought that maybe, God help me, I'd be better off without them. And they would be better off without me.

I've never felt more at peace than I did when I was in Heaven, despite my demon side trying to claw its way back to Earth. I wanted to cry because I was so happy. There was no confusion as to what my purpose was in life. There were no worries that they would miss me, because if they truly loved me they would know that I was in a better place. And I feel awful for even feeling that way.

The clearing of the wooded area is only a few feet in front of me, and I don't know how I made it here this fast. My breath is steady and I still don't feel the cold. I run a few yards into the woods and fall to my knees.

"God, please," I whisper, wrapping my arms around myself as huge tears begin to blind me. "I can't do this. I can't be here. Please, please…"

I close my eyes and wait. Someone has to answer me. I'm the fucking Angel of Death and I know God has to hear me. Doesn't He?

"Lilith? Why did you let this happen? Why did you let *me* happen?" I just want to go home. "Make it stop, please God, make it stop." My heart feels like it's breaking over and over again, and there is nothing I can do about it.

Haines' comfort won't help, my mother's arms won't help, and Rita's words of wisdom mean nothing. I can't do this. This only just started a few weeks ago and in my heart I know I can't do this.

"I give up," I whisper. "I can't do this. God, please don't make me do this."

My head is throbbing, and I can't breathe through my nose. This has to stop. I have to stop. No more.

"They all reach this point, Lady Bug. They all get to the point where coming with me is mercy." I look up and see Samael kneeling in front of me.

"I can't do this."

He opens his arms and as foolish as it seems, I fall into his arms. He embraces me and I begin to cry again. Huge sobs that wrack my body take over and I begin to scream empty words into his jacket.

Samael seems sane. "And you don't have to. Shh, it's all right. It doesn't mean you're a bad person if you give up. You're doing the right thing. Your family and friends will be safe, and you will know peace like you've never imagined." His voice is so sincere.

I pull away from him and look into his lavender eyes and everything is all right with my life. Because it will soon be over, and I can go home and be happy. Be at peace. Never in a million years did I ever think I would get to this point. But I'm here.

He smiles and gently pulls my hair out of my face. "Perrian, you just have to say the words. Give into me and I can help you move on."

Nodding, I pull my arms from around him and run my fingers through my loose, curly hair. "Thank you for calling me by my name," I say, smiling. It almost makes me feel better.

Don't do this, Perrian.

I shake my head. "What did you say?"

"Your name, it really isn't so bad." His smile is angelic. "Are you ready?"

Hold on, Perrian. You needed help and it is coming to you.

Is he messing with me?

"Yes," I say, nodding my head and feeling a little unsure. "I am. And you'll leave them alone? All of them?"

"I give you my word."

This is better. It all works out for everyone this way. It is finished.

As I open my mouth to tell Samael he can have me, two strong hands wrap around my upper arms and I am yanked back and thrown into a pile of fallen leaves. Something falls around my shoulders and I look down to see the satchel that Aunt Rita gave me. Instantly, my head clears and I look up to see Haines and Aunt Rita standing over me.

"Never take that off," she says, chin trembling, fingers spreading out and balling up over and over again. "It was a summoning spell he used on you."

Samael is still on his knees, that crazed look creeping back into his eyes. "I almost had her!" His eyes scan the area in front of him. He can't see us.

"Why?" Haines asks. "Why did you take it off?"

I look down and wrap my hand around the little, powerful, brown satchel. "I—I didn't mean to. What just happened?" It must have come off when I pulled off my sweater.

"A summoning spell," she says again. "Your satchel protects you from him completely and when you took it off you heard his call. That and your feeling of hopelessness added to it. You were ready to leave us. Though how his call was able to breach the barrier…"

That bastard tricked me. Maybe I felt shitty to begin with, but his added shit-stacker made it worse. It made death seem like the only thing to do.

This ends now. "No more." I put my hand to my hip and feel my sword manifest. "You'll be fine, Haines. Blended with Hell's Fire, Heaven's Flame won't hurt you. Both of you, get back."

I pull out my sword and see that the hilt is already wrapped around my wrist.

"Oh," Samael says. "There you go. I was getting a little wor—"

His eyes are priceless. Almost like he's dropped the soap in a jail shower. His skin, normally polished and luminescent is now pale, and his full lips are pulled into a thin line. The small look of triumph drains from his beautiful face.

"How can he see you?" Haines asks.

"It's the sword," Aunt Rita and I say in unison.

Samael smiles. "Got into Hell, did you? And Heaven? Which one made you ready to come with me? I bet it was Heaven."

"Yeah." I shrug. "That and your summoning spell. Stooping to using magic to get me to give in. Sounds like you're scared." With my sword at my side, I take a few steps toward him.

He stands his ground and straightens his jacket. "Who's here with you? Your mother? Is she still mourning? Maybe your lover-boy. Is he cheering you on?" His voice is contemptuous.

Lunging toward him, I raise the sword and slash downward. It skims the front of his coat and leaves a trail of burning fabric.

"I am going to run you through, you son of a bitch." I snarl and lunge again, this time turning in the opposite direction so that my back faces him for a few moments. When I bring the sword down it just barely misses his neck.

He falls backward, eyes wide with fear, and he begins to crab-walk backward but his retreat is ended by a large tree. "I will kill them all!" he says, and he disappears.

I stare at the empty space he once occupied. "Not if I kill you first."

My sword vibrates, as if reminding me it's still in my hand. I move to put it back in its place but I'm stopped by a wave of clarity. I can *see* the summoning spell he used on me now dissipating, almost like a thin trail of blue light, tinged with red. It trails from my chest, through the satchel, and back into the air. He used my blood to make the summoning spell. From my parents' room. The blood on the floor from where I sat bleeding.

A bright bang of light hits my eyes and I see…the truth. That's what my sword helps me see; the truth in the world. The truth in the life of others. Those whose souls are ready to move on. I don't get to choose where they go, but I can see why they're going where they will end up. And I see the truth of this world.

There was no Big Bang, not in the sense that creation *just* happened. God said, 'Let there be light,' and there was an explosion of light and evolution began, overseen by God. It wasn't seven days. Not our days. Peter, the apostle, had it right. One day to God is like a thousand years to us. Try a few thousand. God set it all in motion.

Another flash of light hits me and I see me; my purpose. I am duality in its most pure form. The dark and light within me helps me not to judge. Most people aren't just good or bad. We've all got a little of both in all of us. But in me there are equal parts, so much good and so much bad that sets me apart from everyone else. That's why I haven't been able to form bonds with too many people. Deep down they see me for what I am. A perfect judge who does not judge. And that's why Haines was given to me. He sees it in me and does not hate me for it. He loves me, and that love keeps me grounded and sane and whole.

Now you see.

"Yes," I say out loud. "Now I see, Mother. Thank you."

It was Lilith, our Goddess, whose voice spoke to me when I was ready to give in. *Thank you so very much.*

I turn around to look at Haines and Aunt Rita, and I see the truth in them. Haines loves me more than anything and will help me in any way he possibly can.

Aunt Rita loves and fears me, but she loves me more. Her heart is pure light. The kind of light that only shows in ones like Rita. And my father.

I give another silent *Thank you*, and put my sword away. "I'll try to never let that happen again," I say, jokingly. "With or without the satchel."

They both look pretty pissed off. Aunt Rita's hands are on her hips and her bottom lip is shaking. Her eyes are glossy with unshed tears and her breathing is ragged. She's trying not to cry. Or kill me.

Haines runs his tongue along the inside of his jaw, lips slightly parted. "Never. Take that off. Again. Do you understand me, little girl?"

Does he know he's turning me the hell on? Wrong place. Wrong time, Perry.

I try to hide my smile, feeling almost giddy for getting past something that could have been devastating. "Yes, sir. I will never take it off again." I look at them both and manifest my sword. "I feel pretty bad ass. This thing is awesome, isn't it?"

Chapter Seventeen

"Why didn't one of you wake me up? She could have been killed. One of you should have said something." My mother is not happy.

Aunt Rita rubs my mother's back and pats the kitchen counter. "Well, I for one did not want you to do something silly like offering yourself over in Perry's place. I'm sure he would have taken you, and then come back to get her anyway."

"Not your decision!" My mother slams her fist on the counter, and then covers her face with her hands.

Her anxiety is palpable. She just laid my dad to rest, and now she has to worry about losing me. Up until I got the first part of my sword I was almost certain she was going to.

I get up from the kitchen table and go over to her, pulling her hands away from her eyes. "Mom, I'm fine. I'm not going anywhere. None of you are. Samael is afraid. Of *me*. I don't think he thought I was capable of getting this far, but here I am." I shake my head and run my fingers through my freshly washed hair, feeling it go pouf and curly as it dries. "I just need a little more time. The sword can kill him, but I don't know how I can get close enough to do it. When I pulled out my sword the shields from my satchel disappeared, and he saw me. That does away with my 'I'll sneak up on him and kill him' plan. We'll come up with something."

I cut my eye and watch Haines butter and jelly two slices of toast. He stirs his tea, lifts it to his mouth, softly smiles, and takes a sip. I think he feels a little relieved. For the first time since he and I—I don't know, started liking each other—there seems to be a light at the end of this shitty tunnel.

He looks at me and motions toward his toast, silently asking me if I'd like any.

I shake my head and go to open the freezer. "Anyone up for frozen pizza? It kind of does taste like delivery." Silence. "Good. More for me. But just for the record, once this thing is finished cooking, no one even think about asking for—"

"Perrian?" Haines says. "Who were you thanking? Back in the woods?"

Smiling to myself, I open the oven door, put the pizza in, and set the temperature. "Lilith," I say, turning back to them. "I was thanking Lilith. She spoke to me. When I thought of giving up another part of me kept asking for help. And then I heard a voice telling me to hold on. To wait. She said that help was coming and then, Haines, there you were." I walk over to the breakfast bar and sit next to him. "I don't think I have ever felt so hopeless in all my life. So useless. And then you were there and you made me stronger."

My mother pokes me in the back of the head. "I guess I *do* know how to pick them, don't I?"

"Thanks, Mom," I say sarcastically. "Your humility knows no bounds. He and I would have ended up together whether you chose him or not."

I look at Haines and wonder if he's thinking what I'm thinking. Do we feel this way about one another because we genuinely love each other, or because we're supposed to? I think I'll save that conversation for later.

After Haines and I stare at one another for a few moments my mother and Aunt Rita take a hint and get the hell out of the kitchen. I lean in, kiss his nose three times, and begin to turn away from him.

He gently grabs the back of my neck and pulls me to face him, rubbing his nose against mine. "What we feel is not fabricated. Never let that be one of your doubts."

This gentle interaction makes me smile. He loves me. And I love him. "How—"

"You wear your emotions on your sleeve, and I've grown to notice the subtle changes in your expressions."

It's the truth. Hiding how I feel has never been a skill of mine. Time to work on my poker face. Being the Angel of Death must require a poker face.

I cross my arms and turn my head away from him. "You have no idea," I say, playfully. "I am very skilled at hiding my emotions."

Haines pulls me closer to him until we are nose to nose. He slowly teases my lips with the tip of his tongue. "Open," he says, releasing the hold on my neck and bringing his hand to rest on my cheek.

Was I trying to play hard to get? I surrender to his kiss and lean into him, turning my head to make the kiss deeper. I inhale and feel a surge of power as lust fills my senses. Feeling a pull low in my belly I smile against his lips. He's feeding from me.

"Please, stop it for at least five minutes," my mother says from the other room. "Rita and I are going out to lunch. And maybe a movie." She lowers her voice. "I have to go back home," she says to my aunt.

"Do you know how unpleasant it is when those two…"

I laugh and pull away from Haines, taking a slice of toast with me. "I'm pretty sure I can wait five minutes." A tug plays at my insides and I kiss Haines on the cheek. "Or an hour. The angels are here."

"An hour? Those two always come with news that leaves us all distracted." He groans and reaches his hand down to adjust his erection.

Will it be like this forever, even after the crazy dies down? Sexy games of lust and random carnal feeding that makes us fly? One can only hope.

"That looks like it would have been fun," I say, glancing at the growing bulge in his pants.

He smiles and picks up his toast. "It would have."

Feeling the wards drop I walk into the living room just in time to see Ari-el and Adkiel come into the house. Goddess only knows what those two are here for. To help me or make me want to pull my hair out? It usually comes down to one of those.

"Hey, guys." I walk over to the couch and sit down. If I get too close to them Ari-el will try to hug me. Which is a small price to pay for them helping me and the rest of my family not to die. "Please tell me you have anything but depressing news."

Ari-el comes over and sits down on the far end of the couch. "Nothing new. We just wanted to confirm that you have the weapon." Her eyes are wide as she bites her lower lip. Very human gesture.

I don't want to but I can't help myself. Leaning in, I hug her and pat her back. She looks a little relieved.

"Yes, I have it. How are you two doing?"

Adkiel stands near the window and looks out. Lately, he makes me uneasy. He's risking his safety to help me, but he looks at me like I'm the one responsible for all of this. Are his thoughts on the prophesy about me being overshadowed by his apparent dislike for me? I look at him and see nothing but disdain. He didn't look at me like that when we first met. Guess he didn't know me well enough. It seems as though he's starting to dislike me, and I'm pretty sure I haven't done anything to him.

Yet.

There's already one angel trying to kill me for no good reason. I hope I don't have to add Adkiel to the list. I'm pretty sure I could take him.

Ari-el takes off her jacket. She usually keeps the thing plastered to her body. "We are waiting for this to come to an end. To keep us safe from Samael, Rita set up a sanctuary for us. It's warded so that only Adkiel and I can enter. We can't go home without the threat of Samael's retaliation."

Ari-el is completely transparent. I know exactly how she feels and what she wants. She thinks I can do something to help, and she believes it whole-heartedly. She's becoming more and more comfortable around us; friendlier. She looks at me like I'm her friend, and I want to keep her safe. But her buddy is another story.

The only reason Adkiel is still welcomed here is because Ari-el always brings him. His safety is only by association. He and I need to talk. Welp, there's no time like the present to address the elephant in the room.

"That must really piss you off, Adkiel," I say, getting up from the couch and walking toward him. "Being limited to where you can go. Having to watch out for someone like Samael must make you angry."

Lips tight and looking like he just ate a lemon, he

glances at me and feigns a smile. "It is not so bad." Gradually, he makes his way to the recliner. On the other side of the room from where I am.

Won't give me direct eye contact. Doesn't like being close to me. Looks like we're going to have a confrontation. It's better to get it out in the open than have the fear of betrayal looming over us.

I walk over to him and sit on the arm of the chair he's sitting in. "Not so bad? I'm sure you're used to your freedom. Now you have to stay in a sanctuary so Samael can't use you as a play toy."

Clicking his teeth twice like an uptight cannibal, he looks up at me, eyes fluttering as if he can't see straight. Do angels sweat?

Smiling sweetly, I lean down and rest my hand on his shoulder. "Adkiel, you don't know how much this means to me. You two are risking everything for me and I don't even know how to repay you."

"You are our friend," Ari-el says as she shoves food into her mouth. "It is the will of God to have you take your rightful place. Are those filled with caramel?"

I look down at Adkiel and grin. He looks ill. Looking at Ari-el for possible help, he grabs the pillow from behind him and puts it in between us. It's so subtle I'm almost sure he hasn't even realized he's done it.

Ari-el busies herself with a desert plate full of cheesecake bites and doesn't acknowledge his silent plea for help. If I didn't like her so much I would hate her ass for not gaining a pound.

"I believe I'll get some cake," Adkiel says, attempting to stand up.

Catching everyone off guard, I swing my legs to the other side of the chair so that I'm sitting on Adkiel's lap. My mother, Aunt Rita, and Ari-el all stop talking and focus on us.

Grinning like a fool, I get comfortable and lean back. "You can have cake in a minute, but there's something we need to talk about and you better be real fucking honest."

"Perry?" Ari-el says.

Patting Adkiel on the shoulder I grab his chin and pull his gaze to meet mine. "Why are you helping me if you can't even stand to look at me, let alone be close to me? And before you begin let me share something." I pat my side where my sword sits, invisible to everyone including me. "This here shows me truths, and the longer I'm around you the more I see that you can't stand me. Don't get me wrong, I can be a bitch, but I haven't done anything to make you dislike me. I mean, don't get me wrong. I am quite capable."

He looks to Ari-el, then to Aunt Rita, and then back to Ari-el. I give his chin a little shake to remind him I'm still here.

He's squinting his eyes and swallowing over and over again. If I didn't know any better I'd say he was going to throw-up. "I'm attracted to you and it makes me severely uncomfortable." Word vomit. He spits out the words so fast it takes my brain a few seconds to catch up. "The way light dances in your eyes. The swell of your breasts and the roundness of your bottom. Your legs are plump, and your fingers are…breathtaking. I've never noticed fingers before, but yours are perfect."

Attracted to me? Is he lying? It'd be a great way to distract us from the truth.

Haines speaks up. "Perry, I don't know what just

happened, but I would appreciate it if you were to stand up. Adkiel, please take your hand off my wife's ass."

Adkiel and I both look down at his hand. Sneaky bastard. I hadn't even realized he'd copped a feelskie. Yep, he likes me.

"I'm attracted to you and it bothers me. I'm an angel, and angels falling for women seem to be our downfall. Samael bedded Lilith and those other women, and now look at him. He's even more unpredictable than the Morning Star. Your father fell in love with your mother and now he's dead. Will I be punished, too?" His words are fast but measured as if he has had this conversation with himself.

Inhalations speeding up, he leans closer and smells my hair. He closes his eyes and takes a deep, steadying breath. Adkiel almost looks defeated. "Will my demise or insanity come at the hands of a powerful woman who doesn't even know her own strength? I'm starting to feel all these things that I've never felt before and I don't know what to do." His voice trembles and his eyes are pleading. Sweat beads start to cover his nose as his breathing increases.

He wants to make it stop. Adkiel has never felt lust before and he probably wants to punch a hole through a wall. Or at least get me as far away from him as possible.

I stand up and walk over to the dessert tray, pulling my shirt down over my hips. Mmm, mini-éclairs.

After I shove four into my mouth, I chew slowly to give myself a few moments to think. Adkiel is attracted to me. To me. And he's being completely honest. He's also extremely terrified. As far as I know, the only angels who've fallen prey to their desires have ended up with the shitty end of a stick. I'd be afraid too.

Everyone's eyes are glued to me and Adkiel. Am I supposed to say something to make him feel better? Now, I feel uneasy.

"Dude, listen. I understand that this makes you feel a bit awkward, but you don't have to feel…like this. Angry, scared, sickened…it'll be fine. I'm half sex demon so you're probably being drawn to that."

Violently, he shakes his head and begins to wring his hands. "No, Perrian. It's not that. I'm immune to your powers as a demon."

"But apparently not your powers as a woman," my mother says, a giggle playing at the end of her words.

"Mommy, you are so not helping." If she weren't my mother I'd tell her to shut her yap. But she's slightly crazy so I'll keep that to myself. "Adkiel, I'm sorry you feel this way. It must suck."

He laughs lightly and pulls his jacket around him. "You have no idea. But it has helped me come to a decision. I will help you, Perrian. I believe the prophesy and if the Lord says that you are to be the Angel of Death then I will see this through. With or without me, it will happen. But I'd rather be a part of performing the will of God. And when this is all over, I'm going to fall. I want to find someone who makes me feel this way all the time. Someone who is mine and mine alone."

Two things that pop into my mind about what Adkiel just said, and I'm not sure which one is more appropriate—*I'm sorry* or *You're welcome*. How could he want to give up Heaven for this? This life. I look at Haines, to see him giving Adkiel the stink-eye, and smile. He wants to fall in love. And, I suppose, that is Heaven.

"I'm moving out," my mother says.

What? "Mom, you can't go back home."

She shakes her head and bites her bottom lip, which is beginning to tremble. "You're right, Perry. I can't go back there. The memory of your father is rooted in that place, and I just can't. For now, I'm moving in with Rita."

Why? Isn't there safety in numbers? We're all supposed to be close to one another so that if—when—the shit hits the fan we can be together.

Shrugging, she says, "Perry, I can't be here with you and Haines. I feed off of lust and you two make me uncomfortable. Rita and I will be safe with one another. Don't worry."

Don't worry? How could she even form her lips to say the words 'don't worry' to us? To me? I need her close. She's my mommy.

"Well," Ari-el says, standing up, "since we're sharing… I love to swim. It makes me happy." She smiles, showing a lot of teeth. "The fluidity of the water, the feeling of flying even though you're not. It makes me happy. Thank you, Rita, for allowing us to stay in a place that has a pool."

I purse my lips, one eye slightly closed, and take a deep breath. "That's great, Ari-el. Thank you for sharing that."

She beams and takes a sip out of her mug. Looks like hot chocolate. "And though I will miss you, Adkiel, I know you will be happy, brother. You've exhibited human emotions since you first met Perry. I knew you would choose the fall. You will make someone a wonderful husband." She takes another sip and smiles. "This is wonderful. Being around all of you is so freeing. Rita, Barbara, would either of you like to share?"

Aunt Rita looks around and shrugs. "No, dear, I'm fine."

My mother just laughs it off and shakes her head.

Okay. That was interesting.

The front door swings open and Ryan walks in with Roman. They both stop and look at everyone. Ryan's eyes widen as his gaze settles on me, a silent question of *Should we go home?* on his face.

I wave my hand at him and run my fingers through my hair. "We're just sharing our feelings. Anything you want to add?"

Please, God, don't let Ryan say anything that will drive me screaming from the room. Only a special select group of people can garner that kind of reaction from you. And then it hits me. These people are my family. Ryan, Roman, Trent and the angels included. We've become this little odd faction that completely understand one another and want so desperately to keep the other safe. Angels, demons, humans, and witches.

Yeah, I'd die for them. I'll fight for them. And, unfortunately, they would do the same for me.

Aunt Rita clears her throat. "More hot cocoa, anyone?"

All except Haines raises their hands. He still has his tea cup. Who the hell still has tea cups?

Roman takes off his coat, drops it on the floor, and walks over to me. He smiles and I see he has a tooth missing.

"Dude," I say, stooping down to his height, "what happened to your tooth? And did the Tooth Fairy pay you handsomely for it?" I reach in my pocket and give him a ten dollar bill.

Pushing my hair to the side, he leans in and whispers in my ear. "I built a toboggan. The Tooth Fairy gave me a quarter, but I like this better," he says, waving the ten dollar bill in my face. "Thank you."

A toboggan? I mouth to Ryan.

He walks over and pats Roman's head. "That's why we're here. He's bored to death being cooped up in the house and has taken to doing things that kids do when they are bored. He used a storage bin top as a toboggan. There is now a Roman-face sized dent in the wall at the bottom of the stairs."

I look at Roman who instantly turns red and averts his gaze. Once I catch his eye I give him a thumbs up and point to the dessert tray.

"Anything new?" Ryan asks.

Taking a deep breath, I grab a cup of cocoa and take a sip. "Adkiel wants to be human. My lady parts made him realize how soft women look. My mom is moving in with my aunt, and I have to figure out a way to get close enough to Samael to shove my sword through his face. I have no doubt that he would go after Adkiel once he's human and kill him just like he did my dad. I think that in Samael's mind, my father gave in to his weakness to be with my mother, and that Adkiel would be doing the same thing. Not to mention that you all are easy pickings to him. Oh, and Ari-el loves to swim."

Ryan takes a deep breath, sighs, and puts his hands on his hips. He looks tired. "No pressure, but what are you gonna do?"

I shrug. "Stand in an open field, take off my satchel, say *'come get me, you crazy bastard'* and get ready to fight? That's too obvious. He's insane, not stupid." I look over and wink at Roman. "I'm working on it."

Aunt Rita comes back into the room with a tray of sandwiches. Ever the hostess with the mostess.

My mom and Rita can protect each other. They'll be safe. So will Haines and me. And so will Ryan, Trent, and Roman. Everyone is doing everything they can to stay alive. We'll be fine. I know it.

And when this is all over I'll be the Angel of Death. Crazy job title. I have no clue what the hell I'm supposed to do as the Angel of Death, but I'll try my best to be good at it. I can't be any worse than Samael.

But no matter, I've got tons of support from the people who drive me crazy. Part of me wants to feel sorry for Samael, but all feelings of sorrow for him flew out of the window when he killed my father and drove a bedpost through my stomach. He can rot in Hell for what it's worth. Will he go to Hell? Do they have some kind of jail in Heaven that will teach him his lesson and then set him loose on the world again? Will he be destroyed? Recycled? God only knows.

Well, right now isn't the time to think about all that crap. It'll still be here once we've all finished enjoying each other's company, and this feels good.

My family.

Ari-el comes and stands next to me. "I can replace his tooth if you'd like?"

"Really? You may want to ask his father first."

She shrugs and then kisses me on the cheek.

"You're not attracted to me too, are you?" I ask her.

Ari-el laughs and sits down on the couch. "No. Not

so much." She grabs half of a grilled cheese sandwich, slowly pulling one part from the other, watching the cheese separate. "This is what you are fighting for. These people, in this room. And I am blessed to be part of that."

I lean down and kiss her on the cheek. Damn angels! They've pulled me into their touchy-mcfeely crap. "I know."

We all sit around eating and drinking, talking and laughing. We avoid the topic of murderous angels and impending doom, and I'm pretty sure Roman has collected at least fifty bucks for his tooth. Tooth Fairy, Schmooth Fairy. That bitch has nothing on family.

Chapter Eighteen

It's bright and it smells like vanilla and wildflowers. I hear a babbling brook—it really sounds like babbling—and feel the coolness of the wind that floats over the water. The grass is lush and the sky is so bright and clear it looks white. The flowering trees are beautiful, colorful. I've only seen scenes like this in paintings. Paintings where women lie in the grass in white dresses and white hats with pink or blue bows; where children in knickerbockers run through fields as their kites fly behind them.

I feel loved and warm. Safe and free of cares. The wind blows my hair, and when I lift my hand to move it from my eyes I see that my hand is luminescent. A gray flowing gown billows around me, and my silver wings are strong and beautiful. I let them flutter behind me and watch as the feathers make room for themselves. I stretch them out to their full capacity and see them high above my head. Lifting my arms out to the sides, I see that my wings span at least ten inches from my fingers. I flap them as if meaning to fly and feel the freeness of this place.

"Watch where you put those ghastly things."

"Holy shit. Damn-it! You're making me curse in Heaven." I look over at Samael and slap him with one of my wings. "How did you bring me here?"

Stumbling backward, shocked by the strength of

225

my wing, he rights himself and comes to stand in his original place. "I didn't. I *met* you here. Didn't think I'd see you scrapping around. Ohh!" he says, jumping up and down, his white wings fluttering behind him. "I've always wanted to say this." He clears his throat and turns to fully face me, trying desperately to hide a grin. "Fancy meeting you here, Perry-girl."

"My God, you are insane. Why am I here?" I start to walk away from him, but think better of it. Not smart to turn my back on the angel that wants to kill me.

In his confusion I study him in his beauty. His lavender eyes are wide and his beautiful white wings are spotted with gold flecks. His pale blue gown flows around him, and his porcelain skin glows. And he looks taller.

"I've been waiting around for your angel pals. We've got some business to take care of, and I know they are missing home. I guess that's why you're here." He slides closer to me and bumps me with his shoulder. "Admit it. You love and adore this place just as much as you despise it. It makes you realize all the things you settle for on Earth. You want me to take you. I would be giving you peace if you came willingly. That's the only reason I haven't gone on a murdering rampage. You will come to me. Willingly."

My wings shudder as I give him a sideways glance. It's true. Everything he's said about me is true. I want to give in and give up. Come home to Heaven and be happy. Be free. A very minute part of me wants to, but that part of me is so small it doesn't matter. My family and friends mean more to me than what I want. Heaven will come.

"Your silence speaks volumes, Perry-girl."

"How did I get here?" Great way to change the subject. Yes, it's lame. But it's all I've got right now.

The sound of laughter pulls me from my denial. I turn around and see a group of people standing at a bridge. There are at least ten of them. Their clothes are colorful and the joy of being here in this place is written all over their faces, in their posture. They haven't noticed us yet.

"And who are they?" I ask, taking a few steps toward them. I feel drawn to them. A pull in my chest pushes me forward. I look back at Samael, waiting for an answer.

He touches one of my wings and then wipes his hand on his gown. "Freshly dead. Souls who are about to be ushered unto the light. And to answer your first question, you got here the way you did the first time. You shifted here. All angels can. I'm amazed you're capable, being half demon and all."

Though I am completely offended by his repulsion to me I smile at the people on the bridge. A woman with deep olive skin and bright brown eyes walks toward us. She waves and then gets the attention of the others who are with her, grabbing one other person by the hand. With her leading, the whole group trails behind her.

Unable to stop myself, I follow the pull inside me and walk toward her and reach out my arms, welcoming her into a sincere embrace. "Hello," I say, gesturing for all of them to come closer. "It's beautiful here, isn't it?"

I feel compelled to welcome them, to let them know that everything is okay and that all will be made clear to them.

The woman in front of everyone else wraps her

arms around me and holds on tight. Sobbing, she kisses my cheek over and over. Her words are garbled by her tears and her entire body is shaking as if she were freezing.

I rub my hands over her back and through her hair. "Shh, why are you crying? This is not a place for tears, Cynthia." How did I know her name?

Samael leans in and whispers, "After a millennia of tears and sobbing, it gets real old." He raises his voice and feigns a smile. "The Gate is over there, everyone. Go to it and don't look back."

Looking at him like he's even more insane than I thought, I slap him with my wing as hard as I can. He flails backward a few feet and grimaces, barely catching himself before he falls.

"Cynthia," I say, pulling her head up, "it's time to go home. All of you." I wipe away her tears and kiss her cheek. "You should be laughing. Not crying."

She sniffs and wipes snot off her upper lip. "This isn't Heaven? It's so wonderful."

I smile. "It is wonderful, isn't it? But no, this isn't Heaven. It's the entry way. You were sent here first to prepare. Heaven is a wondrous place, a lot to take in. Coming here, which reminds you of all the beauty the Earthly plane has to offer, helps you get ready. And you are ready, aren't you? Because you should be."

Cynthia finally calms down and smiles so brilliantly. "Thank you. Thank you so much for…"

I shrug. "Don't thank me. I didn't do anything. But let's get you all home, okay?"

Everyone agrees in some way; some shaking their heads, some saying, "Yes" or "Please."

An older woman looks at Samael, who is looking

off toward the sky, no longer paying attention to us. She looks back to me and reaches out her hand. "Thank you for meeting us here." She looks back at him, a hint of fear playing in her eyes. She's smart.

I grab her hand and pull her attention back to me. "You're welcome. Let's get going."

Gathering everyone, we begin to walk toward a Gate that no words can describe. It's made of light and love. Pearl and gold and silver.

Soundless, the Gates open and everyone begins to walk in. When I stop walking, Rosamond, the older woman, tries to pull me along.

I let go of her hand. "No, Rosa, this is as far as I go. I still have things to take care of."

She nods, pulls my hand to her mouth, and kisses it. "Thank you," she says, and then disappears into the light beyond the Gate.

I stand there and look, trying to catch a glimpse.

"Go on, Perry-girl, take a look. You'll never want out again. Your family would be a distant memory."

Damn him for being right. "No, Samael." I take a deep breath and turn around to look at him. "I'm not leaving. It's time for you to move on." He is supposed to be the fucking Angel of Death but he treated those people as if their mere existence annoyed him. Inconvenienced him. "You have a choice to make. Retire to the fifth Heaven and be at peace. Or die by my hand and be stuck in Purgatory until God pulls you out at the end of this age. Those are your choices. There is nothing else. You've lost what it takes to be the Angel of Death." I shake my head and run my fingers through my hair. "This requires love, compassion. You have vengeance and hatred in your heart. And I can see it, because I see the truth. God makes no mistakes. And He ordains that I take your place. Make your choice. Or I'll help you move on."

I sit straight up in bed next to Haines and instantly reach for my back. I try to feel my wings. Why did I think for a moment they'd still be here?

"Perrian?" Haines says. Sitting up, he reaches and grabs a glass of water sitting on the bedside table. "What's wrong? Can't sleep?"

For a moment I think of telling him that I'll be fine and to go back to sleep. Maybe tell him that I had a bad dream and that I'm going downstairs for something to eat. Why would I lie to him about it? Maybe because I don't want him to know that I longed for Heaven so badly that I shifted there in my sleep. That I'd been doing it off and on but didn't tell him because I didn't want him to feel threatened. Didn't want him to think that for a few seconds every day I want nothing more than to go to Heaven. But I don't. I don't tell him the whole truth, but I tell him what went down between Samael and me. I tell him how those people needed to be told where to go, and if I hadn't been there, I don't know what would have happened. They probably would have found the Gates anyway, but they needed a friend to let them know that it was all right to go in.

"He's got three days, dearest husband. Three days to choose, and then I'm going to make the choice for him.

****

"Mmm, corned beef hash and caffeine." I lean forward and smell the cup of coffee my mother just set before me, blocking out the aroma of bacon and scrambled eggs with cheese wafting through the kitchen. "I don't know why you're doing this, Mom, but I'm for it." I reach over and grab the creamer and pour gobs of it into my cup. "So, Mommy, what's up? Why the big breakfast?"

She comes over and dumps more hash on to my plate and then sprinkles scrambled eggs over it. "Rita and I are leaving today." She puts four slices of bacon next to the mountain of goodness. "I know it makes you uncomfortable to have me leave, but I can't stay here. Neither can your aunt. Whatever happens is going to happen whether she and I are here with you two, or not."

Point taken.

"If Haines and I making googly eyes at each other makes you uncomfortable, we'll stop."

She butters a slice of toast and puts it on a napkin next to my plate. "I can deal with the eyes. It's the other bits I can't deal with."

"Then we'll stop!" I take a sip of coffee and add more creamer. "No sex, no kissing, no thinking of sex. Haines and I will be innocent as lambs."

"I'm sorry?" Haines says, walking into the kitchen. He grabs a mug and pours himself some coffee. "I'll make no such promises, Perrian."

"Haines, shut it. My mommy is leaving!"

He makes himself a plate and sits down next to me. Ignoring me like I don't even exist, he begins to eat his food, keeping the eggs and the hash separate. Blasphemous. Eggs and hash belong together!

We eat in silence for a few moments, my mother adding coffee to my cup or eggs to my plate as my supplies get low. I need her here. Her and my aunt. I need to be able to see the people I care for, with my own eyeballs. No phone calls. No texts or emails. Eyeball to eyeball contact. Don't they understand the shit is about to hit the fan, and I don't even know how to start the fucker up to get the ball rolling? How to get the shit flying?

Aunt Rita comes in and sits down next to me. "How are you taking it, dear?"

I frown and shove a whole piece of bacon in my mouth. "Doth it mather?" I say through a mouth full of food.

She smiles sweetly and wipes crumbs from my chin. "Not really. You are an adult."

"Am not."

"One of the most powerful beings anywhere. And now you have the weapon you need to defend yourself. And your family. We don't need to be here."

Shrugging, I take a sip of my mom's orange juice. "I still don't know how to get close to him to end this. I need counsel. You three are my council. Counsel me, darn-it!"

Haines chuckles and shakes his head. "You are acting like a child, Perrian."

"Dude, let's not take our relationship back to the point where I tell you to shut your face every time you open it."

He bites his lower lip and then runs his tongue along the inside of his jaw. I love his mouth. His teeth. His lips. His tongue. And all the deliciously hot feelings that come with them.

My mother slams more toast on to my napkin. "This. This is what I mean. You insulted him, he got pissed, and then you both got the hots for one another. I'm leaving."

I look at Haines and wink.

Yeah, I guess it is time for them to go. Knowing my mom knows when I get the lusts for my husband is kind of gross. But I can't control it. My husband is hot.

Covering my face with my hands I begin to chant, "I am an adult. I don't need my mommy here to take care of me. I am an adult. I don't need my mommy here to take care of me."

"That's right, dear," Aunt Rita says, rubbing my back. "Yes, you are."

"I don't need my mommy here to take care of me. I'm a powerful, bad ass, demon-angel type person. I'm *the* Angel of Death." That does not sound good. "I am the Angel of Death, and I'm going to throw up."

"Yes, dear," Auntie says, still rubbing. "Yes you— what?"

I jump up and run for the kitchen trash can, knocking over my chair and giving my aunt a run for her money as I try not to knock her down in the process.

My stomach begins to give up the ghost. Dizzying waves of nausea crash over me and the room starts to spin. My mother comes over and holds my hair out of my face as I empty everything I just ate, and probably last night's snack, into the trash can. A churning in my stomach makes me heave. There's nothing left for me to throw up. It's getting hot. "Something is wrong," I say, heaving until nothing but empty noises pour from my mouth. "What is that sound?"

A hand appears in front of my face. It's Haines, wiping the remnants of dinner and breakfast from my lips. "Your ears are probably ringing. I'll get you some ginger ale to settle your stomach."

A loud scratching echoes in my head and I grab my ears to block the sound. It sounds like a fork rattling around in a garbage disposal had a kid with another fork that enjoys being dragged down chalkboards. "God, what is that?" I look up at my council—their new name!—and see them looking at me in confusion, not knowing whether to help me drown out the noise, touch me, or stay away from me.

My mother is the first to come to my side. Her lips move but I can't hear her voice. She signals to Aunt Rita who comes over and grabs my face, forcing me to look at her.

It's a summoning spell! she mouths. *A very strong one.*

Alternating between holding on to the wall and covering my ears, I try to block the noise and think of what day it is. "Has it been a week? It's been a week!" I scream at them. "That bastard is calling me to him!" He said I'd know when my time was up. I strip off my sweatshirt and am left in my tank top tee-shirt and pajama bottoms. Battle gear? I am so going to hand Samael his ass back to him on a golden platter. Once I figure out how to. "How do I make it stop?"

Aunt Rita starts pointing at the door and then back to her lips. *Follow it.* She grabs my face again. *Kill. Him. Don't flinch, just strike!*

I nod my head, still trying to hinder the sound by covering my ears, but it's coming from inside of my head.

Haines grabs me as I start walking to the front door. He gently holds my chin and kisses me, and for a brief moment the horrible sound stops. "Come back to me."

"You bet your sexy ass I will!" I look around at my mother and aunt. "I probably don't need to scream at you guys, do I?" Trying to lighten the mood while the sound of ten thousand lawnmowers ride over a million chainsaws as an archaic, insane angel calls you to your death is not easy.

My mother and aunt shake their heads, trying to look at ease, but I can see the fear in their eyes. Making my way to the front door and opening it, fighting through the screeching sound, I look back at them once more. My mother holds on to Aunt Rita just as she held me the night Samael killed my father—her eyes glisten as she fights to hold back the tears. Her nails dig into Aunt Rita's hand, but neither seem to notice. They are terrified. I don't blame them. This is supposed to be a showdown of epic proportions and... "It stopped," I whisper. "I don't hear it. It's gone."

"And here you are, Perry-girl."

I look up and see something I never thought I'd see. Something I inwardly prayed I'd never see. A chill descends over my insides and all the snarky comebacks I'd stored just for this moment have dried up.

On our lawn a small unconscious, God please let him be unconscious, form lies at the feet of Samael. Still wearing his pajamas and little cartoon character slippers is Roman, laying in the grass that is still wet with morning dew.

"Imagine my surprise when this little cad came on to my radar, outside of the protective barrier and with no satchel. And you wanna know what he said? 'Come get me, you crazy bastard. You killed my friend's daddy, and she's gonna get you.' I can only imagine where he would get that from."

Right now, there isn't enough oxygen in the world. I close my eyes and feel tears fall down my cheeks. Roman heard me say it yesterday. This is my fault. Really, really my fault.

My words are garbled and rushed. "Please. I'll do what you want. I give. No more fighting. Don't hurt him." I put my hands up and begin walking toward them.

This isn't going to turn out well. Samael has me, and he knows it. He knows I would never risk the safety of my friends, especially a child. Walking closer to them I can see the rise and fall of Roman's chest. Thank you, God.

Samael picks up his foot and places it on Roman's chest. "Come closer and I will crush him."

I stop walking and keep my hands up. "What do you want me to do? I'll say what you want me to say, just don't hurt him. Please."

He taps the tip of his shoe on Roman's chest and his entire little body jerks. "It would be easy to kill him. He wouldn't even know it happened. He'd wake up at the Gates. Wouldn't you rather him go in peace than to have him watch you *try* to hurt me?" He taps Roman again with his foot, showing me how strong he is.

Watching his little body jerk just from the sheer force of a gentle tap from Samael's toes make me want to scream, cover my ears, and roll in to a ball and pretend that Roman's life isn't on the line. I don't know what to do. The plan was for everyone to stay safe and hidden while I figured it out. But he's going to kill Roman if I don't…

"I give in to you. You can take my life. I give it to you. Just don't hurt him."

Don't give in, Perrian.

"Really," I say out loud, talking to the disembodied voice that apparently only I can hear. "You can't give me a heads up before this stuff happens?" I shake my head and throw my hands up. "Sorry, sorry. That was discourteous and I shouldn't address you that way." *Please, Lilith, help me.* "I said it, Samael. Now let him go."

Eyebrows raised, he looks around, and then back at me. "It doesn't count if you don't mean it. And who were you talking to?"

"An old girlfriend of yours. She says the sex was a bore, and you suck." How the hell am I supposed to mean it if I really don't mean it? I don't want to die. And I can't let Roman die. I won't. What am I supposed to do?

"Lilith," Samael spits out. "She's a dead deity. She speaks to no one." His entire demeanor changes. That normal insane look has moved on to wily and downright frightening. "She speaks to you? Who else speaks to you, you mutt?" His teeth are bared, and spittle drips down his chin. One eyelid twitches, and he takes a step toward me.

Samael knowing that Lilith speaks to me pisses him off. Does he feel more threatened because he knows it's not just me, a half demon whose only favor could be earned in Hell? That I have just as much grace as he does? My being able to shift to the Gates of Heaven wasn't enough. He's starting to see, really starting to see that his time has come to an end. And that will make him desperate. Desperation makes us do terrible things.

"What the hell is...Roman? Trent, get out here!"

With a pure look of terror, Ryan runs toward Samael and the still prone body of his son.

Without even looking at Ryan, Samael flicks his wrist and Ryan's body goes sailing backward smashing into the shrubs near his door. He rolls over onto his knees and tries to get up, but falls back down.

The woman who lives next door to Ryan and Trent opens her door. All gazes fall to her to see if she notices what's happening, but she's talking on her cell phone and turns her back to us to lock her door.

"Getting crowded, Perry-girl. Me and small fry here will see you later. I'm going to put him somewhere safe until you get your sweet-self ready for me. Don't make me wait." Without taking his eyes off me he bends down to pick up Roman.

I've got nothing. No plan. No grand idea to save us all. But if I let Samael leave with Roman we may never see him again. I break into a run as Samael and Roman begin to shimmer out of focus. God knows where he's taking him, but he won't be going alone. Jumping into the air just as Trent comes through the front door, I see a look of dread on his face as I make contact with Samael's quickly disappearing form. As I connect with him I feel like I am being sucked into a vortex; weightless and terrified as I spin out of reality with them.

After what seems like hours of spiraling in mid-air I finally feel like I've made physical contact with Samael. Everything still looks out of focus, but I reach out for Roman and feel his small hand latch on to mine. I pull him closer, wrap my arms around as much of him as I can, and start kicking any body part that's not wrapped in my embrace. And in my wings?

We finally reach our destination and I slam onto the ground, still shielding Roman's body with mine. I shake my head and take a deep breath, trying to get a grasp on where we are. The silence is deafening, and it smells like someone's been sick. An acidic stench invades my senses, and I almost gag. Where the Hell are we?

"Roman, are you—ow! What the…?"

Roman just bit the crap out of my shoulder. I open my arms, and my wings, and see a tiny version of Trent. Small purple horns protrude from either side of his head and yellow eyes stare back at me. Taking a moment to look around I see…nothing. An empty void that goes on forever. But it won't stay that way. Not while Samael and I are here. There will be things lurking around us in no time. They must be close. The smell here is overwhelming.

Roman scampers away from me and looks around. His face holds and array of emotions ranging from pure fear to rabid hunger. "I'm sorry, Perry. I—I don't know why I did that." He covers his mouth, closes his eyes, and starts to cry. "I don't like this, Perry. I can't see anything. W-why do you smell like…like food?"

I thought they used Ryan's junk to have a baby. My mother told me when I was a child that the longer you feed someone, the more they start to look like you. Ryan is a great cook, and Roman looks just like him. Well, not now he doesn't.

"It's okay, kid. You didn't mean to hurt me." I turn around and look at Samael as he stands there smirking. "Keep your eyes closed, Roman. Don't look." I wish I didn't have to look. This place is scary. Standing up, I switch my focus to Samael. "How could you, Samael?

You'd bring him here? You were going to leave him at the Gates of Hell?"

I take a closer look and see a deep gash that runs across Samael's chin dripping blood. His eyes look swollen and he's breathing hard. He shrugs his right shoulder and then smiles. "It's not like he wouldn't fit right in. I think you...yep." He reaches over, grabs his left shoulder, and gives it a hard tug. "You, you violent thing, dislocated my shoulder."

I go to manifest my sword, but the small sobs of Roman brings me back. Let me see how formidable I really am. With one hand on my sword and the other reaching out to Roman, I close my eyes. "*Lorem diligere.*" He shimmers out of this terrible place and back home to his family. Our family. "And now you, you douche bag. *Adiuro vos ad locum istum, et consilium meum.* I bind you to this place, and to my will." I pull out my sword and smile. "Time to dance, bitch."

"Well," he says, backing away from me. "Until next time." He begins to shimmer out of focus, but confusion blankets his face as he realizes he can't. After a few more tries, a sheen of sweat breaks out on his nose. "Why..."

"'Cause I'm a kick-ass 'mutt', you sick bastard. Did you know that this sword that was made just for me links me to the Great Hall of Records? I didn't know that until just now. Every spell, every potion, every *thing* that anyone has ever known is available to me. It's the truth of all truths. So, you're kind of stuck here at the Gates of Hell until—"

The force of a garbage truck slams into me as I am tackled from behind by something large and filthy. Its skin is the color of a rotting avocado, black and brown with splotches of green. Rows and rows of small jagged teeth fill its mouth, and silver beady eyes stare down at me. It is tall, and its skin feels like sticky, hot rubber. I shove and push to keep it at arm's length as it snaps its wicked mouth at me, inching closer and closer each time. Pulling my right arm back as far as I can to gain momentum in my supine position, I hit the demon in the neck and cause it to jerk its head toward my left arm.

Terrible, horrible mistake. It wraps its long, grainy, pink tongue around my wrist and I feel tiny painful bites. This bastard has teeth in its fucking tongue! I scream and punch again, over and over until its tongue unravels from around my wrist. It snarls and snaps at me, getting closer each time. Jerking my knees up as hard as I can and using my wings as leverage, I flip us over until I'm straddling the demon. Quickly, I pull out my sword and bury it in its chest.

A bright light flashes and the demon's corpse turns to cinder. I look down and see a few teeth sticking out of my wrist. Pulling them out and trying not to throw up at the thought of that thing's tongue on my body, I try to catch my breath. This is not what I expected when I woke up today. I was going to eat a hearty breakfast, research stuff, and do my eyebrows, but now I'm pulling teeth out of my wrist. Ew. Where the hell is Samael?

As I turn my head to look behind me Samael grabs one of my wings and pulls, almost ripping it from my back.

I scream in agony as Samael pulls my other wing, but my shouts are cut off as he wraps his long arm around my neck and cuts off all circulation. He pulls me close as he chokes the life out of me.

"Let me out of here, you repugnant half-breed, or I will leave you unconscious and unable to defend yourself against the hungering hordes of demons."

I beat at his arms, hoping he'll loosen his grip so I can take a breath, but it seems to piss him off even more. He's so close I can feel every breath he takes and every beat of his hateful heart.

"They will feast on you as you scream in voiceless anguish. And know that I will kill each and every member of your family," he growls. "Release me from this place."

His lips are so close to my ear I can feel every syllable that pours from his mouth.

My vision is going in and out. But I can't let him go. This is my only chance. My body begins to go slack, and even the close sound of his panting is getting farther and farther away. In a last ditch effort to save my family I choose to truly let go, just like he wanted me to. No remorse. No feelings of what I did or didn't get to do. Just peace. I'm okay with letting go now. I grab my sword and with my last bit of fading strength, plunge it into my chest knowing it will go right through his.

Samael's body convulses and his grip loosens. Taking huge gulps of air and pulling his arms from around my neck, I try to get away from him but we are stuck together by my sword.

But I don't feel anything. No pain. No pressure. Just sweet gobs of sulfur smelling air.

"You've killed yourself, Perry-girl," Samael says as the blood from his mouth drips onto my shoulder. He laughs. He thinks he's won. "You love them so much that you would kill yourself."

Umm, I don't think so. I grab the hilt of my sword and pull. Samael's body hits the ground as I stand up and look at my chest. Nothing. No blood. No hole. Not even one in my gown.

I turn around and look at him. "I thought I *was* killing myself. But it eluded me that the sword, my sword, can't hurt me."

He lays on the ground holding his chest, blood pouring from his wound. "You gonna leave me here and let them consume me? I'd do that to you." His body begins shaking and more blood covers his gown. His eyes dart around, looking to see what's coming for him.

"You don't need to worry about them. They can't see us. Not until I wish it so." I walk toward him and pull my gown up a bit higher so that it won't get tangled if Samael tries to fight back. "You have something that belongs to me. I didn't know how I was going to get it from you, but I do now."

I lower myself and straddle him, my hips settling over his stomach. Bending down, I place one hand behind his head and the other on his chest.

Trembling beneath me, he tries to fight but is too weak to do anything. Placing my lips right above his I inhale and use the succubus within me to feed from him. He tries to close his mouth but I grab his chin to hold it open. Inhaling deeper, a light begins to form between our lips, and I pull it into my body. It's sweet. It tastes of death and life and love and hate. It's the duality that Samael couldn't embrace coming to find a home within me. Swallowing and feeling the light pulse through my body, I try to stand up but fall backward.

Life fills my body and it feels almost orgasmic. Both angel and succubus within me are full to bursting.

The Rite of Death moves through me, and I can feel every reaper angel connect with my essence. All over the world, on every plane of existence, I bond with them and feel their relief that I've finally accepted my place among them.

We both lay there at the Gates of Hell gasping for air, only inches from one another but unable to fight. Well, he is.

I feel powerful. Chosen. The light and dark in me have finally made peace.

I sit up and look around, noticing that demons skate around the perimeter of my holding spell. They can't get in but they sure as hell want to. "I'm not as cruel as you think, Samael. I won't leave you here so they can devour your light. I took it. Your light. Your grace." I crawl over to him and stare down into his glazed over lavender eyes. "They will hunt you. Just like you hunted sex demons for the last seventy years. They've lived in fear of you. And now you will live in fear until your penance is over." I place my hand over his wound and heal him.

He screams out as flesh knits with flesh, and muscle links with muscle. "Don't...leave me. They'll kill me," he chokes out, eyes darting around to see what's coming for him. The look of terror in his eyes is priceless and fitting.

"Then it looks like you'd better find a nice place to hide." I shimmer out from the Gates of Hell and back home to my family.

Chapter Nineteen

"Oh, Perry," Ari-el says, shaking her head. "You shouldn't have done that. If the demons devour his grace…it would be bad. Unspeakably bad."

I shrug and swallow the last piece of French toast Ryan brought me. "I took it. His grace is now roaming around at the Gates of Heaven until he's ready to claim it. And when were you going to tell me that my sword gave me access to the Great Hall of Records?"

Once I shifted back to my family and told them how I handed Samael's ass to him, the party has been nonstop. French toast, coffee, and mini-éclair's for everyone.

"The what?" Ari-el says.

"Really? You don't know what that is?" I ask, scootching over so Haines can sit next to me. He's warmed up more French toast and bacon for me. Love him!

"Well," she says, eyeing my breakfast, "beneath the Great Sphynx there sits a library that—"

I shake my head. "Wait. What? No! The Great Hall of Records. The Akashic Records? The freaking Collective Consciousness? Don't you watch Discovery?"

She still looks confused. Hell, I would be too.

"It's the collective consciousness of everything. Everyone."

She tilts her head back as her mouth forms a perfect 'O.' "*The Magna aula experientia*! Yes, I know of it. But your basic angel does not have access to this. We are to live life as angels and be separate from everything else."

That doesn't make any sense. Every experience, even those of angels, is in the library. When I'm holding my sword I feel like I know everything. It's wonderful. It's scary, like a drug. Every now and then I find myself pulling my hand to my hip. I don't make it manifest, but having my hand where it would be if I did pull it out comforts me. I'm supposed to bring order to the Reaper Angels. That shit sounds hard. My sword makes me feel better. As if I have all the knowledge I need to do the job. Sheyeah, not that simple.

"So, Ari-el," I ask, moving my hand from my hip to my coffee mug. "What am I supposed to do now? How am I supposed to do whatever I'm supposed to do?" Probably should have asked that question a few days ago.

She bites the inside of her lip and frowns. "I wouldn't know where to begin. Maybe you should read the scrolls that contain the prophesy concerning you. What I do know is that I will be your personal Messenger Angel."

"What the hell is that?" I ask.

Ari-el smiles and looks almost giddy. "When you are unable to do so I will deliver messages from you to the Reaper Angels. If a message were to be handed down by Him I will be your messenger."

Him. Does she mean *the* Him? "You mean I could get messages from God? Like…God?"

"Oh, yes." She takes a sip of her cocoa. "You are

the Angel of Death, and you wield one of the most powerful weapons in existence. Did you not think that the Almighty communicated with us?" She smiles, picks up a fork, and then takes a piece of French toast from my plate.

I stare at her blankly as she chews. "When did you and I get here?" I ask. I don't share food.

Just because she's my new PA doesn't mean she can take liberties. My food is my food, and if she tries it again, I'll poke her with my fork.

"We've been here all morning," she says, shaking her head.

Let it go, Perry. She's learning.

This feels good. Everyone is so at ease, not worrying if they are going to die today. I don't remember ever feeling like this.

I glance over at Haines. He has barely said a word all morning. Furtive glances let me know that he's waiting for everyone to get the hell out, but he's being patient.

Aunt Rita comes in to the kitchen and grabs a slice of bacon. "Well, you two. Since this has all died down and you seem happily married, are you going to take a honeymoon?"

Haines pats my hand and pulls me closer to him. "Perry goes back to work in a few days. Maybe we'll take one in a few months."

Biting my bottom lip, I look at him and shrug. "Umm, I'm actually going to submit my letter of resignation, effective immediately. No one knows how being the Angel of Death, and apparently overlord to the Reapers, is going to affect my life. Being a physical therapist is hitting the back-burner. There are too many things for me to learn and deal with." I elbow him in his ribs. "Besides, you're loaded. I can mooch off you for a while. As for a honeymoon, I'm thinking New Orleans. I've been like eight times, but I love it. Will you take me?"

He tries to stifle a smile and clears his throat. "Of course. I haven't been since the 1930s."

I'm a lady of leisure! Hell yeah! I'm going to buy a smoking jacket, sit around the house, and eat bon-bons. Well, when I'm not doing Angel of Death related stuff.

After sitting in the kitchen with everyone and eating all day, Ryan, Trent, Roman, and Adkiel walk in through the front door.

Adkiel has decided to stay an angel for a little while longer. He's promised to watch over Roman to make sure he doesn't have any residual effects from being so close to Hell. He's half demon, and for a cambion the traits don't usually kick in until puberty. We just want to make sure he's all right. I cast a spell to make him forget, but magic and people's minds don't always cooperate. I'm hoping and praying that he doesn't start having nightmares.

Finally breathing a huge sigh of relief, I stand up and get more coffee. Everyone is so relaxed, and it makes me feel good. Overjoyed.

I add more water to the tea kettle, making sure to splash my hands with water and place the kettle on the stove. Trying to go unnoticed I pretend as if I'm shaking the water off my hands and splash it in the general direction of everyone in the room.

Waiting until everyone is preoccupied and not paying attention to me I whisper, "*Et operui in praesidium. Volo id igitur*," and then splash more water toward them. I grab a steak knife from the block, grab an apple from the fruit bowl, and begin to cut in to it, making sure to cut my finger. Without lifting my eyes I turn on the water and let my blood run down the drain, making sure to squeeze my finger a few times to get the blood flowing. Turning off the faucet I splash more water in their direction and then whisper the protection spell again. As my cut heals before my eyes, the protection spell is cast.

Aunt Rita's head snaps up and she catches my eyes. Getting up and walking toward me, she bites the inside of her jaw. "Walk with me," she says, wrapping her arm around my waist.

We stand on the front porch, her shivering and me taking off my sweater to give to her.

"No, Perry," she begins, trying to push the sweater back toward me.

I push a little harder and wrap it around her shoulders. "I don't feel the cold." I wink at her and smile. "Something you want to talk about?"

She pulls the sweater around her. "How did you do it? You cast a protection spell over humans, angels, demons, and half-breeds all at the same time. They all require separate spells and you did it all at once. How?"

Shrugging, I push a curly lock of hair behind my ear. "By word, water, and blood. Don't worry. It's just a cautionary spell. The Rite of Death and my sword make me pretty invincible. It'll hold."

She shakes her head. "That's not what I'm worried about. You cast a protection spell over seven people of many different bloodlines. Even the most powerful witch can't do that." She looks me up and down. "You keep your hand there quite often," she says, looking at my hip.

I pull my hand away and run my fingers through my hair. "I'm scared. The sword makes me feel better. God made it just for me, and touching it makes me feel closer to Him." And it makes me feel powerful beyond the telling of it.

"Be careful, child. With great power comes—"

"Great responsibility, I know. But you don't understand. I don't know what to do, and Ari-el seems like she's pulling this shit out of her ass. She's scared too. For me. For the Reaper Angels. For all of us. This sword makes me feel that if I was good enough to receive it then I'm good enough to pull this off." I reach over and pull the sweater around her neck to block out the freezing wind. "I won't go crazy. I won't end up like Samael."

She sniffs and shivers again. "Why didn't you tell them?"

I rub my hands up and down her arms and steer her toward the heat of the house. "Because if I tell them I cast a protection spell on them they'd want to know why. They'd think I knew something they didn't, and I don't. We can tell them if you'd like, but they all look so peaceful."

Aunt Rita smiles and then turns the knob. "You're right, dear. Let's go inside."

****

"New Orleans? Are you sure you don't want to go to Ireland? You've always wanted to go." Haines puts the last of the dirty dishes in the dishwasher and adds in way too much detergent. "I'll take you anywhere you want to go."

I wipe down the kitchen counter and center the

fruit bowl. It feels good to have a normal, non-death involving conversation with my husband. "Maybe later. New Orleans has always felt like my second home, and I'd like to experience it with you."

He smiles and grabs two glasses, filling them with water. I love his smile. It didn't appear until a few days ago, and I love it. He has seemed so light and carefree today. But he's still all tall and big and sexy.

It's good that everyone felt safe enough to go home without looking at everyone else as if it were a final good-bye. My mom has moved in with Aunt Rita, Roman has gone back to school, and the angels finally got to go home without worrying about being accosted.

I turn around and run in to a wall of warm muscles and soft flesh. Wrapping my arms around Haines' neck I wrap my legs around his legs and begin to climb, not stopping until we are eye to eye. "Thank you for sticking by me through all of this. You could have walked away and I wouldn't have blamed you." I kiss his nose and grind my hips against his and feel his cock begin to rise.

He growls and uses both hands to grip my thighs and pulls me closer to him. "I am yours, Perrian, and I'm not going anywhere. You are mine." He runs his nose along my jaw and bites my earlobe. "I'm going to make love to you tonight."

"I'd like that."

He sets me on the kitchen counter and skims his long fingers up my legs and under my skirt. Clamping his hand along my panty line he balls his hand into a fist and roughly rips them from my body. "Right after I taste you, fuck you, and feed from you right here in our kitchen. In our home."

He pushes me down on to the counter and makes good on his word, over and over again.

This is awesome.

****

Haines lays snoring lightly in bed, the sheet sitting just right so that I can't see his man-parts, but that perfect V-shape is almost begging me to rip off the sheet, hop on, and say 'Hello, nurse!'

My body feels deliciously sore from the past few hours with Haines and I should be tired, but my mind is fully awake. Grabbing my robe from the closet I head downstairs so that I won't wake Haines.

I lied to Aunt Rita today.

I don't know what's coming but I know something is. With all the powers I've been given I am a formidable ally. It's already been proven that threatening my family will make me do anything to keep them safe. It's also been proven that I'll turn into a vengeful bitch against anyone who tries to harm them. But what worries me most is Haines. Severing our link will make me lose my humanity, and that's the one thing that will keep me linked to everyone else. I can feel it. I know it.

If someone or something wants to turn me into big bad Perry, all they'd have to do is kill Haines and bide their time. As long as I live and breathe, that spell will keep all of them safe. It will keep him safe. Someone can try if they'd like. But woe to that man who would try. I'd rip this world apart to keep my family safe. That is truly what frightens me the most. I don't know how far I'd go to keep them safe. And I don't know how far I am capable of going. It might not end well.

A humming sounds off in my head as a light knock

on the door takes me from my thoughts. It's an angel.

I peek through the curtain and don't recognize the person standing on the other side of the door. I ready myself for a fight. I'll invite him in and end him just to make it clear that I am not to be toyed with. "Who the fuck are you?"

He's tall, bald, and damn scary. He looks like he could be a WWE wrestler's larger twin brother. His eyes are such a light brown they are almost yellow. Pale blond brows and lashes make those eyes almost hard to look at. His black leather jacket looks threatening, but the aura of light emanating from him calms me down. "I am Mael, your second in command. A Reaper Angel."

I back out of the way and let him in. I'm not afraid. I'll send him crying home to Daddy if he tries anything. "What's up, Mael? It's almost midnight."

He clears his throat and gestures toward the breakfast nook, silently asking for permission to sit down.

I nod and he sits, looking extremely uncomfortable and cramped in.

"I was waiting for you to contact me but after talking to Ari-el it seems as if you wouldn't know how to."

He is huge. And a Reaper Angel? Would I go with him if I were newly dead? Sure. I'd be too afraid to tell him no.

Shrugging, I grab a bottle of water from the fridge and give it to him. "I know how."

He laughs. "I could sense your unease. You have no reason to worry. We will follow you. You have been chosen, and we have waited for you. Though you're not what I expected. You're short."

"Maybe you're too tall, Mael."

"I am exactly as God wanted me to be."

"As am I." I click my teeth together a few times, mulling over how he feels about me. "We're not going to have a problem, are we?"

Mael pulls himself out of the nook and kneels down on one knee. "No, Perrian. We will not. I'm sorry if I have offended you."

I take a deep breath and move my hand to the counter, just realizing I've had my hand on my hip the whole time. "You didn't. It's all right. Please stand."

Fluidly, he stands and then bows at the waist. "On behalf of all the Reaper Angels, we pledge ourselves to you. You have been chosen and we are honored." He stands. "I shall take my leave now." He gives me a crooked smile that shows perfect teeth. "Let me or Ariel know when you are ready." He turns and walks toward the door.

"Mael? I'm glad that I have been chosen and I vow to…be good. Thank you."

He bows his head, opens the door and leaves.

That was fun.

After a few minutes of staring at the door, I grab a can of soda, sneak out the back door, and sit on the porch swing. I rock back and forth, sipping my drink, and look up. The night sky is clear and the crescent moon shines brightly. The wind whips by, lifting the bottom of my robe and tossing my hair in my face. I can tell I should be cold but I'm not. The cold bench feels room temperature to me.

I close my eyes and take a deep breath. "Thank you, Father. Thank you, Lilith." I exhale and relax.

You are welcome, child. The voice sings in the wind. It's soft and feminine. *Always remember, though you are born of light and dark, the light will always shine brighter. You love, and you are loved. Be ready, Perrian. Blessed be.*

"Thank you, Lilith," I say into the wind. "I will be prepared. I already am. Blessed be."

Smiling, I stand up and walk into the house. I've been chosen to be the Angel of Death; the Death Bringer. Never would I have imagined in a gazillion years that would be my calling. Hell, up until a few weeks ago I thought I was a human-demon hybrid, not the offspring of a demon and an angel.

But I am. And it feels more right than anything I've ever experienced. God made me this way so who am I to doubt His actions. He says I can do it, so screw anyone who says I can't. I may be from the Line of Lilith, but I am a child of God, demon blood running through my veins and all. And I am prepared for anything that anyone has to throw at me.

Bring it on, bitches.

Blessed be.

About the Author

R. A. Boyd is a writer and reader of paranormal romance, horror, and urban fantasy. She lives in Maryland with her husband, daughter, and her massive collection of books.

She loves all things paranormal but dabbles in romantic comedies and hockey fights. When she's not writing at three in the morning she's binge-watching Netflix or plotting random scenes from her novels in the voice of her characters. It makes her daughter giggle but worries her husband.

~*~

Visit R. A. Boyd at
http://raboyd.com
~*~

To chat with R. A. Boyd and other Wild Rose Press authors of erotic romance, join us at
www.groups.yahoo.com/group/thewilderroses.

Also Available
Bite Thy Neighbor
by Esmae Browder

Some neighbors suck…literally.

Quirky Maisy Harker spends her time daydreaming about her sexy husband, Jensen Helsing. Though their marriage is one of convenience, Maisy wishes the sparks of heat she feels around him were reciprocated. Sexually starved, she also lusts after her mysterious neighbor, Adam. True, his incisors do look a bit sharp, and he never seems to drink or eat anything—but hey, maybe that's how he keeps that yummy, drool-worthy physique!

Yet Maisy knows something's not quite right, and it isn't long before she learns Adam is a centuries-old vampire embroiled in a gypsy curse placed on the women of her family. All her female ancestors have been drawn to the vampire and bound by his desires, experiencing a terrible side effect of the curse and resulting in death.

It's up to Maisy to find a way to break the curse once and for all before she, too, falls under his spell.

Also Read

The Mating Game
by Melissa Snark

Two males...two friends...a competition for the right to claim The Heart of the Iron Stone Pack.

An alpha female at her core, Theresa Sanchez struggles to protect her young daughter, but rivalries and politics create volatility in the pack. As Theresa comes into heat, lust and need rule her body. Her pack demands only the most virile male have her. How can she choose only one mate when her body craves two—the virile beta and the man she loves?

Zachary Hunter will do anything to take Theresa as his mate, even if it means killing his best friend. However, Robert Blane is just as determined to ascend to Alpha. Both their beasts howl to mark her flesh, but only one can survive to claim her.

But with enemies circling, they must fight...for the pack, for Theresa, and for a future together.

www.ingramcontent.com/pod-product-compliance
Lightning Source LLC
Chambersburg PA
CBHW070334260626
47160CB00003B/1040